PRAISE FOR

THE MARK OF NOBA

2016 New Apple Summer Ebook Award Medalist Winner for Young Adult Sci-fi/Horror
(Highest honor in the category)

"From the very first page, I was hooked and couldn't stop reading."
NYT and USA Today Bestselling author Ellie Ann

"The world is refreshing, as is the conflict setup. There's more ahead for Sterling and Tetra, and I can't wait to see where their journey takes them."
Author Kiran Oliver of Daybreak Rising

"In *The Mark of Noba* by G L Tomas we are presented a story that is part fantasy myth, part high school drama and all adventure from beginning the end."
"Judge, 3rd Annual Writer's Digest Self-Published eBook Awards."

"Sterling is a likeable high school boy; Tetra is a true gem, and the story really came to life with her viewpoint!"
~ 5 Star Review

"A breathtaking YA adventure!"
~ 5 Star Review

"The world-building in this book is among the best I've ever seen.
It's a very well-written book I would highly recommend."
~ 5 Star Review

"This is a very diverse book that includes many characters of color. I think readers of all races will appreciate the ethnic diversity this story offers. Readers will also appreciate the character development between Tetra and Sterling. Their relationship is complicated because their power is connected to their feelings for each other. But it is more than just a plain romance. This is about trust and belief."
~ 5 Star review from Reader's Favorite

"All the characters in this book are some of the best written characters in YA."
~ 5 Star Review

"There are lots of elements I care about in a book to give me the final impression and this one mastered them all. When I finished the story, I was truly amazed."
~ 5 Star Review

"Storywise, this is the kind of fantasy adventure story that doesn't waste time on backstory, but just pulls you along for the ride."
~ 5 Star Review

"There are a lot of great moments and details in this book and I highly recommend to any avid/YA fiction reader, strong/independent/smart/athletic female protagonists, diverse and relatable book seeker out there."
~ 5 Star Review

"Oh man, it's one of the best books I've read this year! SO GOOD. Can't wait for more."
~ 5 Star Review

THE MARK OF NOBA

G. L. TOMAS

First paperback edition August 2015
Second paperback edition November 2016

Cover by Najla Qamber Designs
Line editing by R.A. Weston
Copyediting by Novel Ninjitsu
Interior Design by JT Formatting

Library of Congress Cataloguing-in-Publication Data is available

ISBN-13: 978-1-943773-34-3

To discover current and future publications by
Rebellious Valkyrie Press, check out our official website
(http://gltomas.net/)! If you want awesome book recommendations, or
just want to talk books, join us on our review sites Twinja Book Reviews (http://twinjabookreviews.blogspot.com/) or Rebellious Cupid
Book Reviews (http://rebelliouscupidbookreviews.blogspot.com/)!

To those who wish to become their own stars.
Never forget to shine bright.

CHAPTER 1

Sterling

The ride home was…eh, *almost* quiet. It was always tough muffling the sounds of a crazy night, when the neighborhood you called home was sound asleep with no sign of life but the blinking streetlights. Kip lowered the volume on his blaring music, as he always did when we were approaching my house. Didn't want to hear it from the neighbors.

"Hey," I called from the backseat. "Let me out right here."

He turned back to give me the look that said he thought I was nuts. "Dude, are you sure? It's like six blocks away. I don't mind driving up a few extra streets."

"Yeah, what's the big deal anyway? It's not like your folks have heightened vision or something," said Grey. Grey never rode in the backseat of Kip's car, not since this one time he sat in something he'd rather not admit to. It was the backseat of a car. The backseat of *Kip*'s car. It was to be expected. Since then, Grey always rode shotgun. *Always.*

"What's two blocks, man?" Grey said. It was tempting to take them up on the offer, but I couldn't risk getting sloppy. It was five weeks into the school year, and I couldn't afford to be careless. Not with all my social privileges on the line. It wouldn't kill me to walk up a few blocks.

I'd made a promise to myself this summer. To be my own entity. To not be lost in my best friends' shadows. My first three years of high school, I hadn't done anything remotely relevant or memorable. I was always that kid that Kip Matherstein hangs out with. Or Grey Singh's wingman. My goal wasn't to be popular—I just wanted what was left of my high school experience to not feel like a complete waste. If that meant sneaking out five times since the start of the school year to hit up a few parties, well then, dammit, I had to.

With all the back and forth debate we'd engaged in, I was four blocks away from my street.

Way too close.

"You guys, I'm serious. Let me out!"

Kip groaned before finally pulling over. It was close enough that I could endure the brisk night air but far enough for my parents not to hear a car running. *Perfect.* I hopped out onto the sidewalk, and Kip made a U-turn, driving in the opposite direction. His car lights flicked on when he reached the end of the street, my cue to start walking. My intended destination: home.

The part of *City* where I lived was pretty domestic. Your typical quiet residential neighborhood, where during the day you purposely avoided your neighbors and at night it was so dead you had to wonder if the symphony of crickets that plagued other regions, like *Borough* and *Province*, skipped our sector of *City* altogether. That made sneaking out the house ten times more difficult. It also convinced me that either my folks were slipping in the patrol department or I was getting damn good at sneaking out. The walk home was easy. The getting back in … that was the hard part.

A buzzing vibration went off in my pocket. My cell. There were a few text messages from various people—Kip, Grey, and some others from school—but the only one I opened was from Waverly. Waverly was pretty much the only girl I'd ever wanted since junior high. It wasn't like I didn't date other girls—I did—but none that came close to how I felt about Waverly.

It was heading into creep territory, but I never deleted any of her texts. Even if they only said *Crappy Party >_<*, like it did tonight. The crappy thing about going to parties of people you didn't know was you couldn't count on them to, y'know, not suck. Part of my grand plan was to go to every social event I managed to hear about, even the ones not worth bringing up the next day at school.

What could I text back that would sound smooth and suave? I started to type, *Yeah, I know*, but before I could finish, a hard force slammed me to the ground. Something—no, *someone.*

He wore a pair of baggy sweats and a shapeless hoodie and scrambled back away from me when I reached for my phone on the ground (*kind of glad I bought that phone cover*).

His hood fell back, and what I assumed was a he was actually a she.

Dark hair, dark skin, dark eyes. Familiar. She went to my school.

"Here, let me help you," I stood up and held out my hand to help her, but she sat there motionless. Her eyes were focused on my wrist, the home of my bizarre, odd-shaped birthmark. It must have freaked her out because she didn't take my hand. I pulled down the sleeve of my shirt as she stood, apologized, and took off into the night. It was late for a girl to be going out for a midnight jog, but this sector of *City* was, as I mentioned before, ordinary.

Nothing ever happened in *City*. Hell, nothing ever happened in *Province, Borough,* or *Suburb*, the regions that neighbored *City*. If I managed to pull my grades up to get into a decent school, I would move somewhere cooler like *Megalopolis, Geo*'s capitol. Or somewhere where girls walked around like it was spring break all the time, like *Seaside*. Now that sounded like a plan.

When I'd made it to my house, I was careful to stick to the side to get lost in the shadows. It was dark, but you never knew who might be up. Just because our neighbors avoided each other didn't mean they didn't gossip. All it would take was a quick "Guess what I saw *your* son doing last night" to open and close a conversation that would lead to my ruin and I couldn't have that after making it this far.

There was a tree that grew outside my bedroom window. Its limbs were long and sturdy, making climbing in and out a simple task. I knew better than to walk in the front door. If there was a foolproof way *not* to get myself caught, my bedroom window was it.

I made it to the branch that sprouted close to my window, attempting to open it slow and with great caution. Another successful breakout.

The light flicked on as I was halfway through my doggy door. My foot slipped on something plastic—probably some leftover plates of food—And I was down on the floor in a pile of DVDs and mixtapes, faced with 135 pounds (or was it 145?) of angry mom.

She pressed hard on my chest with her foot, wearing an expression that could only be described as a woman's fury.

"Sterling Wayfairer, you, my friend, are in a *whole* lot of trouble."

When my mom was pissed, her auburn hair exploded like a volcano erupting around her and her eyes glowed like a pair of scary blue marbles. Was it even possible for someone's irises to grow bigger and consume the entire pupil? If not, my mom was having some scary, screwed-up, sci-fi episode. I tried to come up with a lie creative enough that my mom would actually believe me. Not that it would matter—when she was this mad, she saw right through my bullshit.

"Sterling, do you even understand the severity of this situation?"

I guess I kind of did.

"Do you realize what time it is?"

Of course I knew what time it was. Why did she think I was climbing in through the window?

"Mom, if you just let me explain—"

She cut me off, repeating the words "Let you explain?" no less than 10 times, her face contorting in a variety of pissed-off expressions.

"It is one-thirty in the morning on a school night. What is there to explain? This is just ... You are just—*urgh*—*unbelievable*!"

If my mom wanted to get technical, I'd gotten back at one. But she'd spent the past half hour pacing around barefoot in her bathrobe, rambling profanities with the constant repeat of *"you haven't earned it"* and *"so irresponsible."* I knew when my dad heard about it, one thirty would suddenly become two.

She went into her go-to argument that I could recite verbatim. "Sterling, how hard is it for you to not break curfew? You can't just come and go as you please. We have rules, Sterling, we have rules."

So the need to defend my honor kicks in right about ... now. "Mom, I wouldn't have to sneak out if I didn't have such a ridiculous curfew. Ten on weekdays, eleven thirty on weekends. What am I—fourteen?" Maybe it was immature of me, but my argument harbored some truth. I would be eighteen by the end of the school year, but my folks treated me like a five-year-old.

"Well, maybe I'd stop treating you like a kid if your weekly progress reports from school didn't make me want to pull my hair out. You're already averaging somewhere between a high D and a low C. How is that even possible so early in the year? Feel free to jump in any time, Sterling."

I couldn't. Aside from chemistry, I was doing wasn't exactly a model student. I even almost stayed back last year. If it hadn't been for summer school, I probably would have. These days, I always had so much on my mind that school was never a top priority. But it wasn't like I didn't want it to be.

"Are you even listening to me?"

It had come to my attention that my mom was still talking. Most likely planning out every possible way to make my next punishment severe enough to make me feel it for weeks. It went like this.

Grounded for two weeks. *I could've done worse.*

No Grey or Kip over unless it was to study. *Yeah, like that would happen.*

Absolute kitchen, lawn, and laundry duty for the remainder of my sentence. *Shit.*

And after I got home, I had to turn in every electronic device that kept me close to society. My cell, my laptop, my tablet. How prehistoric. I threw myself face-first on my bed, not bothering to take my clothes off.

"Ugh, Mom, I'm really tired. Can I just go to bed now?"

She didn't argue, making her way to the door, but she turned on her heels to add one more thing.

"I know you think I'm being unfair, but we don't set rules to solely inconvenience you. We set rules to make you more responsible and to keep you safe. You don't know how lucky you are to be sitting here having this conversation with me." The anger left my mom's voice for the first time tonight, her overbearing tone now replaced by a delicate exchange of words.

"Over the summer, a kid from one of the *Megalopolis* high schools went missing, and just earlier today, some parents went public that their son also went missing two days ago. He goes to your school. Neither one has yet to be found. Can you imagine the hell their parents are going through? I don't know what I'd do if anything like that ever happened to you."

As strange as it sounded, this was the version of my mom that I loved. That I preferred. She was a bit of a hothead, but…she recognized me. Knew me. There were a lot of days out the year that my mom couldn't remember who I was and had to be reminded that I was her son. That was the version of my mom I feared. I flipped over to face her, but she had already flicked off my light, headed for her bedroom. There was nothing left for me to do but go to sleep.

CHAPTER 2

My phone on the nightstand woke me up. Mom must've left it. I knew I'd only have it for the school day, but I was glad to have it back. I texted Grey and Kip a quick, *Got caught. Grounded 2 weeks,* then got up to take a shower. I got back to my phone flooded with notifications of tagged pictures of me on my timeline. *Who the hell took these?* I regretted that keg challenge this morning. I looked like crap.

My wheat-colored hair was just two months' shy of needing a haircut and my eyes? They were the only thing I ever got complimented on. To me they always looked ordinary, but girls seemed to be fascinated by the dark ring where my iris and pupil met. They were blue, but the central heterochromia made them look freakish in a good kind of way. I was sort of pale, so I looked like a ghost in photographs. Man, I hated when my friends tagged me in pictures.

I told Grey to meet me at the train stop around 7:15, but I should've said 7:25. It was a seven-minute bus ride, plus a four-minute walk to reach *City* Center, where we met up to take the train to school. Grey lived in *Borough*, a metro region, so it was rare when he took the bus. Even when I was running late, he'd wait until 7:35 so we could ride together.

It wasn't hard to spot Grey in a crowd. While everyone ran rampant to get to their next train, Grey was always too immersed in a comic book to pay anyone any mind.

Grey had finally gotten his latest prize: the most recent edition of Allan Hightower's A World Unknown series. It was a science fiction entertainment franchise about aliens that came from the planet *Denom*, settling in the *Geotic* modern world and adapting to our way of life or I don't know; something like that. He'd waited in line for two days for that copy. I should know—he'd guilt-tripped both Kip and me into going for team morale.

Grey Singh was what you might call a hopeless "*Denominator*." It was a nickname given to any lost soul who fell for the far-fetched storylines and second-rate acting. I didn't care exactly—I wasn't a fan. But Grey, he lived and died for this series.

Grey possessed big dark eyes and long thick hair most girls went nuts over. With his even toned brown skin, he was the only guy I knew who could pull off facial hair and still manage to look seventeen.

He was the main striker on our school's football team (the only team that mattered at our school, City Collegiate Institute). He should've been swimming in girls, but if there was any reason Grey would be labeled un-dateable to anyone other than underclassmen for the rest of the school year, this little *A World Unknown* obsession would be it.

That wasn't fair. He was also a conspiracy theorist with no job or car, and I'd come to learn that no girl would put up with one without the other. That, in *addition* to his obsession, would be why he would stay single.

He stood up, after securing his baby in seal-protected plastic. "What a ride, man. What a ride," he said, placing it in his bag. "Hey, sorry about last night. Did you really get grounded for two weeks?"

I nodded. Words made the punishment hurt more and I didn't want to talk about it. My friends rarely understood my pain. Grey came from a family of eight, and while his older brother and sister were away for work and school, he was the eldest of the remaining five. Because he was the eldest and his folks were huge football fanatics, he was never plagued with this thing called a curfew.

My buddy Kip? Well, he was a different situation altogether.

The train pulled up to the station, and like always, it was packed with people. Nothing like the morning commute to remind me why I needed a car and my license like yesterday.

When we got to school, Kip was parked in his usual spot, the space we met every morning. He rolled down his window, drinking what looked like ten of the nastiest foods I'd ever seen disguised as a smoothie. Kip was one of those guys whose life was dominated by sports. He always experimented with foods rumored to improve performance, no matter how disgusting. And he'd already mentioned that it was football/baseball/rugby season at least thirty-two times this semester.

"Sorry about last night, man. That party was way too whack to do time over. Dude, I'm surprised your mom caught you." Kip was like me, an only child. The difference was that his folks had money. I wouldn't be surprised if his car cost as much as two teachers' salaries combined. I'd only met his folks one time. You couldn't have a curfew if your folks were always out of town.

Kip Matherstein was what I referred to as one of the Golden Ones. A transfer student from *Suburb,* he was popular the second he stepped foot in CCI. He was actually kind of smart and played nearly every sport known to man, and he wouldn't deny that he was a little bit of a pretty boy.

Kip was naturally tan, and shared the same black eyes as Grey did. What separated Kip from Grey and me was confidence. He had a natural presence, and managed to date almost every hot girl to go here in the past four years.

Grey and Kip were teammates. Had been for the past six years, even before high school when they ended up playing for the same district in the junior league. But they weren't friends until sophomore year. Kip stuck to his crowd, the popular crowd. The Golden Ones.

Grey rejected the need to be popular and stayed loyal to me even when he secured the main striker spot. Some people looked at Grey and me as and wondered why Kip was even friends with us.

It happened a few years ago. I was at a grocery store with my mom, and she was having a few…*issues*. She suffers from residual schizophrenia. Most of the time she's fine, but when she's not, she isn't always easy to handle. I was mortified when I ran into Kip Matherstein, who I was sure would rag on me. Instead, he spent the next twenty minutes helping me calm her down.

The next day at school, he sat down with Grey and me at lunch and stuck around ever since. I found out later that his grandmother, Zulay, suffered from a severe case of dementia before passing a few years ago. We didn't exchange war stories, but I knew the real reason we were friends. We separated Kip, the person, from Kip, the Golden One.

There wasn't a time we didn't give each other shit, but I couldn't imagine having better friends than Grey and Kip.

When the bell rang, the lower classmen raced to their classes. We seniors knew better. We all took full advantage of the six-minute grace period we were allowed before we were late for a class. We'd spent the last four years wasting away in this prison; we were entitled to a measly six minutes.

"Hey, did you hear what happened the other day?" I heard a girl speaking beside me. "My parents talked about it all morning. Did anyone know him?" It was Waverly. That voice. I'd know that voice anywhere.

What could I tell you about Waverly Matherstein? (*Yeah, you read right. She just so happened to be Kip's cousin.*) We've gone to school together since the third grade. We managed to remain cool with each other over the years, until she took an interest in sports, and her circle of friends shifted into the Golden Ones. Nothing about her changed, but it made it harder to stay connected. One of the perks of Waverly and Kip being related was that Waverly was the one girl Kip *couldn't* date. And it provided me a way back into her inner circle.

"Yeah, my mom was talking about it last night. Tristan Sorensen, right? I think he was a sophomore" I said. I didn't actually know much about the situation, but I jumped at any chance to talk to Waverly. Even if it was to discuss a tragedy.

Since freshman year she had dyed her dark brown hair a vivid red in an effort to stand out in a sea full of blondes and brunettes. I could never figure out why she wore makeup when her face was flawless with or without it, but I did notice that when she did, it made her hooded eyes appear wider and a tad more dramatic. Either way, she always looked smokin'.

The final bell rang, a sign to disperse and get to our first classes. Although I dreaded school with a passion, under the current circumstances I'd rather be here than at home.

The morning announcements were centered on the kid who went missing from our school. He was a sophomore so I didn't know him, but I still felt horrible. My tablemate Rebel Lee scribbled down an array of unintelligible notes, probably both profound and meaningful. Rebel was someone else I've known since junior high, and even though we were pals, he didn't talk much. Which was odd because he seemed to be understood by everyone. *Correction.* Everyone except Grey.

A sea of sorrow surrounded my classmates. No one was in the state of mind to be here, and the cheerless announcements added to our already despondent moods. Man, I really hoped they found this kid.

The teachers opened up the floor to talk about the situation, prolonging any collections of homework assignments that I *didn't* do. The more others talked about it, the lower our spirits got. Why didn't anyone have any more information on what had happened? Was it connected to the other boy who disappeared? Did they run away? Were they abducted? Were they going to be all right? Thinking back to what my mom said earlier, I *was* lucky to be sitting here. I listened, but didn't contribute. I had too much on my mind.

My attention drifted across the room until I settled on someone I hadn't noticed at the beginning of class. She wore her hair in a high, messy bun and had on gray sneakers with three blue stripes. She felt familiar. Did I say felt familiar? I meant *looked* familiar. Looked. *Because how does someone feel familiar?*

She had this faultless dark brown skin that made me question how no one else seemed to notice her. Judging by her face alone, she was one of the prettier girls at school. She didn't seem interested in the discussion we were having in class, and she, like me, faded into the background. I'd never given it much thought before but...I always kind of looked for her. There was just something about her...

CHAPTER 3

"Sterling Wayfairer? Would you please come to the principal's office?" I heard my name over the intercom announce. I grabbed my bag, heading toward the door.

There was a pop quiz, so half my classmates burned a hole through my skull as I walked by. It wasn't my fault I was being called to the principal's office. Something must've happened. Kip waited for me at the door of his class. He faked a smile and gave his usual thumbs-up, his way of wishing me luck. I would need it.

I should've been accustom to this kind of thing by now. I had to wonder what it would be this time. Did Mom break all the windows again? Dad would struggle replacing them on his own. My parents shared a car, so she didn't drive. Last time she attempted to drive during an episode, she'd totaled a neighbor's car. Since then, every time the person two houses down catches my mother behind the wheel, we can expect a police report to follow. It doesn't carry much weight since Mom's license got reinstated, but still.

There was no way of knowing what might've happened. I only knew that if I was being called to the office, then something was wrong.

When I reached the office, the vice principal led me to one of the old rotary phones on the secretary's desk so I could call my dad. I looked around the room as I waited for him to answer, and recognized two students sitting at the round table on the opposite side of the room.

Douglas Glover, who I knew through Kip and Grey. He was attractive, popular, and a rarity amongst the jocks because he was also gifted academically. We weren't the best of friends, but we got along well. He was one of the few guys on the football team who'd ever acknowledged me. None of them bothered to remember my name. We hung out a lot, because of Kip and Grey, so I knew he could be a total buzzkill sometimes. He cared about keeping his marks high and spread his time so far out, he never had time to get drunk or stay out all night, especially if he had a game or test the next day. He was also Treasurer of the Student Council. The student body's budget was in good hands with him, another trait of his that was annoying. *Being trustworthy.*

The girl who sat next to him was Margaret Alvarez. She was recording secretary on CCI's Student Council, in charge of council meetings and contacts, which seemed appropriate for her. She was also popular and an athlete, so she was great at making students enthusiastic about school-related events. Did I forget to mention she was Waverly's best friend? They were inseparable, so any chance she had to remind me how basic I was, *she did*.

Margaret was cute, but she wasn't my type. Like me, she was pale, but had raven hair, dark eyes, and a face full of freckles that orbited across her nose and cheeks when she scowled at you. Which was a whole hell of a lot.

They must've been waiting for the Humphries twins for their meeting. Both of them provided distractions as I waited for Dad to pick up his phone.

"Dad?" I tried to sound detached and withdrawn.

He sighed in relief when he recognized my voice. "Kiddo? Why didn't you call me from your cell?"

I rolled my eyes. "Not allowed to use it at school, remember?"

Dad was sure to be nodding on the other line, followed by an "Oh yeah." Everything that followed was pretty routine. He was on his way to pick me up. We were going to the hospital.

The car ride was quiet. It always was. Dad and I didn't talk about Mom's schizophrenia. Part of his way of dealing with it was ignoring it until something happened. I wish it were that easy for me.

What would he do without me? He didn't handle Mom when she struggled. He didn't have the detailed knowledge of her mental health. It was always me.

Don't get me wrong. I didn't blame my dad for not doing more. He worked full time since Mom had stopped working, so I wasn't ungrateful. But I went to school for the same parts of the day, and the problem didn't fix itself by the time I got home. If something was wrong, it was up to me to get Mom through it, often without help. Sometimes I just wanted a break from everything, too.

We were briefed on her condition once we reached the psych ward. Dad had no idea, so I let the doc know the Zyprexa she'd taken in the past helped her more than her current medication, Lurasidone. It made her gain weight, and she refused to take it.

She hadn't been taking her medications for two weeks, which explained her episodes lately. Mom didn't hate taking the pills if they helped her cope easier from day to day, but she didn't like how the recent ones made her feel. She wouldn't take them if she didn't want to. I didn't appreciate the evil eye the doctor gave us upon writing out a new prescription.

I was sure a doctor's life goal at one point was to help people. It was a shame that dealing with so many patients desensitized them from actually giving a crap. People with nueroatypical disorders never got the treatment or attention they deserved. Hospitals should use the tagline: "Once we fill the prescriptions, you're on your own."

We were in for a long night.

Mom surrendered to the couch once we got home. Her eyes and nose were red from non-stop crying and sniffling. That was normal. She'd spent an entire car ride apologizing for things beyond her control.

Dad told her it was okay, prompting her to stop talking. He wasn't always home when she broke down. He volunteered for kitchen duty, to make hot tea or soup or whatever it was that he wanted Mom to down her medication with.

I raided the kitchen before booking. I was afraid Dad would ask for help. She was my mom, but she was still his wife. We both cut our days short and made sacrifices. Only I was often the one doing all the sacrificing. Just once, he should have to deal with what I had to. I did feel bad. It sucked that Mom was on the couch crying all afternoon, but it was Dad's turn.

Flames danced all around me. Black smog painted the sky grey while smoke invaded my lungs. Peppery shards of ash fell down to litter the ground.

People are running. No ... some are running. Others are fighting. Go further?

No!

A shiver crept through my entire body. I jolted up, soaked in my own sweat. I must've fallen asleep. The clock on my nightstand read 2:36 a.m. *Great.* I hadn't finished any homework. Not that my method of attempting to finish it just before actual class hadn't been working.

With all the madness earlier, my parents hadn't confiscated my phone. I reached for it. The battery had twenty-seven percent left, and I'd gotten nine new messages. Two were from

Grey. One from *City*'s BBQ Grill asking me to confirm my text subscription. Five from Kip. Oh? One from Waverly?

You alrite? o_0

I typed and deleted my original message multiple times before I settled on a simple *"Yup."* I'd text something longer in the morning; right now, she was probably sleeping.

I opened Kip's messages next. Half of them asked me what happened and was I okay. The other two? Heads up that Waves would text me. I knew I should have opened his messages first.

Sometimes I hated that my dream girl was my best friend's cousin. They were the kind of cousins who, because they didn't have siblings, compensated for that with each other. He told Waverly freaking everything. I'd text something longer in the morning; right now she was probably sleeping.

I was tired, but too spooked to go back to bed. My dreams were so vivid lately. I'd wake up assuming my dreams had actually happened, and there were times where I was downright scared of what my mind would make up. It was like I was losing it.

And it was only whenever I'd dream about…the burning forest.

It gave me a bad feeling. Not because of what I dreamt but how real it was afterward. There was always a tear, a scar, in the middle of a gray sky, and yesterday marked the first day I saw it even when I was awake.

CHAPTER 4

My day wasn't off to a good start. I was up earlier than usual, clothes conveniently laid out on random spots on the floor. I prayed that the bathroom door wouldn't be locked when I turned the knob.

Locked.

I didn't have time for this and couldn't miss another day of school. Knocking once with no response, I leaned my ear to the door.

"Mom?" My voice didn't *always* calm her down, but sometimes hearing me calm was the first step to comforting her. "Come on, Mom. This isn't funny. I have to get ready. Don't do this to me."

She was in there. Her shaky breathing and muffled sniffles echoing behind the door made that evident. She was crying. There was no way I was getting in there.

Picking up my clothes off the floor, I got dressed and grabbed my stuff. I didn't have time to call Grey to tell him I'd be taking an earlier bus. I needed to get to school before the masses poured in so I could make use of their facilities.

I'd made it to the locker room by 7:17. Not bad on timing. That left me with more than twenty minutes to shower and get ready before the first bell rang for homeroom.

This rarely happened so early in the school year. Waking up to find my mom in a *mood*, rushing to school to get ready. Sometimes I wished my mother didn't suffer so much.

I knew it wasn't my mom, just her mind betraying her, but it was something that took a toll on me. I'd spent most of my adolescence learning to deal with it. I was tired and secretly resentful. Most seventeen-year-olds had going off to college and moving out to look forward to. I wasn't so sure that was in my future.

I finished just in time to catch Grey and Kip at our usual spot. Grey met me halfway down the hallway. He'd left me a dozen text messages and called me four times. No wonder he'd come looking for me.

"Dude. This morning. What happened?"

I ran my fingers through my thick, stringy, wet hair. "No big deal. Had to take an earlier bus. Started to call you, but…you know…" Grey nodded. By now, he knew not to question if I'd gotten to school earlier than him. He wasn't exactly the uncomfortable conversation kind of guy.

Despite the day getting off to a rough start, the time between homeroom and fifth period flew by. Things were finally looking up…until PE.

It'd been an event that had been postponed because of the 2nd disappearance, but the fitness test could be put off no longer.

I tried to slow the clock in the locker room, but believe it or not, changing slower did not help. A sense of relief washed through me at the sight of my friends. Hearing their petty argument always took my mind off things. *Temporarily*.

"Singh? Why the hell is that smell coming from *your* locker?"

Grey's mouth turned into a grin between pride and arrogance—you could never tell with Grey. "Lucky football socks, bro. Haven't washed them in, like, two years. Coincidence? I think not."

Grey's locker definitely reeked of something beyond anything *Geotically* produced.

"Ugh! No wonder we've been winning. No one'll go near you. Those smell like my dead grandpa!" Kip said.

Grey laced up his sneakers, not appearing the least bit affected.

"We win because I score goals," Grey said with conceited smile. Kip reached over to hit him, but Grey moved quicker. He was the main striker for a reason. Kip parked it next to me, giving me a rough pat on the shoulder.

"So is today the day you're finally going to impress Waves?" he asked. By asking, he was being completely sarcastic and annoying.

"Shut up, Kip."

Kip shrugged. "What? I mean, you're going to do better than last year, right? Didn't you start working out?"

Having two athletic best friends reminded me every day that recreation wasn't my calling. I'd skated through the physical fitness test with excuses two years in a row. Between doctor's notes and early dismissals to tend to a sick mother, I'd been in the clear. Last year, I ran out of excuses. I finally had to face my fear. *The result?* I couldn't run a mile without passing out.

Incorporating fitness in my life became a necessity after that. Not to compete with my friends or to impress girls. It became a new distraction. Something to do when home wasn't an option.

My poison of choice was swimming. It was free, I could do it after school, and I didn't even need to be a pro to do it. It was better than jogging, my second choice, but there was only one track at school and Waverly was usually on it. The last thing I needed was for Waverly to see how out of shape I was.

I didn't lift weights, which explained my lanky frame, but when the weather was good, the trails in *Woodlands* made for a great workout. Although, because of the multiple bus trips it took to get there, it wasn't an everyday option.

"Don't think I'm impressing a track star anytime soon," I said.

"Sterling, you've had so many chances with Waverly. Starting to think it's me you got that crush on, Wayfairer."

I laughed under my breath, middle finger soon following. "You wish."

I always had this fear that Kip would be one of those guys who took you to the side with the whole stay-away-from-my-cousin lecture. Yeah, never happened. Kip was protective of his cousin, but she was the type of girl who made decisions for herself. In other words, he had no real influence on who she could date.

"Why do you care, Matherstein? Are you a matchmaker now?" Grey said.

Kip threw a jockstrap at Grey before standing. "Singh, this is why no one talks to you about girls. You suck as a wingman; therefore, you suck with girls. Sterling sucks with girls, but at least he makes me look better."

"Eat me, Kip."

Kip wasn't one hundred percent wrong about me, but he was totally wrong about Grey. Maybe he wasn't the best wingman, but girls liked him, just not his interests. Grey was too picky, he liked to have conversations that transcended reality television and mall visits, but at CCI, that was all girls cared about.

The beloved fitness test. *We meet again.*

Let me be clear. I've always hated PE. All it did was separate the dexterously gifted from the rest of us.

Maybe some jocks were cool. My friends were. Sometimes even Marge. But the beginning of the year fitness test brought out the blockhead in everyone. Especially the athletes.

Every year we were tested on three things: cardiovascular endurance, flexibility, and strength. Margaret and Waves often always took the first one the most seriously. I wish I could call them arrogant, but they were very much the "Kip and Grey" of the track team. Translation: CCI actually started winning when they joined the track team.

I paced myself for a smooth run. I saw both the girls go by me twice before I went around once, but I was grateful I didn't collapse. Many didn't have the same urgency to finish as fast as Marge and Waves, but we were so busy in our own worlds, we didn't notice someone else had actually placed before them.

With the senior class, that didn't happen. No one ever outran Waverly.

It was that new girl.

Until today, she'd never shown any strong signs of athletic ability. Margaret shot her an evil eye, and everyone seemed to have something to say about her. I didn't. All I cared about was that I did better than last year. My mile run had clocked in at eight minutes and nine seconds. Not too shabby. For me, at least.

Flexibility is kind of a given for most the girls. Not to say guys aren't flexible, but at five foot ten and mostly leg, touching my toes was a long way to go for me. It sucked stretching the muscle *after* you'd done the work. I was glad to get it over with.

Until the strength test. CCI didn't have a sane PE teacher (who ironically was also the football coach), therefore we didn't have a sane fitness curriculum. Mr. Ruiz believed in pushing us to our limits. We could've lifted weights to see how long it took the individual to cry uncle, but no, our measurement of strength had to be the most obnoxious, most difficult, nearly-impossible-to-be-good-at activity of them all.

A rope climb challenge.

Mr. Ruiz demonstrated several different climbs. A basic climb, which consisted of grouping one hand directly after the other. *Easy enough.* There were even five ropes, so anyone who wanted to volunteer could get theirs over with.

Doug, Margaret, and Kip fought each other on who would make it to the top first. I was just praying not to fall.

The first climb wasn't so bad, considering we were allowed to use our legs. I was a slow climber, but my pace was steady and careful.

"Go, Sterling!"

Was I hearing that correctly? That *sounded* like Waverly. Cheering me on. Kip was in the background, clapping and boosting me to go forward. *Yeah, I could do this.*

"Fall, you loser!"

And like that, the moment was gone. I'd have to remember to thank Marge and Grey later for that. I wasn't sure if Waves was psyching me up on her own accord or because of Kip. It didn't matter; the high felt too good to fail.

The second climb was *waaaay* more challenging. Same as the first, only we couldn't use our legs. I volunteered to be one of the first to get it over with. Margaret volunteered, too, along with two students I didn't know very well. Including that new girl. As luck would have it, she positioned right next to me.

I thought she'd be taller, but close up she only came up to my neck. She shook out her arms, and when the whistle blew, she waited. I braced myself and attempted the climb.

Without the use of my legs, it was much harder. If I rushed it, I'd fall. I was only halfway up when I noticed the empty rope next to me come alive. You know new girl? She moved quicker than a flame on an oil-stained curtain.

She distracted me. Not because she was faster, but because she looked at me. I mean, really *looked* at me. Her dark, glassy eyes were so mesmerizing, the world stopped mattering and nothing else was worth worrying about. I didn't even notice when I let go of the rope.

The sharp yank on my wrist finally woke me back up. There was a struggle above me. The new girl—she was trying to hold onto me.

"Wayfairer, you crazy?!" By now, my friends' faces screamed worry and fear. I was too busy swearing and spurting obscenities—y'know, the only thing one could do while dangling twenty feet in the air.

"Wayfairer, don't look down!" Kip yelled at me.

"Why the hell would you tell me not to look down? It's just going to make me look down!" I screamed back.

"Reach for the rope, Sterling!" Grey shouted.

It seemed so far away. I couldn't expect her to hold onto me forever. The girl performed a dyno in an effort to help me back to my own rope. After I took hold, I admitted defeat. Screw proper technique. I climbed down, grateful to feel solid ground beneath my feet again.

Grey patted me on the shoulder, crawling in closer to me and whispered, "Hey, Ster, who is that girl?" We watched as she restarted her climb, making it all the way to the top.

I motioned but couldn't say anything. Outside of our classes, I didn't know her. Not really.

The last climb wasn't a requirement, so didn't get a lot of volunteers. Hmm, *I wonder why?* Maybe because it required a ballistic pull-up method?

The ballistic method required two ropes and a method of pulling yourself up with both arms, letting go, and grabbing the rope before falling down. In order to gain height, you had to lose some in the process.

Douglas was the first guinea pig. Even if he couldn't do it, he wanted to try. He pulled himself up twice before giving up. "I can't hold it for that long," he said, before dropping to the floor.

Of course Margaret stepped up to the plate. "You wimps. Does someone really have to show people how it's done?"

After that encouraging outburst, I really hoped she would fall. I wasn't so lucky, but she didn't get far before switching back to the intermediate technique. She reached Douglas's point before slumping down next to Waverly. Grey wasn't a fool, so his butt was glued to the floor, but I knew one of my friends would want to try it.

Kip stood, moving toward the ropes. He gave it a once over, but the fear of letting the rope go quickly garnered an "I can't" before sitting back down.

The new girl stood up. For the other two climbs, she'd worn a sweater that made her look cartoon-like, like that marshmallow dough boy you saw on commercials. Now, she lifted her sweater over her head, and I swear, she was in the best shape ever. Her entire upper body was concrete definition with the sickest abs I'd ever seen. The sweat shone off her physique, making her appear even more defined. She was muscular and feminine at the same time; two things you didn't see very often in seventeen-year-old girls. It was either one or the other but new girl was like…*whoa*.

She picked up two ropes. No one assumed she'd make it any further than CCI's finest, so when she made it all the way up without pause, there wasn't a closed mouth in the room.

Someone tapped my shoulder. Waverly sat at my left, her weight resting on her hand on the floor.

"This is going to sound weird but…do you know that girl?" she asked. I shook my head. I wasn't sure why she was asking me. She leaned over to whisper to Margaret.

What? It wasn't a lie.

I saw the girl all the time, but didn't know her. I couldn't even remember her name. If it were something common, like Amy or Rachel, chances were it had just escaped me. I *did* remember one thing. The new girl always wore the same sneakers. Grey ones, with three blue stripes.

My nickname for her was Girl With the Three-Striped Sneakers, but that was a mouthful. Eventually I'd have to learn her real name.

I was relieved when no one brought up the mishap in PE. By school's end, I'd been abandoned by my friends for football practice. Man, I hated sports. That left me little to do before heading home. I thought about swimming but in my rush to get out the door that morning I hadn't packed for it. The library was another option but eh … I'm a strong believer in homework being for home. What else could I do to avoid going home?

I'd have to face my mom eventually, but not right now.

I roamed the abandoned halls. CCI's hallways were enormous without the mob of students usually present. I used to think I'd never get used to the gray walls and burgundy lockers, but four years in, I was starting to think I'd actually miss them.

City Collegiate Institution was the largest public high school in *Geo*. There were close to four-hundred-and-fifty students in each class. With those kind of numbers, you didn't always know the lower classmen.

"You got somewhere to be? I'm buffing the floors." Our school janitor.

"On my way to the pool." I had no intentions of heading to the pool, but that was none of his business.

"Lousy kids. Always making more work for me."

He murmured something that, during school hours, would have been highly profane, but being that I was the only one there, I ignored it. I didn't dislike the guy, but he was a bit of a prick. It was his life's mission to catch students in the act of doing something scandalous.

I slipped through the corner, entering the West Hall. The West Hall was notorious for its seclusion. Grey'd even nicknamed it the Institute's "Sepulchral Dungeon."

The West Hall had been shut down because of budget cuts. Outside of a few alternative classrooms that were still useable, it only ever officially held afterschool meetings, detention/in-school suspension, though occasionally the students would seek out a private, dark room to make out in with little surveillance.

The vending machines throughout the corridor were broken or empty, but there was one that was widely known to anyone who'd been going here for more than two years that would take any amount equal to a quarter before spitting out the goods.

I'd almost walked by it until I noticed someone standing in front of it. It was a girl. That was clear. She was small, her hair tied into a high bun.

Before I could stop myself, I walked toward her. My feet communicated with my legs before my brain could stop me.

"That machine's broken."

Her reflection was visible to me against the glass. She wore a faraway expression I came to recognize as her go-to glance.

"I should really be thanking you about earlier," I said, rubbing the back of my neck. I bit my lip, hoping I wasn't being a complete doofus. "I'm a little embarrassed. Somehow I got distracted. So um…thanks."

She wasn't in a talking mood, and since that was all I really wanted to say, I thought it wise to make an exit before I made an even bigger ass of myself.

"Wait."

I stopped and we faced one another. She stalked over to me, making my heartbeat increase with every step she took. Our eyes met.

I froze.

I was drowning. Lost in her trance-inducing gaze.

Her name… It was at the tip of my tongue. If I could only reach out for her hand… I'd just…

CHAPTER 5

"Whoa!"

I shot straight up. I was drenched in sweat. Nearly naked, I tossed around a bit, my feet meeting the floor.

I was in my room. In my boxers, like I'd been here all night. 6:22 a.m. My alarm hadn't even gone off yet. That couldn't be right. Last thing I remembered, I was at school… I had to have been.

What had I been doing? Roaming the hallways? Had there been something else?

I edged off my bed, standing, rubbing my eyes. I hadn't taken anything, but I headed toward the mirror to be sure my eyes weren't red. Or black. Drugs were never my thing, but I checked anyway. A black eye would've been completely noticeable on my fair skin.

Nothing out of the ordinary.

Sterling, pull yourself together. It's only been a few hours.

Maybe I'd just been studying. When I couldn't remember stuff, it was something I blamed on studying. Yeah, that was it. *Or was it?*

Even if I'd been studying, it didn't account for not remembering taking the bus home, eating dinner, or showering.

Wait a sec. I bent down and sniffed. *Hmph. Better scratch that shower part off.*

There was still a lot I couldn't account for, though. I tried to remember, but nothing came. Where did those hours go?

Sterling, you're not losing it. Get it together.

I was just on edge. That had to be it. I was failing three classes, my curfew sucked, and I wasn't any closer to getting Waverly to know I was into her. On top of that, I still had to cope with the responsibility of being the carer to a parent in the early stages of schizophrenia.

I rubbed my face and collapsed back in bed. I laughed out loud. Of course I forgot stuff. I was dealing with too much not to. One plus to losing hours I didn't remember? It was the first time in a while that I hadn't had that dream…

I got up for school, preparing myself for the ridicule and banter after the debacle in PE the day prior. I expected snickers and stares behind my back anytime I walked by or into a classroom.

First period? *Nothing.* Third period? *Nothing.* By the time fifth period rolled around, I was sure that any minute now, some blockhead on the football team would crack a sardonic smile the minute I walked into the locker room. But they just carried on the way they normally did. Ignoring me.

No one messed with me, or at least not after sophomore year. Grey wasn't a conventional athlete, but he was still a jock. He was CCI's strongest main striker, so even if his teammates wanted to, they wouldn't rag on him. I didn't exactly have the same immunity but it did help who I was friends with. Before Kip started going to CCI, I'll be the first to admit, I'd gotten stuffed into a locker or two.

Outside of snide remarks or cackling, none of the Golden Ones bothered me. *Much.* Marge bullied everyone, except for Waverly. That was the extent of it though.

I was a senior, so I wasn't on the bottom of the food chain. But that didn't mean I couldn't be a target for ridicule, especially after PE yesterday, so it was weird that not a single person mentioned it.

When PE ended, I saw her. I hadn't thought about it, but up until then, I hadn't seen her all day. Not even in PE. Granted, she wasn't "*new*" new. She'd been attending CCI since the beginning of the school year. But she was one of the few students who'd started at CCI as a senior.

She didn't seem to have any friends. I didn't know anything about her. Maybe she was an athlete at her old school. I didn't know many girls who could hang onto a rope and another person else at the same time.

It was weird, but whenever I thought of her, it was like she knew. She'd look in my direction, and every time she did, my throat would catch fire. Something happened to me. There was a strange sensation to be near her.

Like right now. We were in the hallway, but it was like it was just us. She shot me a sharp expression before she walked into a classroom.

Bam!

I went face-first into a locker. Just great. With my luck, I walked straight into the locker of the last person I wanted to seem like a dork to.

"What do you make a habit of looking like a dweeb, Wayfairer?"

It was Margaret. Waverly stood with her, a passive grin on her face. I knew Marge wouldn't let me go an entire day without ridicule. I rubbed the back of my neck, looking for any sign of the new girl, preparing for the worst.

"She's pretty," Waverly said.

I didn't register the comment. "What?"

Margaret rolled her eyes and glanced over her shoulder. "Oh, come on. She's not that cute."

Waverly laughed and rolled her eyes. "You're hating on her, Marge. She must be pretty."

I let my eyes wander to hide the fact Waves and Marge had caught me ogling her. "I mean, she's cute. If you like odd, silent types. I wasn't really…you know…she's…" I needed a response to save myself. It was only a matter of time before someone brought it up. "Just…after gym class, y'know? I've been looking for an excuse to talk to her. To, I guess, thank her."

Margaret shrugged. "For what?"

As if my answer hadn't been enough. "You know? Yesterday? In PE?"

Waverly smiled, but only her mouth moved. Her eyes didn't match, making it seem forced. Margaret's face distorted in an angry snarl.

"What the hell are you talking about, Sterling?" Margaret asked, more impatient than before.

I squinted, as confused as they were. "You remember? That girl? During the rope climb? That ring a bell?"

This time Waverly and Margaret shrugged.

"Wayfairer, you're weird."

Margaret walked off to her next class. Waverly stayed behind, but I wished she hadn't. There was pity in her eyes; she wasn't the best at hiding it. She reached for my wrist and hesitated.

"Are you doing okay, Ster?" Always concerned. She probably thought I was losing it.

"I'm fine. Thanks for asking," I said with a fake smile. She returned it, then joined Marge halfway down the hallway.

Something was off; I needed a second opinion. And just as I'd put the image of both of my friends in my head, I'd experienced a strong pull, my legs leaving the floor as I felt myself flying backwards. I was moving faster than anything *Geotically* possible, the trail of the lockers moving in a blur in front of me. One minute I was in the hallway, chatting it up with Waverly, the next I was…

…hurled into the table Kip and Grey had reserved during lunch. If they hadn't looked at me with such shock in their eyes, I would've thought what had just happened was only a figment of my imagination. But I knew I hadn't been sitting here the whole time, and the last time I remembered, I was on my way to my fifth-period class.

"Uhhh, where did you come from?" Kip said, taking items out of his thermal lunch bag and placing them on the tray in front of him, one by one. I had half a mind to tell them what I really thought happened, but what was I supposed to say? That I friggin' flew from fifth period to lunch period? I answered the next best way; resorting to lying.

"Ehh, I was just in a rush when I heard they were serving that goat-cheese pizza in the café again. I must have been running so fast, I wasn't looking where I was going."

"Okay, so where is it then?" Grey laughed, referring to my empty hands. Next time you have to sell the lie, try having the product in your hand first.

"Uhh, turns out they ran out. Enough about that though, I wanted to ask you guys something."

It was the perfect opportunity to ask, without the fear of a concerned response. I didn't always see her, but I did *always* remember her. I wanted to make sure other people did, too.

"Hey, Singh, trade my rice pudding for your Jell-O?"

Grey's brow furrowed. Without hesitation, he threw his Jell-O onto Kip's tray and snatched the rice pudding before Kip changed his mind. We knew he wouldn't. Kip always ate clean when he played. Maybe it worked. He was a great second striker. I envied that sports was that "thing" my friends were in on that I wasn't.

I had different reasons why I had two best friends. Grey was a combination of history and plain brotherhood. We'd been friends since the dawn of time, and he didn't try to force unwanted conversation out of me. So we clicked.

Kip on the other hand? He unapologetically forced me to discuss my home life, even when I didn't want to. Grey cared, but I knew he didn't have experience approaching the subject. You'd never know it, but Kip was more of a "feelings" guy. He knew how to manipulate that when it came to getting girls.

Both of them notched numbers I'd never reach in the girl department. I wasn't ashamed or anything, but I'd only had sex once my entire life. And it'd been great. *All five minutes of it.* But I was comfortable in my skin. All that toxic masculinity crap was for the meatheads anyways.

Grey and I weren't on the same wavelength when it came to girls as Kip and I were. There's no way Kip didn't notice the new girl; he never missed a new face.

"Hey, anyone notice that girl in gym class the other day?" I leaned my elbows on the table and checked to ensure no one was listening. Grey and Kip's faces distorted in confusion.

I popped open an extra can of soda Grey had nearby, but didn't take a sip. Everything I was about ask required my complete concentration.

"What girl?" Grey asked.

"You know?" Neither of them caught the hint. "The one from the fitness test? Hot. Dark skinned. Athletic?"

Kip groaned under a muffled laugh and scooped Jell-O from his cup. "I think I would remember a girl with that description."

I studied the cafeteria. It was a good thing lunch period was split between two periods. Fewer people to look through. She wasn't hard to find. She was the only person sitting by herself. That was a form of social suicide, so it must've been by choice. I leaned forward, pointing.

Grey laughed. "What—the new girl?" He shoved a scoop of rice pudding in his mouth. The smell of coconut, cinnamon, and vanilla overwhelmed me. I should've brought something to bargain with Kip. It would've been mine if I had.

"Yeah, if by new, you mean since a couple weeks ago."

Grey dropped his spoon, and met my gaze with dark eyes. "Dude, she just started like yesterday. I think we would've noticed if she'd been going since the start of the year."

Huh?

Kip studied her from a distance. He was never good at hiding when he was attracted to a girl. "She's definitely nice."

I hoped I didn't have to spell it out but I was wrong. There was no way they'd only just noticed her. Surely this was an oversight.

"You don't remember yesterday? During the fitness test? She was the only person who finished the ballistic climb."

That got a reaction out of Kip. He interrupted me, waving his hands. "Hold on, Wayfairer. There wasn't a person in class who finished that climb."

"Uh, *ya-huh.* One person did." *Jocks.* They never let you get away with challenging their loss.

Grey stopped our arguing, hoping to get to the point. "What is this about, Ster?"

"You guys don't remember her from gym?" Kip and Grey shook their heads, denying any claim to the new girl or what happened in class.

Grey laughed and picked up his pudding. "No, that's what I've been trying to tell you. Dude she just started like, yesterday. I think we would've noticed if she'd been here since the start of the year. *Yesterday.* Get a grip, buddy." Grey reached out to shove my shoulder.

"So you guys don't remember her from PE? Or anything?" I asked. I wasn't letting it go. This had started as a friendly inquisition but was turning into a full-fledged debate.

Kip shrugged. "Well, if she's been going here all year, what's her name? Oh, uh, and what's her number too? I might need that come Homecoming." Kip laughed. Neither of us found him funny.

I wanted to answer, but I didn't know it. She didn't speak to anyone, she never handed in assignments, and every person I asked had no idea who she was. It was as if she came to school every day to make sure we'd cross paths and exchange awkward stares.

Something about it now seemed…spooky.

"I don't know. But the fact that none of you remember what happened yesterday weirds me out a little."

Grey pursed his lips and looked over my shoulder. He widened his eyes as he finished off his dessert.

"You know what's spooky?" Grey asked, as my body tensed.

"What?"

"She's staring at you right now. Either she's got supersonic ears or maybe you're right. Maybe she's spooky," Grey joked.

Kip laughed with him as I turned around. Grey wasn't wrong. She was staring right at me. And she *kept* staring. I don't know why, but…

And like before lunch, I was ripped from the table, crash landing into Geo-knows-where this time around.

"Ahhh," I hissed as I found myself slamming front-first into a locker inches away from my last class for the day. I examined the halls and realized I was the only one standing there. Everyone else was most likely already in class. I couldn't explain how I'd gotten here, or if I was just too tired to find myself drifting off to sleep and waking up in the oddest of places.

Wait…what had I been doing before this? With only twenty-two minutes left in class, I was bound to face some sort of trouble for entering class late, but it was better than skipping altogether.

I walked in only to have all eyes on me, including my chem teacher who would most likely tell me after class that a detention was in order for the nearby future. Trying not to make too much of a fuss, I took my seat next to Holly, my lab partner and planned not to make another peep until the last bell rang for the day.

I was disoriented. Holly gave me a strange look, followed by something she mouthed that was either "*Are you okay*?" or "*Pay attention, dumbass.*" Blinking a few times, I got my vision back, but my hearing was off. And my brain.

Hadn't I just been sitting in the school's cafeteria? Grey, Kip, Rebel … No, wait. Not Rebel. That was the day before. Kip and Grey were there. But what was it we were talking about again?

I clicked a pen I hadn't realized I was holding, and caught Holly's attention. This time I got her message loud and clear. Definitely was the second one.

I almost dropped my pen when I looked at my notebook.

Symbols. Or actually, the same symbol, drawn in repetition. A circle with three curved tadpole lines meeting toward the middle. As if they were chasing each other. Why would I be drawing it?

This has happened to me before. Losing hours. Think, Sterling. What did other moments like this have in common with right now?

CHAPTER 6

"Seriously, Sterling, you've been staring into space for five minutes. You're starting to freak me out." Holly's purple glasses had been replaced with disposable safety goggles that made her amber eyes look double their usual size.

"Here, you'd better put these on," she grabbed an identical pair for me from her book bag. She hated using the ones at school. I put them on, awaiting my next instruction and noticed she'd already completed half of the work for me.

"Sorry, Hol," I huffed. "I can't seem to focus today."

Holly mixed vials of liquid and watched the colors blend upon contact. She jotted something down, prompting me to hand her the next sample.

"Sterling, I don't think anyone can focus with what's going on. My mom won't even let me take the bus by myself anymore. It's getting annoying."

Everyone at school was dealing with the disappearances differently. I was scared for my parents, the parents of the missing boys and anyone who knew them. But I dealt with so much already that I didn't join the majority bothered by it constantly. Now I was just making things up in my mind, when all I probably needed was a good full night's rest.

"Sorry you had to start without me," I said, followed by a faint smile. She'd been doing most of the work since the school year started, so I should've been apologizing for the whole semester.

"Someone has to be the brains around here," Holly said, sticking out tongue.

Holly wasn't a cheerleader or athlete and wasn't the girl guys brought up in sleazy locker room conversations, but she was kind of cute in a nerdy, I-have-a-crush-on-my-math-tutor sort of way. She never went to parties so I was curious what she did after school. Something about our laidback attitudes made us click. Plus, she was hella-good at keeping me in check.

"Hey, did you still need help with that lab work?" Holly asked. "Because I'm really pressed for time today. I have to go straight home after school to babysit my little brother." She had this look of worry on her face like she was sad to disappoint me. Holly was the only reason I was passing this class, but I hated that she felt obligated to help me.

"It's fine, Hol, Get out of here. I was going to go swimming anyway. We could go over it during the week."

The last bell rang, and the remaining students cleared out from the chem lab. "Thanks, Sterling. I promise I'll make it up to you, okay?" she said. Holly made good on her promises, so I wasn't worried. Besides I didn't want to spend the last hour at school studying.

I considered trying out for the swim team but couldn't get past the uniforms. Waltzing around in nothing but a Speedo while others laughed and pointed at my pasty chicken legs wasn't on top of my to-do list. Competing would've taken the fun out of it anyway. I swam because it helped me take my mind off everyday life. Making it a competition would only add to my stress.

There was something about being submerged underwater. I didn't worry about test scores or taking care of my mom. Down here, it was just me and the soft, gentle waves of a manmade pool.

Most days, I set goals to see how deep and long I could hold my breath under water. The longest I'd made it was thirty-six seconds. I'd come up breathless and crying for air, but I'd never been more at peace. The idea was to never overexert myself. When I swam up, I didn't take the aggressive strokes, just calm, relaxed movements.

I made my way to the top and timed myself at thirty-one seconds. Not better, but not bad considering the days I took off. I thought it might help to freestyle a bit, to feel as though I'd worked. I didn't brag about it, but it was euphoric to swim a fifty-meter lap in less than a minute. Guess that's what happened when you kept at something. You got better at it. *Who knew?*

At my tenth lap, my lats started burning. Time to take a breather. I was nearing the pool's edge, about to call it quits, when a vacuum-like pull dragged me back under the water, much like the other times when I'd thought I'd dreamed it up.

What on Geo was going on with me? Maybe I still was dreaming.

I swam with war-like effort, but with every stroke, I seemed to sink deeper … deeper …

Don't panic, Sterling, you can do this!

But no matter how hard I went, I'd reach a certain point and get sucked back down. I must be losing sanity points on top of oxygen because the next thing I saw was something I couldn't believe. Shadows of what looked like two people. I was too deep to see features, but it looked like they were fighting…on top of the water.

Torpedoes of water shot toward the pool's surface with violent quickness. There'd been two gusts of waves at the beginning, but now I counted eight at a time.

I had to get up for air and I had to do it *now*! The closer I swam to the top, the stronger the waves became. I was sure I'd surpassed my current record of thirty-six seconds underwater, but that wouldn't mean much if I was dead.

I used whatever strength I had left in me to break through the surface. No use—it was hard like a metal door. I wouldn't be able to break it open, not with my bare hands.

I was going to suffocate. I took one deep exhale. It gave me a few seconds, but my lungs cried for oxygen.

A strong force hit the water. Someone was sinking with me. It was so fast, but seemed like slow motion. I couldn't make out her face, but I reached for her hand. My mouth opened and water flooded my throat, burning into my lungs. I couldn't fight it anymore. At least I wouldn't die alone.

I woke, coughing up streams of pool water, fighting to get off my back. Crap—how did I get here? The last thing I remembered was being underwater and then … Damn it! Why couldn't I remember?

I stood up to find myself wearing no more than my swim trunks, so I had to have been swimming, right? I walked to the boys' locker room, eager to get into some dry clothes. There was a message painted on the entrance in a black, sticky substance.

I wouldn't go in there if I were you

I froze in place. I knew they were just words, but something wasn't right. I powered through my fear, as curiosity willed for me to touch them. I pulled away the moment I did. Whatever the words were written in, it burned. It was official—there was no fucking way I was going in that locker room, soaking wet or not.

I was so spooked I didn't notice someone walking up behind until they crashed into me.

The school janitor. The one who hated nearly every kid that went here. He surveyed the writing, then me, furious. It dawned on me that my hands were covered in the crap on the wall.

Great. As if today couldn't get any worse.

CHAPTER 7

"THREE MONTHS? That's completely unfair!"

It was way past dinnertime, but my parents and I had been arguing since that afternoon. Why was I being punished for something I *didn't* do? It didn't make sense.

Sure, I'd been there. There were things about those oh-so-short moments that I couldn't explain. But I hadn't lied about anything. By the time I'd gotten there, the doors were already vandalized. It was a wrong-place, wrong-time situation, and I was being chastised by my parents about whether three months of grounding was enough.

"Two thousand dollars, Sterling. Do you know much damage that is?" Mom said, rubbing her left temple like she was the most stressed. Dad just sat there, arms stretched out over the couch. As useless as ever.

"Sterling, you're getting suspended from school for an entire week. It's a wonder they didn't expel you. So no, I don't think being grounded for three months is unfair."

Pacing in a nervous panic didn't help. What bothered me most was that I couldn't tell the part of the story that mattered. Telling that part of the story would mean…

"I can't believe that, of all things, I'm getting blamed for something I didn't do."

"Sterling, you sneak in and out of this house. Your grades are *laughable*. And you have the nerve to raise your voice at me? Everything you've done has earned this three months. Get your act together and grow up!"

I pulled at my hair. I was in trouble either way, but seriously? Mom was telling *me* to grow up.

"You guys are ruining my life! I swear, you are the worst parents in the world."

Dad sat up for the first time in the argument. "That's enough, Sterling. We don't do things to make your life harder. You do that on your own."

Mom started going on about personal accountability and responsibility. Anger and frustration burrowed its way into my psyche. Even when I wasn't to blame, things were still my fault. I was drained, confused, and a mental wreck. I wanted to stop myself, but the words just came out.

"Well, I wouldn't have to do all that stuff if you weren't so fucking crazy!"

The room fell silent. I regretted the words the moment they left my mouth. There wasn't enough damage control in the world that would take them back.

"Mom, I'm—"

"Go to your room."

A lump in my throat prevented me from speaking. That was the *one* word we didn't use in our house.

"I didn't—"

"I said go!"

I'd broken the unspoken rule in my house.

Don't call Mom crazy. That was the *one* word we didn't use in our house.

I hadn't meant it literally—I was angry. Angry for not hearing a thank you or a sorry for all the sacrifices I made. I didn't expect a parade. A simple *"Thanks, kiddo"* would do. I knew I wasn't the perfect son. But was *there*. I tried. I sacrificed.

I wished sometimes, just once, I'd get a break thrown my way. For someone to be in my corner.

A knock came at the door. I sank my face down into my pillow. The door opened, and I prepared myself for an early grave.

"Ready for your conjugal visit?"

The side of my mattress caved and I raised my head. With all that had happened, I was surprised my parents even let Grey and Kip inside the house, let alone my room.

"What are you guys doing here?" I asked.

Kip sat at the desk station I *didn't* use and tossed a football in the air. Grey caught it as Kip threw it toward my head.

"Dude, your mom called my mom. Wanted to make sure you got the homework. Obviously, Kip's the ride," Grey said, bouncing the ball on his fist. It didn't take two people to bring my homework, so clearly they'd had an agenda.

"Ster, I have to know. What happened?" Kip asked. *Of course.* Tossing and turning on my bed, I threw my back onto the mattress, painting the air with my hands.

"I'm grounded. For three months on top of the two weeks I already had for sneaking out."

Both my friends grimaced; clearly they knew my pain. "Dude, that's rough. I almost hope you *did* do it. At least then it'd be worth it," Kip said, leaning back into the chair.

"That's the thing. I didn't do it." It was one thing for my parents or the principal not to believe me. How could my friends assume I was guilty, too? Grey's shoulders sank into my bed.

"Well, it's kind of hard to know what to think. I mean, the evidence isn't exactly in your favor," Grey said as I finally stood.

Of course, the evidence was against me. I vaguely remembered what happened before I saw the words, but there was something about that moment. I hadn't been the only one there, but I didn't remember who was with me.

"I'm sick of everyone blaming me for something I didn't do. Don't you think if I'd done it, I would've been more creative? Seriously?" I said, throwing my head back in a fit.

Grey laughed. "Whether you're guilty or not, the football team totally wants your head right now. Everyone thinks it was the senior prank.

The senior prank was a rite of passage. Every year, there was no saying who would be responsible, how many would be involved, or even when it'd happen. All we knew was that we only got one shot. Waiting until the end of the year would risk prom, so if it happened, it was before the new year.

Now everyone thinks I did it.

"I didn't."

"Well, if you didn't, who do you think did?"

My mind grappled for clues, answers, anything.

"Listen, Sterling, I'll be by tomorrow to drop off your work. We just wanted to … see how you were holding up."

Both my friends stood. They cared, but all they really wanted to know was if I'd done it. The appearance was unnecessary. A text message would've sufficed.

"See you later," both said practically in unison. They were off to freedom. Me? Just another day as Sterling Way-fairer.

Two knocks on the door in one night. It wasn't Grey or Kip, and Dad didn't knock. *Much.*

"Come in," I yelled.

Mom. She paced across the room, avoiding me, and lay a plate on my desk.

"Thought you'd be hungry," she said in a hushed, impassive tone. She wiped off her face, until her fingers met her hair, pushing the loose fly-aways from her red eyes. She'd been crying—or trying not to.

Mom dropped into the chair in my room and spoke.

"We don't…do things to make your life miserable. We care. Caring does not mean we are perfect. I know I…I care." Mom's eyes were serious and heavy. She wiped her runny nose and stood.

"You're grounded for three months," she said again before slamming the door behind her.

The heat of the flames seared my eyes as they danced around me. The fumes and smoke worked their way through my throat, resulting in a fit of thick coughing. I was grateful for the cloth concealing my mouth.. She'd thought of everything.

I was moving, faster than I could on my own, passing the trees that were losing the battle with the fire. People fought bravely. Their screams became louder as we reached the south end of the trail. Bodies lay scattered across the savannah, lifeless ... defeated.

I had to move. No, we had to move. There had to be a quicker way out of the holocaust that engulfed us. We headed toward the water—she was stronger near the waves—but something told me to pull back. The leviathans...they moved faster underwater.

There had to be another way.

We took another route. Wildfire surrounded us and didn't slow down our pursuer. She knew every bend, every fork, every turn. We couldn't afford to head down an unknown trail. We needed an advantage—any advantage would keep us alive longer. How much longer would we have?

You're tired. Your fear washes over me. You tell me don't worry, that you'll protect me, but I know. Its eyes are the eyes of a demon. Green slits become visible as it closes in on us. Frightening, primal, inhumane.

They tear open the sky. They slither into our world in droves. Our world is dying. We have no way out.

You can't run any longer. You don't think we'll make it. You know your power—now I must find mine. Alone we don't stand a fighting chance, but together our powers merge. To-gether we are strong.

Together we Ride...

My eyes flew open. I was shaken, grabbing the first thing closest to me. A wrist. A girl.

The girl. I remember! We held hands like this before. I never made out her face, but I felt her. It was the girl I always saw at school. Her eyes glowed a translucent blue, like some freaky sci-fi shit. She closed them, returning them to their normal black-brown.

We jumped away from each other, frozen like deer.

I reached out but recoiled when a burst of flames coursed through my arm as I fell out of bed and to my knees. My skin was hot from the pain, and I reached out to her. Two beams of energy released from my hands, the pain leaving along with them.

She made a beeline toward the window and did the most insane thing ever. She jumped.

"Wait! Don't go!"

I wasn't dreaming this. It was real. She was real.

I raced to the window. Who the hell could survive a jump like that?

CHAPTER 8

My mind was losing a battle with my body, and I wasn't all here today. Exactly the opposite of how I wanted to feel on my first day back after a week-long suspension. The first three periods were a blur. I probably failed that pop quiz in third period history. If schizophrenia was hereditary, then it was a matter of time before I would follow in my mother's footsteps.

I tried to convince myself last night never happened. What other explanation was there? I spent the first half of school asking around, and no one at school knew anything about that girl. No teachers, no students. All my friends shared a look of pity before confessing that they had never seen a girl like that attending CCI. With my mom's history, I knew they worried I wasn't all there.

Maybe she was a hallucination. Maybe I dreamed her up the way I dreamt up last night. Or all the other times something messed up happened. How long would it be before I was popping pills to get a grip on what was real and what wasn't?

I wanted to believe I was making this stuff up. That was the story—shouldn't I stick to it? But I didn't. The girl was real and held the key to my sanity. The only other option was...

I didn't want to think about the only other option.

By sixth period, I didn't even try to stop my drooping eyes from closing. I let the plush comfy chairs in my astronomy class do all the work for me. I woke up with a teacher in my face and a note ordering me to appear in the principal's office. Probably to add to my detention sentence.

Since the supposed school prank, I hadn't been on her good side. I'm sure after a week-long suspension, my face was the last thing she wanted to see. If Mom was being my mom today, she wouldn't be happy about me getting into more trouble.

It had been my every intention to head to Mrs. Nyugen's office protest-free. There was no way to fight the accusation, so why bother? My mind knew where I needed to be, but my body? It wouldn't listen. My legs followed the magnetic pull leading me away from the office into the furthest regions of the school's West Hall.

I turned the corner. Paralysis swept my entire body. Chilling stare, crossed arms, and daunting presence—it was her. The girl with the three-striped sneakers. We stood there, motionless, eyes locked on each other.

"Sterling Wayfairer, we have things of great importance to discuss."

It was hard to know if I was dreaming. I wanted to know what she planned to "discuss." She knew my name. Why didn't I know hers? There was something she knew that I didn't. Whatever she had to say, I wanted to hear.

We made our way to the farthest classroom on the first floor, the art room, which by now was a ghost town. There was a door on the left side of the room leading directly outside. It offered the best option for ditching.

Me and my friends? We used it *a lot*.

With those two kids still missing, everyone was beyond on edge—

I didn't worry about that now. New Girl was here and real and had my full attention. Even though my legs were longer, I had to power walk to keep up with her.

City's Center was home to the bus, train, rail lines and dozens of shops located on every block. Vendors were already setting up their food trucks by the gravel roads that bordered the *City* Park for the afternoon rush. For the *City*'s Center, it was surprisingly empty.

I followed her into *City* Park. I didn't know what she was waiting for, but I finally bit the bullet, starting the conversation. We'd only have a half-hour before the park was swimming with passersby.

"Can we stop here?" I asked. She faced me, but didn't speak. My guess, she wasn't a talker.

I had so many questions for her but didn't know where to start.

The memories came back to me in fragments, and I was still at a loss to piece everything together. Every time we came in contact with each other, something weird happened. Even if she hadn't been drowning with me, I still saw her last night. In my room. A moment later, lasers were shooting from my hand.

"We have to stop meeting like this," was all I could muster up to lighten the mood. When her eyes met mine, it was hard to explain but … they didn't scream "*stranger*."

"So um … you going to explain the whole breaking-and-entering last night?"

When she spoke, her voice surprised me. It was deeper and more mature than I'd associated with her appearance. Her dialect sung, the pitch heightening in the middle of each sentence. Wherever she was from, it was anywhere nearby.

"I apologize for startling you. I was in search of something."

My face settled into a confused expression. "In search of something? Something like what?"

Her chin dropped to her chest, and she looked defeated. "I needed to see if you remembered anything about the latest boy who went missing."

"The one from a few weeks ago? Why would I know what happened to him?" I was ashamed that I didn't remember his name. He was a sophomore. In my grade alone, there were three kids looked almost just like him. There was no connection to me and the missing kid, but maybe it meant mystery girl was an undercover law enforcer. One that broke into teenage boys' rooms and walked on water. That *had* to be it.

"That much I am aware of, but I wanted to be certain. There are things our minds recall that our eyes cannot. I am desperate for solutions." She finished in her distant accent.

Whenever my nerves got the best of me, my wrist itched like crazy. I didn't realize I was scratching it until she shot me a look of disgust. She probably thought I had hives.

"Your birthmark? Has it changed in shape? Does it become harder to control the flow of energy?"

The flow of what? Wait a second. How did she know about my birthmark?

"Look, I don't know what you're talking about. It's just a friggin' birthmark." *Was I really listening to this?*

"But the shape … has it changed?"

I shrugged. "I mean, yeah, but that's only because I pick at it all the time. It's not anything out of the …" I lifted my sleeve in an effort to back up my story, but at that moment the nick I believed to be a birthmark seared my skin into the shape of a circular symbol with a tri-fold of vein-like lines. It stung every so often, but this time it was like someone had taken a hot branding iron to my skin. The pain only subsided when her wrist came in close contact with mine. We shared the same birthmark.

"I don't understand. What is this? What does this mean?"

"It means that you and I are connected. You bear the Mark of *Noba*."

"You and me—connected?" I said in a cloud full of doubt. "You have to be joking, right? Who put you up to this? Was it Grey or was it Kip? This would've been hilarious if it weren't me at the butt of the joke."

Her face scrunched in confusion. "I have no knowledge of what a Grey or Kip is. Put you up to? I am not familiar with this expression. It means what exactly?"

I laughed. "If my friends didn't send you here to spook me, how in the hell are we connected?" Bet she couldn't explain that one. I wasn't the palest of all pale, but her dark brown skin wasn't making us related any time soon.

"Have there ever been times that things happened that you could not explain?"

Plenty, but only when she was around.

"Have you ever felt…compelled to find me?"

Was she calling me a stalker? She was fairly cute. (Okay, okay. Maybe fairly was downplaying it.) But that didn't make me obsessed with her. *Did it?*

"We've always been drawn to each other. What I am about to tell you may be difficult to understand, but you and I? We are not of this world, of *Geo*. We come from a place called *Noba*."

I grinned. "What did you say your name was?"

"Sai-Liber Tetraphrimaporticheeq."

"Let's see if I understand this…SIGH-La-bear Tet-RAH-fear-ma-porta-chic. Can I call you Sai-Liber?"

She cringed. "Sai-Liber is my family name. Much like Wayfairer. You may call me Tetraphrimaportacheeq. It is much simpler."

To who? I'd barely got it out the first time.

"Okay, so, Tetraphrima-portapotty …"

She cut me off with a somber look. "Tetraphrimaporticheeq," she corrected.

I nodded.

"Right … I think you have me confused with another person. I also think you should go see a doctor or something. The stuff you're saying … it just doesn't sound plausible."

She frowned. Her posture shrunk into oblivion. "You do not believe me?"

Of course I didn't believe her. We were connected? From a place called *Noba*? Both of those had to make the list of top five most ridiculous things I'd ever heard. I was born in *City* on the planet *Geo*. Not some place called *Noba*. So what if we shared the same birthmark? That didn't mean anything.

"Look, Tetraphrimapadame, I'm sorry I wasted your time. I thought maybe you'd tell me something … I don't know, useful? But now I kind of think you could use some help." I hauled my book bag over my shoulder, heading in the direction of *City*'s train station.

I barely made it six steps before her next question stopped me dead in my tracks.

"Are your dreams getting worse?"

I spun around, and my feet didn't stop moving until we stood face to face. "What did you just say?"

What she lacked in height, she made up for in poise and presence. She didn't back down. "I asked whether they were getting worse. Vivid? More pronounced?"

The questions tore me open, left me exposed. My dreams invoked a fear in me so powerful I assumed I was losing my mind. And she knew about them. But how?

"Yeah, but … how do you know about my dreams? I've never told anyone about them."

Her face was hard and stern. "Because, Sterling, they are not dreams. They are your memories."

Tetra

Sterling dropped to his knees, pulling at his hair, eyes glaring. His visions didn't happen when he was awake, that much I knew. He didn't know how to channel or decipher the images. To explore memories, exploit thoughts, and influence minds—it was a skill known back home as Phantom Riding. It took years, perhaps decades, to master. But it was also known to confuse the mind and, without the proper training, drive the disciple mad. While I had not been a recognized *Rishi,* I dedicated my all to its study. In this foreign world, Phantom Riding proved quite useful.

"Ugh, why is this happening to me?" Sterling cried. I kneeled before him, concerned. His suffering was not easy to bear, but he caused it himself. The source of his pain came from his reluctance.

"Sterling Wayfairer, it would be in your best interest to channel the pain associated with your memories. I can act as your guide, but I seek your permission first."

"Fine! You have my permission, just make it stop!"

I eased into a lotus position. "You will need to do as I do."

Sterling lacked the flexibility to enter a true lotus. His ankles, his feet, his hips were all wrong. But it would do for now.

"When I take your hands, you will feel far away, but do not to wander off. Stay close to me. Memories … some people can lose themselves in them. It can be difficult to distinguish what has happened and what hasn't happened yet. Remember you are here. On *Geo*."

He nodded, and we clasped our hands together. The present faded as his pain ceased. Our current world faded to black.

Mentally, Sterling and I were no longer on *Geo*. I was not fond of revisiting this.

Our past.

But there was something about this memory that Sterling would not let go. Evil parted the sky, leaving its mark on my homeland. *Our* homeland. It was the *Day of Scar*.

His interpretation differed greatly from mine. I saw it the way it had actually happened. Him—from the mind of the child he'd been at the time. Riding the memory of a child was not without challenge. Deciphering fantasy from reality was strenuous. The explosions happening in the distance? Not real, for we did not use such foreign technology. The Behemoth that closely followed? Real.

It moved with the speed of the wind, bearing the appearance of a snake. In our world, we had a word for them. *Naga.* Serpent. It opened its mouth wide, nearly solid green eyes locked on its target, snapping its long neck toward us.

With my eyes shut so tight, I didn't realize when the memory changed.

Images of flames, ash, and death were soon replaced by endless pitch darkness. Massive twisting lines of cerulean, tinges of sapphire, and cosmic beryl raced against a legion of stars. In that instant, we were weightless. I was the vessel; he, the True Traveler, the navigator. We would land where he felt safe. In an exchange of thoughts between us, he convinced me where …

Geo.

Sterling

I took a moment to remember where I was. The memory had only been in fragments, but I'd had it for years. Why would I ever consider it to be more than a dream? I was so young, viewing everything from a sling on her back. And her? She looked exactly the same. *Except for her clothes.*

"Can you make sense of it now?" she asked.

I shrugged. "Barely." Our hands were still clasped together as our marks of *Noba* blazed in unison. This was the closest I had ever been to her. I knew this was supposed to be a serious moment, but … *she was so hot.*

I figured I might as well ask my questions to make sense of what I recalled. The *Naga* … I didn't want that part to be real.

"What are those things? The *Naga*?"

Her hands broke free from mine. I noticed the calluses and scars that decorated her small palms. "No one really knows what they are. Only how they first appeared to us. In serpentine form."

"What do you mean no one really knows what they are? What does that even mean?"

"The *Naga* show no allegiance to form. They devour the soul of any living thing. Vegetation, animals…people. As a result, they become what they devour. I am not certain if the serpent is their true form or simply the form they feel most comfortable in."

A question lingered on the tip of my tongue. It seemed rude to ask, but I had to know. "What does that have to do with us? Because a part of me doesn't get this whole connected thing."

She grunted. Guess that was the effect I had on girls. "In numbers, the *Naga* are fearsome. Alone? They must grow more creative to attack and conquer. When we first arrived in *Megalopolis*, I assumed you and I were alone. But that tear in the sky tells me otherwise."

I looked up at the open sky and noticed that scar, the tear in the open sky that I was so terrified of acknowledging. "Wait a minute; you can *see* that?" I asked in a state of panic.

She whipped in my direction violently, as if it shouldn't have been a valid question. *"Of course* I can see it."

I nearly collapsed to the ground, my mind in a whirlwind of emotions. "I thought I was losing it. I asked my friends and they have no idea what I'm talking about."

"That is because they are not looking for it. You know that it's there. So your mind stopped looking with your eyes. But even though that is proof of its voyage here, there is no doubt that its stay has been consequential. Especially since there have been so many missing people."

The missing kids from our schools. They were linked. "This has something to do with the kids who went missing?"

She nodded. "The actions of a face stealer are unpredictable, but there have been many signs." She shook her head, eyes focused. "Concentrated disappearances in one area. Brief atmospheric changes. Some *Naga* are able to manipulate massive heat waves, while others can cause uncontrollable rainstorms. And then there are the plants ..."

I didn't understand everything, but if what she told me was true, it meant I wasn't losing it. As much as I wanted it to be wrong, it made sense. "What happens to the plants?"

She stood and walked, expecting me to follow. "The presence of a *Naga* brings destruction to botanic life. The solid matter of a world is a power source. When a *Naga* encounters herbage, trees, or crops, they deteriorate. When a *Naga* comes in contact with people, we lose a lot more than that."

My ringing cellphone interrupted her story. I thought I'd turned the damn thing off. It was 2:36, so school was over. Everyone was probably looking for me. I pressed the power button hard, making sure it was off. I'd pray for my friends' forgiveness later.

I wanted to know how this connected to me. How she connected to me.

"I have been unsuccessful in my encounters with it. Whenever I find a lead on its whereabouts, we battle…and I lose. I have no way of defeating it. This world, *Geo*? It disabled a portion of my abilities. Most importantly, my ability to wield *helstones*."

"What is a *helstone?* Like, a guard dog?"

She bit her lip and lowered her eyes, trying to find the right words. "A *helstone* is a defensive article with the ability to change for its wielder. It has the ability to shift into any weapon its wielder has come in contact with. As far as we know, it's our only defense against the *Naga*."

I shrugged. "Well, how do you get one to work?"

"It is not that simple. My *shakti* … erm … spiritual link with mine is blocked. Much like the bond between you and me."

Someone jogged by us. The rush of air tickled the skin on my arm, and my wrist itched at the sound of that word.

"There's that word again. 'Bond.' What is that supposed to mean? *Our* bond?"

Her eyebrows scrunched to the center of her face. "*It means that we are bonded.*"

Okay? That answered my question.

"Uh…okay? So what does it mean to be bonded?" The park was now flooded with people. Since *City* was the center of everything, when most people got out of school or work, they switched off here.

"I apologize, Sterling. But you must know I do not hold every answer to all the questions you may have." At least she was honest. "In *Noba,* we believed the land to be spiritual.

That it was the very life force that fueled the air, the water, and its inhabitants. It was not merely a home. It was a connection to all worlds. There were those born to it. Then there were others…like you. True Travelers. Foreigners. Ones the world called to through the manipulation of time and space. A Time Rider."

Now I was mega-confused. True Travelers? Time Riders? Bonds? I still didn't get it. "What does that have to do with you and me?"

She recoiled her fingers, desperate to get the words out. "*Noba* does not call True Travelers through mere chance. You are summoned through a bond. The journey requires a sacrifice."

Now I was worried. Not only did it sound insane, but "sacrifice" never meant anything good. "What … kind of sacrifice?"

She locked eyes with me for the first time since we'd left school.

"Half your soul."

We stood in silence. I tried to force a smile, but it was useless. I understood even less than I had at the beginning. She seemed to sense a shift in my mood and walked forward.

"I sacrificed half my soul as well, but it affects me differently than it does a True Traveler."

"Like how?"

"For a True Traveler, you can do things you wouldn't have been able to do before the bond. For me, it amplifies my spirituality but … hinders my ability to age at a standard rate."

That explained why she looked the same. But I still didn't believe her. How could I? "Say I did believe you—how come I don't remember that?"

She frowned. "You wouldn't. Our bond is underdeveloped. When our souls called to each other, your mother had just given birth to you. You were fourteen to sixteen moons younger than most True Travelers, and I had just entered the first stage of my adulthood. It was seen as unorthodox."

I had always had this weird feeling around her, but how was all that even possible? "So *Noba* is a world outside of *Geo*, and *Noba* is, like, the connection to all worlds? Are you telling me there are more worlds out there?"

Her jaw clenched. "Of course there are other worlds," she spat. "You can't possibly think that this world is the only one that exists. There are hundreds, perhaps thousands more. Possibly even more than that."

Now was a good time to shut up. I'd offended her, assuming no other world existed outside of this one. But could you blame me? Until today, it was what I'd believed.

What if she was wrong? I'd never done anything overtly amazing, incredible, or even interesting. What if I was a regular guy? You know, the type of who just *happens* to shoot beams of energy from his hands?

"What if I'm the wrong guy? You say I'm a True Traveler or whatever it is I am. But manipulating time? That seems way out there. I'm barely passing trigonometry."

Her eyes glanced over. Judging by the sour look on her face, she agreed with me. "I admit, you do not appear to be exceptional, but that has kept you alive." Wow, she wasn't shy.

"There is speculation that the *Naga* never stop hunting until complete annihilation of a race. There are still many of us out there, but we are scattered across the galaxy, waiting to be picked off one by one unless we're able to destroy the threat. It knows what I look like, but I can defend myself against it. You are an unrecognized *Noban*. Your soul is defenseless. You would not stand a chance."

For the record, she wasn't selling me on this whole bond thing. The more I heard, the less I wanted to hear. My forehead wrinkled, stumped on what I should do or say. She continued.

"We have seen them defeated. We can harm them, but only our divine technology has proven effective against their serpent form."

"So how do I factor?" So far nothing she'd said pointed back to me.

"Evil has many faces. I wish to destroy it before it can gain more, but I cannot without you. We've been estranged for some time. We cannot make up for that lost time. However, spending time with you...you may find your initial reluctance fade away."

That didn't sound like a bad thing. The girl whose name I couldn't pronounce was the type of girl who would never hang out with me if not for dire circumstances. She didn't have to yank my collar to become my friend. My hands met each other in a clasp.

"Okay, sounds good, Tetraphrimaportacheck. We'll work on this bond thing first thing tomorrow at school."

I had about seven inches on her, but she gave me a look that made me feel four foot ten.

"No, Sterling Wayfairer. *The bond starts today.* The bond starts right now."

My eyes bulged, and I shuffled back a step or two. "Uh…what are you going to, like, follow me home?"

She crossed her arms in front of her chest. "Will that be an issue?" I would've balled up on the floor laughing if she hadn't seemed completely serious.

"Um … I'm seventeen. I kind of live with my parents."

We continued to walk, and the wind blew her hair off her shoulders. I could smell a harmonious blend of crisp dew, with a hint of an intense rose-like scent. (Cherry blossom, maybe?) In a strange way, it suited her.

"How does that pose as an issue?" she asked.

"I get that this whole bond thing is important, but you can't just follow me around. What do I say to my parents? *'Hey, Mom, Dad? So this girl followed me on my way home from school—what do you say? Can I keep her?'* You know how crazy that sounds? Oh, and a word to the wise, I can't lie for shit!"

The look she gave next was condescending, as if the solution to our problem was obvious. "Why would you have to lie?"

It dawned on me that my parents might know her. "Do my parents remember you?" I asked.

She shook her head, pursing her lips to one side. "Your parents do not remember anything, but it doesn't matter. I have to teach you to control your *ticking.*"

"*Ticking?*"

"Do you or do you not find yourself in one place with no explanation of how you got there?" Okay, so maybe I'd found myself in some odd places lately, but I know I wasn't *that* out of control.

"That is called *ticking*. Untrained Time Riders tend to be pulled in whichever direction your thoughts tell you to go. Be grateful you've never ended up some place difficult to find your way out of. Once you get a concrete grasp of things, you won't find yourself *ticking* involuntarily. That much I can teach you if given the proper opportunity."

Her eyes lit up in an a *eureka* moment. "Do not worry, Sterling Wayfairer. I will take care of everything. We will meet later."

Before I could object, I lost her in the crowd. On my way to the train station, I violated a direct order. I worried.

I was halfway home when a black SUV pulled up. Well before the obnoxious voice called out, I knew who it was.

"Hey, Wayfairer. Get your scrawny ass in here and stop ignoring everyone's calls! We've been looking all over for you." Had to love Kip for that. He was such a sweet talker.

I figured walking home would give me clarity, but getting a ride wouldn't suck. Waverly sat shotgun, so I helped myself to Kip's backseat. It was nice having it to myself. It'd be a packed car for the next few weeks, so I planned on enjoying it while it lasted. *I really needed my own car.*

Kip kept his eyes on the road with an occasional glance toward me. "Dude, where the hell were you? You turned your friggin' phone off when you know what's going on?"

If it was true that Tetraphrimaporticatch was hunting the threat, it sucked I couldn't tell anyone. Like they'd believe me anyway.

"What's wrong—you miss me, baby?" I whined to Kip. I patted his shoulder and was quickly met by a hard shrug. "It's okay now. I'm here."

Kip bit back a laugh. His right hand lifted off the steering wheel to give me the middle finger. I leaned back in the seat and hoped Waverly was too immersed in those magazines on her lap to notice me.

As bad luck would have it, she wasn't.

"Sterling, seriously, everyone was worried. We were like ten minutes away from calling your parents. Everyone denies it, but we're all still pretty shook up." Her smile was small, but still shed light on a less-than-stellar day.

"It's cool, Waves, I had a quiz I didn't study for. Decided to skip last period. No biggie." Unless you overlooked the news of finding out that I was a Time-Riding True Traveler who shared a bond with a super-intense, super-*Geotic* (or should I say super-*Noban*) girl with a penchant for killing shape-shifting serpents. Guess that was no biggie, right?

Kip pulled into the driveway. Certain indicators pointed to whether I was about to have a rough couple of hours dealing with a mother with schiz. A front door wide open? That would be one of them.

I left the car with a sense of urgency, praying Kip would drive off. The car door slammed. The slapping sound of Waverly's flip-flops hit the pavement. "Wait, Sterling. Let me go in with you. Just in case, y'know…"

She didn't need to finish. I did know. Just in case my mom was having one of her fits. "It's okay, Waves. I should be okay."

She hesitated, as Kip gestured her back to his car. "No, I really don't mind."

I should've been mortified, but I'd already guessed Kip let his tongue slip occasionally. Waverly must know all about my mom's behavior. Plus, she worked in a hospital; she'd probably seen worse.

"Mom?" I called out from the living room. She wasn't downstairs. It was clean, and Mom ran through like a hurricane when she forgot to take her pills. She must've been upstairs. "Y'know, she's probably in the bathroom or something. I can handle it from here, Waverly."

"No, Sterling, I want to help."

It was weird having Waverly in my house for the first time since the fourth grade. I'd always hoped it'd be under different circumstances. I reached the bathroom door. No one inside. It could only mean one thing.

That she was in my room. *Not good.*

One time when she didn't take her meds, a trip to my room had resulted in all things I deemed important being thrown into three black lawn bags because "she didn't know who they belonged to."

Because seeing my photographs and my name didn't make it obvious. I'd only had seconds to gather my stuff before the trash man made his weekly rounds. This time I'd catch her before she reached the lawn.

The door was ajar, but I heard voices. She often talked to herself in ill moments.

Looked like Waverly'd be seeing Mom at her worst. *Just my luck.* I swung open the door. My room was different, not at all how I'd left it. Nothing was missing, but it seemed … smaller.

"Mom?"

Mom popped up from the floor. She rubbed her brow, a pinched look on her face.

"Sterling, where have you been? You were supposed to be home an hour ago. Everything was supposed to be ready before she got here." She blew her bangs out of her eyes and faced Waverly. "Oh, hi, Waverly. Nice to see you. Nice hair." Yeah, woohoo. Redheads unite! What was Mom doing in my room?

"Mom? Before *who* got here? What are you talking about?"

With the help of my mattress, she stood up. Then it finally hit me. The reason why my room seemed smaller. Instead of my single twin bed, there were two, separated by an old dusty nightstand my parents kept in the basement. "Sterling, don't tell me you forgot? The foreign exchange program we signed up for over the summer. She's here. You didn't see her downstairs?"

Mom was … somewhat competent, but not making any sense.

Her eyes widened with excitement as she gestured to the door. "Here she is."

I almost passed out. What was she doing here?

"Don't be rude, Sterling. Say hello to our house guest for the school year. Tetraphrimaporticheeq."

ow Tetraphrimaportichess had made it back to my house before me was beyond eerie. She definitely wasn't your typical all-*Geotic* girl next door, that was for sure.

"So, Sterling," Mom began. "You might want to get a head start on that cleaning I told you to have done BEFORE she got here."

At that, my eyes practically leapt out of their sockets. "Wait. *She's staying in here?*"

Waverly inched her way toward the door, her foot catching on something in the process. "Yeah, I'd better go."

I was grateful when the front door slammed shut. That meant she wouldn't be around to witness the Wayfairer residence transform into a full-fledged war zone.

I should have been ecstatic. Not one, but *two* hot girls had made it back to my room, unforced and at the same time. But the excitement vanished at the thought that one would be making herself a permanent resident.

"Make it quick, Sterling. I'm going to get started on dinner, and I could use your help in the kitchen."

My mom excused herself without saying another word. How dare she leave without seeing the reality of the situation?

There she was. Tertaphrima … (*oh you know her name*). What could she have said to make this situation even possible?

There had to be another way. I could not, *would* not share my space with her for obvious reasons—she was a girl.

"Wait here," I murmured to her.

She put a small bag on the bed closest to the door and sat down.

I went after my mom as she made her way down the staircase, practically bouncing all the way. I had to reason with her. This had to be stopped.

"Mom. Mom? Mom!" She faced me, rubbing her brow, her head rattling from side to side. At least she'd stopped. "She can't stay in my room."

"Sterling, please. She's our guest. Are you insisting I have her sleep on the couch?"

Of course I wasn't, but that didn't mean I wanted the two of us to be roommates. "No, but geez, can't she stay in the basement? Or I can stay in the basement. It's just … I can't share a room with her."

My mom pressed her palms against my cheeks and almost looked concerned.

"Sterling, you know it gets cold down there, and it's an even bigger mess than your room is. Plus, there are too many spiders down there." She shivered dramatically. I'd rather wake up to a blanket full of spiders than have my new roomie to catch me with an accidental hard-on. Just the thought made me panic.

"Mom, please." I said through squeezed lips.

Her eyes felt my pain, but her lips curved into something sinister, just to mock me. "Sterling, why are you being so difficult? I thought you'd be happy to make a new friend. Especially since you won't be leaving this house for anything non-school-related for the next few months." For a woman, my mom was clueless. Weren't women supposed to pick up on everything?

"But, Mom, she's a girl. With boobs and legs and girly smells." *Intoxicating girly smells.*

Her mouth flew open as she met me with an incredulous stare. "You know what, Sterling? I hadn't noticed. Let's go ask her if she has a vagina, too!"

How was she joking about this? And why did she think it was okay to say the word vagina? My mom didn't trust me to tie my own shoes right now. Why would she trust me to host a girl in my room for who knew how long? I didn't want to plant thoughts in her head, but she left me with no choice.

I followed my mom into the kitchen as she pulled out various things from the cabinet, placing them on the counter.

"So … you're okay with me living with a girl in my room?"

She rushed to the fridge to remove a thawed-out roast, and placed it in the sink. "Sterling, in a few months you'll be eighteen. Do I have to remind you how to behave in the presence of a lady?"

I rolled my eyes. That usually meant no.

"Just give Tetraphrimaporticheeq some time to herself when she's getting dressed and it shouldn't be an issue." Man, why was it so easy for my mom to say her name? I hoisted myself onto the counter, stuffing a few stale cookies in my mouth from last week's batch.

"So, like, what if she wakes up one night with an uncontrollable need to hook up with me?"

When my mom wiped the tears from her eyes and caught her breath from laughing, she patted my face the way you pet an animal that you might find pathetic but in a cute kind of way. "Sterling, honey? I'm almost positive you won't have that problem."

That explained it. The only reason my mom trusted me was because she trusted that a girl like Tetraphrima … —(why was I the only one who couldn't say it?)—would never be interested in me.

My mom thought I was a loser.

I went upstairs to see how my new roommate was doing, knocking first as I didn't want any early slip-ups. When she failed to answer, I let myself in only to find my worst nightmare.

Tetraphrimaporticreek had violated a major rule in this household. No one—and I mean no one—attempted to clean my room but me.

"What do you think you're doing?"

She was so in the zone she barely looked up. She was too busy ruining my life with her sorting of clothes and neatly stacked porn stashes … Wait, were those MY neatly stacked porn stashes?

"I am cleaning your room. It appeared to be of great concern to your mother."

I slammed the door. She didn't flinch. She didn't stop cleaning. "Okay, first rule of this room: parental figures' words are void as soon as you hit this line!" I pointed to the door way. "I swear, in a week, you'll see that this is the only place in this house that offers an asylum from my parents."

She stuffed a combination of clothes, both clean and dirty, into a garbage bag.

"Wait! Some of those were clean!"

I reached for the bag, but when our hands came in contact, she backed away from me, crossing and uncrossing her arms like she'd suddenly forgotten how to use them.

"My apologies."

I didn't know what she had been through. Maybe she didn't like to be touched. "Hey, I'm not trying to hurt you or anything. It's just ... You don't have to clean my room. Here, sit down."

We sat down on our beds, avoiding eye contact. I was hoping she'd talk about it, but all she did was take a sudden interest in her hands.

"Okay, so you know this is a little weird, right?" It wasn't the most sophisticated way to start a conversation, but I couldn't take the silence any longer.

Her eyes kept examining. "Weird is a term similar to peculiar, strange or foreign?"

I nodded. "I mean, I believe you. We share some kind of bond or something. I don't understand what that means yet, but we have all year to figure it out. Just so you know, our living situation... Guys and girls don't usually sleep in the same rooms together. Did you know that?"

She pursed her lips to one side. It was really cute. "Your parents? Are they an exception?"

I really hoped she was kidding. "Well, I mean yeah, they're married. That's what married people do. We're a ..." I searched desperately for the words. "A different type of situation."

She turned away from me. "I've spent most of my time here learning how to connect to this world. I don't have much experience interacting with its inhabitants, adapting to its customs and culture."

Thinking back, I'd rarely seen her engage at school. People mostly saw past her. "So, um, what did you do in the meantime?"

"Connecting spiritually to a world takes patience. It is achieved by long bouts of mediation. You must prove yourself worthy before it trusts you with its gifts."

Spending time away from people just to be able to do things that were out of this world? I may have had to pass on all that other stuff she talked about earlier.

"Well, the culture isn't that complicated. You could probably learn most stuff as you go. Don't know if I'd be any help with that."

She mimicked the face my mom made when she'd caught a glimpse of my grades for the semester. I didn't know another person could make a face like that.

"It would be helpful as our bond develops for you to learn a few of the ways of our culture. There is much to know, and it'd be beneficial for you to be able to defend yourself if the face stealer discovers your identity. Especially before either one of us is fully recognized."

I tried to swallow the fear that lingered with that comment. *Nope, didn't work.* "Listen, Tetra, I know this will take a *lot* of effort between us, but—"

"Tetra?" she interrupted.

I knew it was super insensitive but I'd given up on trying to say her full name. My tongue was phonetically impaired and rather offend her more by messing it up every single time it left my mouth, I'd come up with the nickname, Tetra. I mean, it was part of her actual name after all. "It's not that I don't like Tetraphrimaporti … *yeah*. It's just *Geotics* don't really have long names like that. Can we just keep it simple? Just for school and stuff."

She sat in silence, considering, finally nodding in agreement. "Tetra is fine. It has been some time since I've been called that."

My mom shouted my name from the kitchen. I totally forgot I'd been helping her and was supposed to be right back. "Guess you better get used to everything around here. Want to help me with my mom in the kitchen?"

Tetra

Dinner with the Wayfairers was immensely different than I had expected. For one, the way Laurel prepared food was less than satisfactory. The meat was so hard it could have doubled as a weapon. The roots were almost flavorless, and the legumes needed to be cooked longer.

Peter, Sterling's father, believed that the tomato-based condiment ketchup made everything taste better.

It did not.

If they ate like this every night, I would have to start hunting my own food again. Although, I never prided myself on preparation.

It was Laurel's mission to ensure my comfort and to learn more about me. We spent dinner time talking only about me. That made Sterling uneasy, which puzzled me. Only when the question of my origin was presented did Sterling become an active participant in the conversation. In *Noba*, it was presumed defiant to fail to acknowledge your parents or any officials, for that matter. But with the Wayfairers, it was a natural occurrence.

After dinner, I offered to assist Peter and Laurel with clean up, but they were insistent on making me feel like a guest in their house. Was I not expected to make contributions in support of this household? In our culture, every person had their role in the community. How was I supposed to do nothing? Sterling signaled my attention on the staircase, and with nothing else to do, I followed him.

He gave me a quick tour of his house, including a stop to the bathroom informing me where his mother kept her important medications should she forget to take them. There were so many, four at least, and because his father lacked the proper knowledge of which pills she took and for what reasons, he thought it best that someone else should know. In any case of Sterling not being available.

"What a night." He plopped down on his bed as I followed suit. It had been a while since I'd slept on something this soft.

"Hey, Tetra, question," he called.

I faced him, feeling tall in my position. "Yes, Sterling?"

"That was you that day, wasn't it? With the water?"

It was true. Many *Nobans* possessed affinities for elements of nature. Mine—amongst many others from the tribe I was born into, the *Oerbans*—had a natural talent for controlling the waves. We referred to it as Wave Riding.

"You almost killed me, y'know?"

I picked away at the calluses my hand developed from being a huntress. "I wouldn't have let you drown, Sterling. The water trusts me as I trust it. You can learn as well. Riding the waves only takes practice."

His head fell back on his pillow, his gaze directed toward the ceiling. "Thanks to you I won't be swimming for a long, long time."

I didn't blame him. The first time I had ridden time, I'd vowed never to do it again. However, once I'd mastered it, I shamed myself for ever showing fear of it.

My body twinged with exhaustion. Most likely due to Phantom Riding Sterling's mind. Because it was my weakest affinity, it took the full extent of the *shakti* I could access to use it. That, in turn, left me drained.

Sleeping in undergarments was painfully irritating. I hated wearing them during the day, but I especially hated wearing them while I slept. It was the one thing I couldn't get used to in all my time in this foreign world called *Geo*. I took my shirt off and reached to rid myself of this unnecessary confinement when Sterling jumped to his feet, his hands over his eyes.

"Whoa, whoa, WHOA! What are you doing? You can't just undress in front of me. Just—whoa!" His voice cracked on the last word.

"Sterling, you are unaware of how uncomfortable these things are. I cannot sleep in them."

He paced around the room in no set direction, tripping over shoes, books, or whatever else was in his way. He made contact with the dresser, scrabbling through what looked like an even bigger mess, and pulled out a pad of paper and a pen.

"Tetra, I'm not going to look, but is your shirt back on?" He sat across from me with his hands still over his eyes until he heard a yes. His outburst seemed uncalled for. After all, I had only removed my shirt.

"I think it'd be best if we set some ground rules. Y'know, a kind of Tetra-and-Sterling –living-together manual. The only way I see this thing working is if we respect each other's concerns." He scribbled the words "The Complete Tetra and Sterling Living Guide" and underneath wrote our names.

His hands skated along the page reaching almost the bottom when he handed it to me. The penmanship was scarcely legible and though only writing for a short moment, he'd compiled a list of twenty-seven rules.

He leaned forward with his hands rested on his bouncing knees. Before I could read to the bottom of the page, he seized it, claiming to have forgotten something. He then added five more rules to the paper.

"There," he said. "Feel free to add as many as you need to."

I scanned the list quickly. The majority of his concerns were easily accomplishable. Heading the list was (in his words), "I'm a guy. You're a girl. No taking off clothes in front of each other."

I didn't know how our genders contributed to that particular issue and why he even assumed I identified as solely female. People acted in parallel roles on *Noba* and the fact that this world excluded so many genders confused me. What was decided for those who did not classify as male or female? I'd only known three True Travelers on a personal level, and they had always found it difficult to relinquish inhibition. I speculated my body made Sterling uncomfortable, an argument I found to be valid but still perplexing. As a *Noban* aboriginal, it would take time for me to adjust to the ways of another world. However, I planned to respect his wishes.

One item would be difficult, so I thought it wise to address it before I officially given my word.

"Twenty-nine could be an obstacle for me as I do not attend school every day."

He looked the list over and focused his gaze on me. "Uh, why?"

"Because I have obligations that rank of higher importance." Any clues that would lead me closer to finding the *Naga*, I had to take. In comparison, school was a waste of my time.

"Uh, no, you don't! If I have to go to school every day, *you* have to go to school every day. End of discussion. Besides, you've been hunting this thing for, like, seventeen years. It's not going to kill you to adjust the search to after school hours. Aren't you going to write anything down?"

I grabbed the list and wrote down a single request. It was all I could think of at the moment. Perhaps more would come in time.

"I wish for you to keep my part of the room free of obstruction."

His eyes blinked in rapid succession, a dumbfounded expression on his face. He appeared entranced. "That's it? That's your only concern?"

I forced myself to add onto my requests. He wouldn't be happy until my list was as long as his. "I meditate daily for a total of four hours, more when time permits. Am I welcome to do so without interruption?" He added it to the list. "If you have any other areas of interest, be sure to add it to the sheet. I'll try to look at it every day."

He laid it down on the nightstand that separated our beds. "I'm going to give you a few minutes to get ready for bed. I'm friggin beat." He picked up a few articles of clothing from off the floor and walked into the hallway.

I didn't need any time. After taking my pants off and curling into my comforter, it wouldn't take much to fall asleep. I was already halfway there.

CHAPTER 11

Sterling

I hit the snooze button for the third time since 5:45. If I ignored the next one, no doubt we'd be late. It surprised me to see Tetra still bundled up in a sea of blankets. I didn't peg her for the sleep-in type.

"Hey, Tetra." I'm sure she didn't hear me. I kneeled on her side of her bed and gave her a little shake. "Tetra!" Her eyes opened to slits, groggy and worn of energy.

"What time is it?"

The clock read 6:20. "It's time to get up."

She rolled over in the opposite direction, taking the covers along with her as if that was enough to stop me.

I pulled back the comforter just to the point of decency. "C'mon, we have to get ready. This was, like, twenty-nine on the list, remember? Let's go, Tetra!"

She grabbed her hair in clumps, raising her eyes to the ceiling. "Will it matter if we are just a few minutes late for homeroom? First period does not start until 8:30."

I thought *I* hated waking up early. "Tetra, you just wasted, like, three minutes trying to find a loophole. Get up and take a shower already. You can go first since I don't take long. I want to get there early so you can meet my friends."

She took a deep breath and got out of bed, revealing two of the most toned, shapeliest legs I'd ever seen in person. I swear, I really tried not looking at her ass when she glided past me in search of a towel, but I shamefully lost that battle. She was nothing short of a visual masterpiece.

Grey got a ride from Kip so they could go to some early morning practice, so I didn't get a chance to brief Grey on the Tetra situation before school. I literally spent the whole train ride planning what I would say to them.

I had different methods of explaining things to my friends. Grey was easy. He didn't ask follow-up questions, keeping the lies I'd have to tell him to a minimum. Kip was different. He had to know every last detail, and nothing was ever elaborate enough to satisfy his curiosity. Sure hoped Tetra was better at lying than I was.

We got off the bus a stop early. I had to make sure Tetra and I were on the same page before we got to school.

"So, Tetra. Do you remember what you're going to tell everyone if anyone asks you anything?" We'd gone over it a few times at the bus stop, but it didn't hurt to have our stories straight.

"That I am a foreign exchange student visiting from *Outland*. I attend *Outland* Sixth Form College and my family name is Pierce."

I nodded, relieved she'd remembered. "Oh, and none of that Phantom Riding stuff. Let people make up their own minds on whether you're worth noticing or not. Your accent might draw some red flags, but as far as I know we should be good. No one around the main sectors really knows anything about *Outland*."

We approached the school grounds. She kept adjusting the weight of her book bag, so I took it as the time to…I don't know…*bond*.

"You okay?" I asked.

She offered a quick nod and continued.

"Hey, Tetra, I could take it for you."

"It is all right. I am not yet adjusted to carrying the required textbooks. I thought now would be the best time to start."

I hated seeing her struggle. My mom would probably kill me if I didn't help a girl in need.

"Give it here." I reached over to grab it, but the weight took me down to the ground. "Geez, Tetra, what do you have in here, rocks?"

She shot me a look of pity. "I told you before—they are my required textbooks."

I huffed and puffed, trying to level her book bag with mine. It took all my strength. "What—all of them?" She nodded. I definitely needed to step my game up. She made it look easy.

"If you find that it is too heavy for you, I have no issues in carrying my own bag." She tried to take it back, but I wouldn't hear of it.

"I got it, Tetra. Just…when you get inside, keep your books in your locker!"

Tetra

An entire day at school would take time to adjust to. Generally, by the fourth period bell, I found no reason to attend my full schedule of classes, but as per our living agreement, I like Sterling would attend school every day.

All day.

There was nothing demanding about school, but I thought my time would be best spent completing tasks of greater importance. My *shakti* was still limited, and due to our weakened bond, the strength of my abilities was modified. If I was to defeat this bottom-feeding face stealer, I had to be strong enough to call on my *helstone*. Otherwise, each battle would end just like the last. Draining and hopeless. Speaking of draining…

"…Ms. Pierce!" Mr. Omni cried. My eyes shot open as he whacked a flimsy stick on the chair in front of me, a look of irritation on his face. I was certain he was displeased with me.

I had disappointed many where I originated from in *Noba*. It was something I was accustomed to.

"Not exactly the best way to start off your first day, is it now?" He walked up a set of stairs that led to the stage of the auditorium. From there, his voice resonated, but from other times I had taken this class (drama, was it?), he had always spoken this way.

"Let's try to make a better impression, Ms. Pierce." He continued his discussion as a familiar voice whispered in my ear.

"Don't worry about him. He's just mad because his lectures are so boring there's always at least one person who falls asleep. For the most part, it's usually me."

A close-fitted hat covered most of his long hair, and he had eyes that expressed innocence and curiosity.

Sterling's friend Grey.

He, along with Sterling's other friend Kip, behaved so bizarrely during our introduction that I'd been eager for the first class to start. Yet under isolated conditions, Grey proved to be pleasant. My favorite of the two.

He spent half the class period talking about who he found annoying. The ones he referred to as the Humphries Twins ranked high on that list. Taylor and Brittany were the senior class president and vice president, respectively, and according to Grey, the smartest kids in school.

The girl Brittany was lost in her brother Taylor's shadow. Being the dominant one, there was nothing he shied away from.

They didn't look like twins. The girl was darker in skin tone, perhaps a few shades darker than Grey while her brother was a sun-kissed light brown, all while possessing different eye colors and facial structures. Grey thought Brittany was "hot." Perhaps she was. She wore many layers, and summer weather was still in reach.

Grey and I were so lost in conversation that I hadn't noticed Mr. Omni when he approached us from behind, furious that we were disrupting his discussion.

"Mr. Singh and Ms. Pierce, I'd like for you both to take center stage and recite the last four passages from Chadna's classic piece, 'For I Have Not Lived.' Since it's obvious that your attention is elsewhere, I take it that neither one of you will find difficulty in doing so." He brought his hands together in a clap and directed us to the stage.

We stood center stage, frozen and reluctant. Grey wasn't able to recite any lines but was successful at evoking laughter from the audience. This irritated Mr. Omni. So much that he gave Grey the permission to return to his seat. I wasn't given the same luxury.

"Well, what are you waiting for, Ms. Pierce? Commence!"

In contrast to what Mr. Omni believed, I *had been* listening to his lesson. I had caught every word and found no difficulty in repeating back what I'd heard verbatim. For *Nobans*, this was a rudimentary skill.

A classmate by the name of Samir Ali approached me from stage left, eyes closed as if savoring the experience. His green eyes peeled open and regarded me with undeserved adoration.

"That was an impressive reading—Tetra, is it?"

I nodded. He had a habit of leaning in close and then away when he saw my discomfort. "That accent you use; it really adds to the character. Mr. Omni, don't you agree?"

Samir always ignored Mr. Omni, but it was evident that Samir was his prized student. It had much to do with the fact that Samir was what others had referred to as "The King of Drama." I'd had the pleasure of observing him my first official month in attendance and to date he was one of the few people I'd come across that reminded me of people back in *Noba*. Not his behavior, but because he'd conducted courtships with people of multiple genders. Physical attraction wasn't something Nobans doted on but when couples were paired, gender rarely played a role in it.

"We should find time to meet, to talk about possibly performing together. I know an actress like you would bring out the best performance in me."

A voice that sounded like Grey's shouted from the audience, "Oh, give me a break." I'd be sure later on to ask him what that meant later.

The end of class bell rang, yet Samir stood eager to discuss future plans. "We should meet during independent study to talk more. I've got to head to my next class so if I don't see you later on, let me give you my number."

He handed me a card that contained several methods to contact him. Unsure of what to say next, I thanked him. Wasn't that customary?

The gymnasium was congested with an overflow of students. Normally, it was solely students from the senior class, but in light of the disappearance of Tristan Sorensen, parents demanded action from the school board. The faculty was expected to exhaust all resources in making the students at CCI feel safe, so for the next two weeks our regular gym classes would be replaced with lessons on self-defense.

A class that was divided by grade would, for the time being, be determined by last name. Pierce seemed like a fitting family name when I had chosen it, but now I regretted ever doing so.

Sterling would be grouped with the T-Zs, while I was assigned to the M-Ss. I would be alone with no one I knew.

The sound of a whistle silenced the ongoing chatter that resonated on and off the playing floor. Students sat together in groups, and it was then I noticed Grey sitting several feet away with Sterling's other friend Kip and the girl with the unnaturally red hair. Social skills were never my strong point, but I was disappointed by Grey's disregard. I thought we had made progress.

The gym teacher, Coach Ruiz, shouted for everyone to pair up into groups of two. Others around me made finding an ally look simple, yet I couldn't help feeling as I once had after tragedy struck my beloved *Noba*. Like an outcast.

Things were simpler when I could use my Phantom Riding to come and go unacknowledged. Now that I had become a viable presence in the senior class, I was faced with people avoiding me or pushing beyond my personal boundaries. Was there not a medium?

I tinkered with my shoelaces when a figure crouched down in front of me.

"You look so lonely over here. Looks like you could use a partner. It's Tetra, right?" I nodded. "I don't know if you remember me. I'm one of Sterling's friends—we met this morning. I'm Kip."

Kip's introduction in the time before school was a moment I wished not to revisit. He was intrusive, even more so than Samir Ali, and had a stare that seemed to assess you in one glance. For that, I couldn't tell if he would be a difficult person. And yet this close, it took great effort to take my eyes off him.

Kip had features most would find preferable in *Noba*. It was hard to evaluate his overall physique in *Geotic* clothing, but it was clear he was well-built.

Back home, those who trained their bodies to their highest limits were the ones who had the strongest spiritual connection to their *shaktis*. Mind and body worked in unison, and surely Sterling's friend Kip would have been one of the admired.

Imagine if he were to bond.

His lips curved into something maliciously playful when he discovered my sudden interest in him. I couldn't remember the last person to genuinely smile at me. There was my older brother, Arindelsoa, who I had not seen in over two decades. And then another—one I still hoped to see again.

"Hello, *Geo* to Tetra. Do you want to be my partner?"

I glanced over at Grey to see him partnered up with the girl with the unnaturally red hair—Waverly.

"Why didn't Grey want to be my partner?"

Kip's eyes reduced to squints with a hard smile. "Aww, you hurt my feelings." His lips stuck out in a pout, his hands meeting together at his chest. "You see, you were my first choice."

I scanned the room to realize everyone was paired up. I didn't have a choice. I was stuck with Kip.

"So today we're going to learn the basic rules of self-defense. For those of you who actually listened to my ten-minute lecture on how to prevent getting into an altercation with an assaulter, you'll come to realize that a display of words doesn't always fend people off when they pose as a threat. Once a person puts their hands on you, it's best to understand that by not reacting fast, you put yourself in a real situation to get hurt. A few seconds might not seem like a big deal to those of you willing to waste hours of your day mindlessly in front of a game console, but those measly seconds can really give you the upper hand in a confrontation."

That, I had learned to be true. Instinct and reaction time contributed to a large part of what we *Nobans* were taught early on in life. Many people of the *Oerban* tribe could not even move forward in their training until first mastering their extrasensory perception. To predict what your opponent would do was no simple feat.

Mr. Ruiz illustrated which body parts that left an attacker easily vulnerable. However, it was obvious that he was no *Rishi*. He demonstrated strikes that would make an unskilled disciple feel incapable of defeat and confident in their stance, though the force in his blows and lack of sagacity left me to wonder if he'd ever been in a physical encounter.

He mentioned nothing about leverage of weight and barely touched the surface in determining weaknesses. And here I'd thought that today's class would be thirty-five minutes well spent.

Coach Ruiz called on the class for assistants to help demonstrate his lessons, and when no one came forward, Kip volunteered us. It would be the two of us in front of everyone. I hoped what was asked of us wouldn't require much skill. In the height of a battle, I found it difficult to downplay my training.

For the next few minutes, we stood face to face—me in my defensive stance and Kip with his arms across his chest, repeating the words "I'm not hitting a girl" over and over again.

I had known my place back home. That is, I had *occasionally* known my place back home. To disobey the orders of a superior…you did not do it. For Kip to stand there and blatantly defy the coach's instruction led me to believe that Kip was to Coach Ruiz what Samir Ali was to Mr. Omni. A favored student.

Geotic law was strange if someone's gender somehow determined how they were to be treated, what abilities they could perform, and which roles they took on in adulthood. While it was true that gender did pose certain limitations for those who were unskilled, this was why we trained—so that our bodies and minds conquered their limits.

Geotics, however, believed women to be incapable of anything physical. Such strange principles.

"C'mon, Matherstein. Stop being a wuss," a less attractive boy with a similar build to Kip shouted.

"Yeah, Matherstein, she's just a girl. Afraid she's going to kick your ass?" another added with a laugh. His face flushed red as he had a sudden change of heart.

"Let's just get this over with."

Kip was instructed to put his arms around me and use all his force to overpower me. He was as tall as Sterling and easily weighed more than I did. He was the perfect opponent to apply my training to.

The next few seconds we tussled, further proving that Kip did have a powerful frame, but I waited. I waited to see how his body moved, where his feet moved. He led with his dominant side, his right side, so I'd have to attack from the left to catch him off-guard.

I hooked my left foot around his left ankle, putting enough force to cause his stance to become unbalanced. He loosened his grip, giving my elbow an open opportunity to meet the side of his face, *hard*. He reached out to grab my arm and used all his strength to pull me in closer. With the force of my body, I twisted my arm out with enough pressure that bent his wrist back, releasing me from his grip. My fist met his right eye, and if it hadn't been for Coach Ruiz coming in between us, I would have tackled him to the ground.

"My gosh, young lady, where'd you learn to punch like that?"

I shrugged. "Erm, self-defense camp?" I said in a tone that almost formed a question. When he nodded, I was relieved that he accepted my explanation.

While it was impossible to cover everything I needed to know about where kids in our age group learned things, Sterling had advised me to keep it simple and, if anyone asked, to say I'd learned it at a camp.

Intuition told me I'd be drowning in camps before the year's end.

Never have I been so eager to disappear to sixth period independent study. I'd garnered lots of talk and stares from my demonstration with Kip, and once word got back to Sterling, I'd never hear the end of it.

Number thirteen as per the Complete Tetra and Sterling Living Guide stated that all avoidable attention should be kept to a minimum. I wasn't the best at adhering to rules, but I had given my word. I'd promised to try.

I took refuge in the school's library. If you could call this place a true library. The first library I'd ever been to was the one assembled by what was left of our people—the Boundless *Noban* Library or Universal, in short.

Now that was a collection of references.

Only those who performed well spent their time in the library, which meant a quiet spot to complete my assignments while the scandal died down. Or so I thought.

Taylor Humphries immediately approached my table, taking great pleasure in formally introducing himself. As luck would have it, he'd been eager to talk to me since first period but I'd always been surrounded by primitive company.

Sigh.

Speaking of primitive….

"Run along, Humphries. Tetra and I are about to have an adult conversation. You kind of have to reach a height requirement. It's okay. Next time, buddy."

Kip didn't have independent study this period. What was he doing here?

"Nice shiner, Matherstein," Taylor said. "Hear you got sized up pretty good. Just let me know if the other one is feeling lonely. I have a four-year-old sister who'll even it out for you."

I disappeared into the aisles, fading behind rows of books. They were so immersed in each other that I believed they hadn't noticed me leave. But I glanced over my shoulder, and there they were, at my heels, still engaged in their ongoing dispute. What did I have that they wanted? Why couldn't they just leave me alone?

With every row we passed, I willed—no, *prayed*—for a means of evasion. Hope was fleeting and surrendering seemed to be my only option until I saw just the distraction I needed within stone's throw.

I recited the passages from my earlier class. Samir, who was cataloging a tray full of books, peered around the room until his green eyes, sparkling even from a distance, settled on me. He met me in a grapple of arms, ignoring the following I'd gained along the way.

I turned back to see Kip and Taylor both sharing a look of dismay and was relieved when they gave up pursuing me, accepting that Samir Ali had won the war in the fight for my company.

Samir wasn't any less obtrusive, but at least with him, I knew what he sought from me.

He wanted a muse.

If reciting a few lines from a piece of paper gave him that, then in essence, he was the lesser of two evils.

Sterling

By the end of sixth period, it was already news that Tetra had breached one of our rules. We shared our next class together, so guess who'd be finding himself a seat next to Miss Rough 'Em Up?

Me.

She sat in the back like she always did, her eyes glued to the table, projecting an invisible shield of modesty. I sat down next to her, the tension brewing as I prepared to address this violation of guidelines. If we didn't have order in our lives, there was no point in having them.

PE? Violation. Not cool.

I passed the notebook to her and watched as she looked over it. She took in a deep breath and started writing. When I got it back, it was one paragraph short of an entire page. Tetra needed help with her note passing.

I skimmed through it, but the gist of it said something along the lines of, *"It was a self-defense class. What was I supposed to do—not defend?"* Afraid to get caught sending notes back and forth, I closed the last note with a declaration that we would talk more when we got home. It wasn't like the rules weren't bendable, but why did I always miss all the cool stuff?

CHAPTER 12

Sterling

Urgh—I'm freaking suffocating! When I wasn't at school, I was home. When I wasn't home, I was at school. How did my parents expect my grades to improve with no freedom? I wasn't going to admit it, but if Tetra hadn't been living here, I would have gone mental.

It wasn't easy, but we were getting along. Our arrangement ran smoother with compromise. Cooking Tetra breakfast became ritualistic, and she volunteered to do the chores I hated. It wasn't a perfect situation, but it worked. It was weird, but the more time we spent together, the less I questioned the bond.

We still bumped heads. When Tetra was good at something, she didn't hide it. She made me look bad, as if I weren't good at doing that on my own. It wasn't even the worst thing. I wasn't comfortable sharing a room with a girl, but sharing a room didn't bother her. Tetra didn't care about or understand gender differences. Needless to say, three more additions made it onto the living guide.

There was still a ton I didn't understand about her. Why she did things, why she questioned everything. I only knew what I saw in my memories, which wasn't much.

The only thing I did know? Was that I'd stopped feeling…lost.

Since there's nothing to do when you're grounded, there was lots of time to finish studying/play video games. There was a history test coming up, and I wasn't prepared for it. I sat on my bed, reading. Carmen Chung, *something, something*. Minor bullshit, *something, something*. Civil suit, improved public school systems…dammit! Level 12 was getting on my nerves. I rolled over on my side. Tetra sat at the desk I never used. Her arms glided over her page. She must've been drawing.

"Hey, Tet, did you write any notes for the history test coming up?" I asked.

Tetra was focused. I assumed she hadn't heard me, but she responded, "Why would I take notes?"

I stood and walked over to peek at what Tetra was doing. Symbols—or runes?—erratically scattered over her page. They danced and jumped, sending me into a trance. The only thing that brought me back was at the corner of the page.

It was a drawing of a sword. It was small, with a three-plate construction style. I leaned closer to make out more.

"What is that?" I asked.

Tetra whipped her head around. "Did you *need* something, Sterling?"

You would've thought I'd been asking her questions all day. I slumped on my bed, defeated but still curious. "Did you finish studying, or are you frustrated like me? Because I don't have any of this stuff down," I said as she leaned her weight on the back of her chair.

"To 'have any of this stuff down'—I do not know what that means. Breaking that sentence apart, it does not make a coherent diction."

It was insanely annoying, but I forgot Tetra struggled with *Geotic* colloquialisms. She took and said things literally, so in my best efforts, I tried to do the same. It was difficult enough explaining why "rite," "write" and "right" sounded the same, but had different spellings and meanings.

"Tetra, how come you never study or do homework, but you still get better grades than me?"

Tetra's face pinched in a grimace. "You mean that coursework they assign at the end of class? I complete many of those assignments during free period. Is that not what it is meant for?" When I didn't answer, she directed her attention back to her project. "I find that once I return here, my time is best used elsewhere."

I dropped my head onto my mattress and picked up my handheld. "You mean drawing?" I said with a hint of sarcasm.

"I am replying to a correspondence, if you must know," Tetra answered coldly.

So that's what it was. Who did she write to, and how did they communicate? If they were words, I couldn't read them. Did she know other *Nobans* in *Geo*?

"If you require assistance, you are welcome to ask. I do perform better academically than you." Tetra was *not* good at subtlety.

"Geez, Tet. Don't hold back."

Tetra faced me, biting her lip, a look of concern on her face. "Is this an example where being forthright translates to insolence?"

I bit the inside of my cheek, my face tightening. "Yeah, kind of."

Her expression was flat, but she spoke with wide eyes. "I apologize."

"I'm just not as motivated as you, Tetra. Stuff comes so easy for you. Every time you try something, you're so much better at it. It's like magic."

Tetra's brows scrunched in the middle of her face and she dangled her coin bead between her fingers. "They tell us things we need to know during class. I remember them. In *Noba*, the ability to memorize information isn't an extraordinary skill. It is certainly not magic. You have books or professors to keep track of *Geo*'s past. Mental muscle memory is how we record things in *Noba*. Things I would have offered to teach you…" She didn't have to finish her sentence. I tried to get the whole "bond" thing, but it seemed so unreal. I always changed the subject if the hints were too close.

"Sterling, there are things that, if you knew, would give you the ability to access your psyche in a multitude of ways. Retaining past and present information wouldn't be as difficult but—"

My face lit up with glee. "That sounds great. Tell me how!"

Her voice cracked into a mocking tone. "Unfortunately, it would not be as simple for you now. You are nearly a man. We are taught much younger, when our minds are most susceptible to memory training. What took me a few days—weeks, at best—might take you months. Years, in your own time."

A knock came at my door.

"Come in!" I yelled. Dad cracked open the door, then walked inside. His fists were balled at his hips, more defensive than normal.

"Didn't want to just pop in."

I pointed in the direction of the door and answered, "Why? You do any other time."

"Sterling, that was before."

Sharing a room with Tetra had one advantage. My parents didn't barge in anymore without confirmation first. Sterling: 1; Parentals: 367.

Dad clapped his hands together. It was dinnertime, and it was his night to cook.

"So dinner is almost ready. Just wanted to get you guys downstairs to help set the table," he said, ending his statement with another clap. My dad worked full time, but he still cooked three times a week. When Mom was in good spirits, she took the other three, but I typically volunteered if she wasn't able to. The last day was left for takeout.

I wondered why no one ever helped me set the table.

We always spent the first fifteen minutes of dinner listening to Dad talk about work. If he didn't talk, only the clinking of forks against plates, Mom's awkward laugh, or absolute silence echoed throughout the kitchen. Dad was always in good spirits after work. He got to leave his problems at home. If Mom flipped out, the storm passed, no thanks to him. I loved my dad, but I tuned out conversations that started with *how the market was going*.

"So, kiddo, how was school?" he asked out of habit, though assumed he didn't really want to know. He rarely followed up when I answered.

"It was okay."

Mom's crow's feet gathered into a half-smile. "I'm sure it was more than just okay."

"I said it was okay, *gosh*!" I snapped, looking for a butter knife. Tetra twirled it between two fingers. I reached for it, but she dropped it, flinging it toward me.

Dad reached for the ketchup. He put ketchup on *everything*. He turned to his left, addressing Tetra.

"How about you, Tetra? Was your day just okay?"

Tetra shifted her shoulders and laid her fork near her half-eaten plate. "I am not sure. What qualifies as 'just okay'?"

Mom clucked her tongue, dropping her spoon on her plate. "A teenager who speaks."

I should've added that to the guide. You weren't supposed to speak in complete sentences with the parentals. *What was Tetra thinking?*

"Why don't you tell us how your day was? Regardless of outcome," Dad said.

Tetra scanned the table and stretched forward in her chair. "I am not proficient in certain topics, and I do not wish to offend…but oral sex? Is that related to coitus?'

My eyes grew to twice their size, and I could barely keep my food down. Mom covered her smug grimace, as Dad scratched his five o'clock shadow. He barely spoke without snorting or a cackling under each breath.

"Laurel…ahem…you want to take this one?" he said.

Mom followed with a long and winded, "Noooooooo."

I was dying. I sank into my chair. Could dinner get any more awkward?

Dad shrugged. "Okay? Um…well…"

"Dad, you are not about to have a conversation about oral sex at the kitchen table. Geez."

Dad chuckled and pointed in Tetra's direction. "Come on. That's rude. Tetra asked a question."

Tetra looked at me, leaning forward over her meal. "Is oral sex bad?"

Mom and Dad caved like two hyenas at the zoo. They both burst into a fit of laughter, as if in unison.

"No, Tetra. It's definitely not that," Mom said, mascara running down her cheeks.

"Did I say the wrong thing?" Tetra asked.

Dad banged on the table and fell back laughing in his chair. Mom leaned forward, clutching hold of her chest. "Maybe we can discuss it later, dear. Sterling is uncomfortable," Mom said, unable to contain her giggles.

"Tetra, I'm putting away dishes. Think you could lend a hand?" I stood, holding my finished plate.

"*You require help with one plate?*"

"*YES!*"

Tetra stood and took her plate as well. She joined me in the kitchen, the door closing behind us. My parents must've been holding in their laughter more than I thought. The moment we were out of view, the chortling grew louder.

"You are not seriously having a conversation about oral sex with my parents. At dinner!" I said, dropping my plate in the sink.

Tetra shrugged. "I was not aware it was a taboo subject," she said nonchalantly.

"It is when it's *my* parents." I pointed to the door, ignoring the sounds coming from the dining room.

"Can I ask you about it then?" Tetra asked.

I wanted to pull my hair out. "No! No, you cannot talk to me about it. FYI, bringing up oral sex is not a normal conversation starter during dinner!"

Tetra's eyes searched the room. "I apologize. Perhaps I was premature in assuming you had prior experience. If you do not know, that is all you had to say."

I had the sudden urge to defend myself. "Well…it's not like I'm a virgin." I knew there were a couple things Tetra would want to know when it came to the things that made our worlds different. But I wasn't used to talking about sex with my parents. I was even more uncomfortable addressing it with her.

"I wasn't suggesting that you were. In *Noba*, intercourse was only used for procreation. Only True Travelers made love for pleasure…and I met a True Traveler. I was just curious to know if my experiences were uncommon here, but…forget I asked." Tetra edged toward the kitchen door. I reached for her wrist to stop her.

"Look, I'm sorry." Tetra ripped her wrist away from mine. Weird. She'd only been here a few days, but she did that a lot.

Mom and Dad interrupted, bringing their plates to the kitchen sink.

"Wow, what a great dinner," Dad cried.

I narrowed my eyes at him, but the moment had passed and Tetra left the kitchen. I rolled my eyes. "Funny."

Dad drowned the sink with dish detergent. "It's not a bad thing to be curious, or ask questions. It wouldn't be the high-light of my day to talk about sex with you either but—"

"Dad!"

"Wait, let me finish. Like I said, there's nothing wrong with being curious. Tetra thinks it's okay to ask. It's uncomfortable, but we're here. We're not going to shame you for asking questions. It's kind of nice to have a teenager who'll say more than '*it's okay*' and '*yeah*.'"

Mom shook her head and helped Dad dry the dishes. "We didn't exactly have 'the talk' with you. We wouldn't judge. All we care about is whether you're safe," Mom finished, as I eased toward the kitchen door.

"Well, I'm leaving now." I said. My parents shot each other a leering glance before I disappeared into the hallway. I was still tense after dinner, but something was off. I didn't want to jump to conclusions, so I wanted to ask Tetra first.

I closed my door behind me. Tetra paced around the room, away from me.

"Are you going to tell me what's going on?"

Tetra stopped, studying me with a blank expression. "In regards to what?"

"You know what." I walked in Tetra's direction, but decided against it the moment she withdrew. She was threatened by my presence. Which was bizarre since we shared a room. I couldn't help feeling like she'd been abused in the past. I didn't have the right to ask, but the situation already strange.

"Tetra? Should we be sharing a room together?"

Tetra sat on her bed, arms crossed in front of her. "Do not be ridiculous."

I rubbed the space between my eyes. It was my only relief. It didn't stop the stress, but it nullified the tension in my head.

"I'm not trying to be ridiculous, Tetra. I'm just trying to get you. You're not the best at sharing."

Tired of asking questions with no answers, I headed for the door. Tetra's voice cracked as she responded. "We are strangers. You and I. We differ culturally and socially." That much was obvious. She paused, then continued. "We are more different spiritually than we have ever been. We have become two different people. My comfort level with you has decreased, and as much as it shames me to admit, my boundaries with you are rather limited."

I didn't really understand what she was trying to say, but it sparked a question in me. "Are you not allowed to touch people?" I asked.

Tetra held her hands in front of her chest defensively. "Not prohibited. But in your upbringing, touch is often used as a tool of comfort. In *Noba*, comfort is a sign of weakness. There are other politics involved, but it also shows a lack of control. I must be more careful. Our bond enables me to perform incredible feats, but it is not without consequence."

I sat down on my bed. "What does that mean exactly?"

"Our bond affects us differently. While it is useful that my ability to age is halted, my nociception is affected as well. It alters how my mind interprets pain, so it views all stimulus modality as threatening. Sometimes even with True Travelers."

That was a lot to process. How did anyone benefit from this? People couldn't touch, couldn't show emotion, or they risked appearing weak? There seemed to be so little room for connection.

"Then why do people bond in the first place?"

"I do not know. I told you I would not always be able to answer your questions. But those who do, see the world through a new set of eyes." Tetra wrung her fingers. "My comfort level around you comes because I do not know you as the man, only the boy."

"So it's because I'm a guy?"

Tetra's brows squished together, followed by a narrowed eye. "Your gender has nothing to do with it. But I look at you, and I do not see the person I feel."

That confused me. If she didn't see what she felt, then what *did* she see? "Well, I don't know how to change that."

Tetra sat on the floor, tousling her shoulder-length hair to the side. She gestured for me, until we sat face to face. "There is one thing I have not been able to do."

"What?"

Her eyes met mine. "There are parts of your mind you don't allow me access."

"What do you mean?"

Tetra ran her hands against her jeans. "I can access your short-term memory, but when I attempt to connect to your long-term memory, your mind has blocks in place. It is why you have the dreams. I tried to ease your pain, but your mind would not allow it. It puts up blocks for a reason, perhaps in an attempt to defend itself, but only you can tear them down."

Tetra reached out for both sides of my face and placed both her hands on my ears. Our eyes met. It was bizarre. I felt myself reflected through her. We looked nothing alike, but she was like a mirror. She closed her eyes and concentrated.

"You're blocking me," she said. I wasn't doing anything. Tetra's chin trembled, her grip growing tighter. She gritted her teeth, mouth tensed in a grimace of pain.

"*Let me in, Sterling*!" Her eyes burned a celestial blue as a ball of energy projected between us. It hit so hard we were pushed back away from each other several feet.

"What the hell was that?"

Tetra clutched her head, collapsing her face to her knees. "You continue to block me. It is so frustrating."

I held my chest, the pain less intense than before. "You did that on purpose? You're freaking psycho!"

Tetra backed out of the room. I didn't know where she was going, but I didn't care. If she didn't come back, I wouldn't lose any sleep.

CHAPTER 13

Sterling

I was *not* in a good mood. The memories? They came back full throttle. When Tetra started living here, they'd stopped. I hoped they'd gone away for good, but as luck would have it, they didn't. It was time to get up. Things were about to get cranky.

I grabbed my stuff and left the room to take a shower. It wasn't that long, but Tetra still wasn't up when I finished. It irritated me, having to wake her every … single … day.

"Come on, Tetra, you do this…every day…" I trailed off. The bed was empty. There wasn't even much sign it'd been in use. Come to think about it, I hadn't heard from her since last night. Since I called her psycho.

In retrospect, it hadn't been the best thing to call her, but in my defense, it also wasn't cool to zap me with her supercharged frustration. I didn't even know what she was looking for. She certainly never let me probe around in her head.

Dodging my parents was difficult, but I managed to make it out without questions. My only challenge now? Grey. He wasn't chatty in the morning, but he'd notice Tetra's absence. Fortunately for me, he had his head stuffed in a notebook. Maybe a day without Tetra wouldn't be such bad thing.

By the time third period came, I started sweating. More than normal. It was flu season, and the beginning stage of winter weather in *Geo* had a bite to it. Only this wasn't like a normal "sick." Whatever it was had to be "bond" related. I ignored the feeling as I went to class. It was *Geotic* history, which admittedly, was a class that didn't hold my attention. Today it was even harder to concentrate. It was a class Tetra and I shared, but since she hadn't showed, I couldn't her ask anything.

When the bell rang, I was relieved. My eyes burned, and I needed to reach a water fountain to flush them out. My vision was so blurry that I didn't notice the three people I ended up bumping into in the hallway. "Sorry" was all I mustered up each time my shoulder ran into another's. I rubbed my eyes until they hurt, and the water from the fountain had provided little relief. I barely made it to visual media in one piece. Today's assignment involved watching a film. Easy day.

The light would be off, so that would be a plus. I hid behind the dark to conceal my continuing struggle. Only five periods to go, right? Good thing I'd sat in the back today.

Something was wrong. I would've ignored it if only my body temperature hadn't kept increasing. I could have even dealt with the blurry vision. But I was antsy. There was a burning in my chest. That never meant anything good.

My head pounded. I rubbed my eyes and temples, but it didn't do much. It was weird, but I smelled fire or burning wood. The smell made me want to lose my breakfast. I had to be imagining it. I was in a classroom full of kids I knew. *Not a burning forest.*

I collapsed onto my desk. My midsection burned like a pit of hell. I was three seconds from a meltdown. I had to excuse myself. I reached up to rub my face, but before I could stop it, an intense pyre blazed out of my wrist. The violent hot stream struck the ceiling. It must've set off the outlets in the room because the walls spit out a series of sparks and it was literally raining ceiling tiles. Students screamed, covering their heads under their desks. I managed to crawl outside with some of the others. I was lucky. No one noticed what had caused the fire. Saved by *A History of the Camcorder*. I put as much distance as possible between me and the classroom as possible.

The hallways were a mad house. My plan was to make my way to the nurse's office to avoid the crowd. By now, the pain had spread to my entire body. I was fortunate to have made it this far. I probably shouldn't have closed my eyes.

I wasn't sure how long I'd been out, but rest hadn't stopped the pain. I squirmed and fidgeted until I my eyes peeled open. My vision was a blur at first, but a mote of dark red came into focus. I wasn't alone.

Waverly leaned over me. Holy crap. Did I have drool on my face? Was my fly zipped up? There was too much room for error at this point.

"Sterling, are you okay?" Waverly asked.

"What are you doing here?" I asked defensively, leaning away from her on the table. Waverly rolled her eyes. It was kind of cute, but she talked with her hands when she was being sarcastic.

"Oh, thank you, Waverly. It's nice of you to make sure I'm okay." Her voice altered, becoming saccharine sweet and dripping with sarcasm. "Oh, you're welcome, Sterling. It's no problem to waste my free period helping you and clueless freshman, who are freaking out over an electrical fire…"

I laughed, suddenly feeling like a jerk. "Sorry, Waverly. You know what I meant." Waverly was a candy striper, so she helped out in the nurse's office for extra credit or something like that. Seemed like the perfect job.

"So were you in fourth period visual media?" Waverly asked, eyes curious.

I leaned up on my left elbow, the one in the least amount of pain. "Um, yeah. But it's not like I saw anything."

"You have a bad burn on your forearm."

"You looked at my arm?" It practically hummed with excitement as I tugged at my sleeve.

"Well, I had to." She leaned in to lower her voice. "Most of the people showing up are, like, faking injuries, to avoid that chem quiz eighth period."

I definitely wasn't prepared for that test, but I didn't want Waverly checking up on me. "Well, I guess I should go—"

Waverly was quick to interject—"You're not going to wait for the nurse?"—but I was already headed toward the door.

"I'm fine, really."

The hallway felt like a labyrinth. I knew where I was, but everything felt like it was spinning. I knew shouldn't leave school, but I needed to get out of here. I wanted to collapse, but it couldn't be here. Not now. Not when I wasn't sure what was wrong with me. What if I started another fire?

The big gray doors were all that stood in my way to freedom. I hadn't felt the weight of the door or pushed it open, but I already felt the air, licking at my skin and hair.

To be honest, that was all I remembered.

He'd pressed his lips against hers with undying need and hunger. They floated along the water, the serene, tender tides caressing their skin and saturating his long hair so that it slicked down close to his scalp. He pulled away, half smiling as he whispered to her in a foreign tongue and yet, not so foreign to her as she returned the smile and answered back in the same language, while he placed his once lonesome lips along the smooth column of her neck.

Both were indistinguishable under all the tribal markings that adorned their faces. It was a wonder they hadn't washed away against the often-ruthless currents. Her gaze felt familiar, no, her gaze was familiar.

"*Tetra.*" I woke up from my dream in a fit of gasps, my heart racing. The fire in my chest was gone; my energy back. Light poured in my window as the last few hours were an absolute blur. And then there was this other *issue*. I didn't know how I'd gotten here or when she'd even gotten back, but here I was in her bed. Our legs were tangled up in one another's, her back pressed too close to a place I *really* wished it hadn't been.

Please don't have an erection! Please don't have an erection! And yet, I'd spoken too soon. Tetra—or my parents, for that matter—couldn't find me like this. They'd think I was a total pervert.

I peeled her leg from mine, but fell to the floor in the process. Tetra was a heavy sleeper—she wouldn't notice. She tossed around like I'd never been there and it was then that I noticed the string on her wrist.

It held a bead that resembled a coin. Like the mark on my wrist, it had a symbol—various circles on the outside and arrows pointing toward the middle. It looked like something I'd seen before, but like everything else, I didn't know why.

Back to more taxing issues at hand. The dream I just had. It felt so…real. Which only led me to believe that perhaps it wasn't a dream, but a memory. And not my memory but Tetra's.

I was never sure if Tetra had had anyone in her life that she'd cared enough about to share her experiences, let alone fantasize about. The guy she was with was more a man than an adolescent, that much was certain. His voice, his build, his presence all shouted "mature male", which would probably explain why high school guys annoyed her.

Who was this mystery man and why did I have to accidently stumble across some cloaked memories to find out even the tiniest detail that would make me understand her better. As much as I wanted to know more about her and how our destinies entwined, that memory, well it seemed private. I thought it best to keep it to myself until she was actually ready to tell me what her life was like before she'd settled in this one.

I was bonded to her, *right*? Even if she and the past weren't on speaking terms, did that mean that we had to be? I wanted so bad for her to fill in the gaps and it sucked not knowing.

I crawled back to my own bed. Clearly on the weekend, Tetra didn't make an effort to wake up early. I'd just have to wait until she was up.

She moaned and lifted her head off the pillow. Perfect timing.

"Long time, no see," I said, an attempt to sound casual. "Look, Tetra. I'm sorry about the other day."

Tetra scrunched her nose, her voice cracking as she spoke. "For what?"

"I don't know. I guess for calling you psycho," I said, running my fingers through my hair.

Tetra shrugged. "You believe you offended me? Your choice of words are always a puzzling matter, but I knew you had not meant to insult me. Though, it is rather difficult to know what you mean most of the time."

I sat up, pointing my arms to nowhere in particular. "You were gone for, like, a whole day. Without anyone knowing. Except me. I thought we weren't doing this anymore."

"I had business to take care of. When I say that, it means it far outweighs my obligations to public high school."

"Well, you should at least tell me where you were. Or let me know where you'll be, just in case somebody asks me."

"Did you have something to ask me, Sterling?" She was a master at avoiding touchy subjects. Why would she be any different now?

"Why? It's not like you'd tell me anyway. When you're here, you avoid my questions. When you're not, crazy shit happens—"

"Has something happened?" It was her first sign of concern since she'd been back.

"No. Unless you consider it normal to emit lights from your hands, then no."

Tetra shook her head. She blinked twice, before holding out her right hand. "Sterling, it is only habitual for light to emit from your right hand. If it is emitting from both hands, then no. That is not normal."

My palm hit the middle of my forehead. "I meant it as a hypothetical thing."

Tetra stood, balled fists at her side. Her midsection glowed and traveled to her chest, then burned through her arm. Her palm produced a powerful light before she her fist, dissolving any trace of it.

"Was it anything like that?" As if it were the most mundane of questions.

"Well…yeah, but…not like…that controlled," I managed to spurt out.

Tetra's eyes moved up and down, considering the options. She paced to the other side of the room. "I did leave the world. It is possible you were resonating." Huh? I needed to backtrack. It sounded like she said she'd *left the world*." As if she could've meant something else.

"So you left *City*?"

She shook her head. "No. I left *Geo*. Did I not make myself clear?"

I tried to form a coherent sentence but could only mutter excessive *ums* and *uhs*

"Did you have something more to ask?" Tetra asked.

I was still on the whole leaving-*Geo* comment. "So when you leave worlds, does it cause you and me to…I don't know, want to share a bed?"

She met me with narrowed eyes and a slack expression. "I do not know what you mean. But if you are suggesting what I believe, then yes. When you and I are separated by long distances, our energies increase in an attempt to find one another."

"So we're like…some sort of spiritual GPS?"

"Perhaps. Leaving one world for another has always affected you considerably. As a True Traveler, you are never in balance without me. That is why *you* bond. Spiritually, the soul exchange neutralizes the energy we host that is imbalanced."

That didn't seem fair. I didn't ask for this. There had to be something to control it, at least at school.

"Why doesn't it happen to you?" I asked.

Tetra addressed me with a dismissive glance. "It does."

The entire room shook—the beds, the desk, the clothes on the floor, all lifted off the ground in unison. Tetra's eyes radiated, as did her wrist. Her feet miraculously left the floor. She joined her right fist into her left palm, causing her and everything in the room to resettle.

"I resonate, but I am in control of it. The understanding of energy imbalance is the only way to harness it. My root *shakti* keeps me from causing destruction."

Why couldn't I hover? I had to have laser beams shoot out of my hands instead. "What else should I know about *shakti*?"

Tetra sat across from me. She threaded her fingers through her hair and held out seven fingers. "*Shakti* is a synonymous term for energy, but they are also points on the body through which those energies flow. The root is located at the base of the spine and represents our foundation, spiritual or literal. The sacral starts in the abdomen and deals with our ability to connect with others and experiences."

She pointed to her upper abdomen and it gleamed on contact. "The solar plexus challenges our ability to be in control. It is the *shakti* point we use most when connecting to elements. You may need work on that one."

Tetra squirmed around to face the wall. "There is the heart. It spiritually governs devotion. We are not encouraged to express our heart *shakti* unless we bond." She shifted and reached for her throat. "Then there is the throat. This is the energy meant to communicate with. It should be used to communicate only the truth."

I'd counted five so far, but still had questions that weren't answered. "Tetra, this information is good and all, but how does it stop me from shooting light out of my hands at school?"

Tetra shook her head and held out her hands in front of her. "This is where you differ greatly from your *Geotic* peers. You mustn't hold energy inside. We use it defend ourselves for a reason. It must leave our bodies, where we are marked, and should never be denied. If you knew your body's spiritual weak points, you would be better at preventing the outbursts to begin with."

Great. Another thing I couldn't do.

"I did not know you still reacted this way. In the past, all your senses would increase, but I assumed now that you would be able to resist my influence, that you'd conquered it."

I shook my head. "I don't think this has happened before. I would've remembered."

Tetra avoided eye contact with me. "Sterling, I had to erase it every time it happened—"

"So you screwed with my mind?"

She stood and sat on my bed, the first time she'd actively closed the space between us. "Sterling, I had to. Releasing energy that makes you vulnerable, and it grew stronger once you found me. Taking your memories of me suppressed your ability. But now that your mind rejects it, I leave you defenseless if we are not together. It would be different if you could protect me, as well as yourself, but you cannot."

What a way to make me feel lousy. I didn't want protecting. Granted, I wasn't prepared to take on crazy snake creatures, but I wasn't defenseless. And why was it okay for Tetra to tinker with my brain when we were supposed to trust each other? That didn't breed trust.

"Tetra, how am I supposed to trust you when you don't tell me anything? You come and go and mess with my head. I don't always know how to trust you." A sense of guilt washed over me for admitting it, but maybe she'd appreciate my honesty. She did prefer the truth.

"I agree with you. Our bond has not been easy, and our time apart has caused a rift between us. There are many things we both need to overcome. But until then, I can give you what was once lost to you." She reached for me, but then stopped. "It is…customary to ask permission to touch someone intimately in *Noba*."

I edged back. "What are you going to do?"

"I cannot manipulate you anymore. But if you allow me, I can give you what I took. Your memories of me."

I nodded. We sat and faced each other as she stretched her hands to the sides of my head. "I can access your Crown, but I should warn you. You may feel me in a way that is invasive. If you can live with that, I will continue."

"As long as it doesn't hurt."

Her eyes began to glow once more. "Ready?"

CHAPTER 14

Tetra

The boy pulled at the woman's shirt, but the rows of canned goods held her attention. Bringing him with her wasn't the ideal situation, but she wasn't the type of mother to hire someone to watch him. He often joined her on a trip to the supermarket.

"Mom. Mooom! Can I get this?" he asked, desperately pulling at her shirt. He held a small case, and his mother inspected its price. Her eyes widened and her mouth dropped.

"This is twenty-five dollars. Absolutely not."

I'd had a very limited concept of value then. It could have been steep; it could've been a bargain. All in all, I'm glad she hadn't given into him. Indulgence was a strong sign of weakness, whereas adamancy was a powerful trait to have as a matriarch.

"Remember the last one you had? You played with it for a day before you wanted a new one."

"But Mom—"

"Don't 'but Mom' me, Sterling. Put it back!"

Sterling.

The sound of the name made us both shiver. It was a sign that neither one of us belonged in that place or time. Names were powerful. The old stories of *Noba* claimed that just the sound of one's name from their bonded was often enough to call a soul into consciousness.

That wasn't the case now. I was feeding a memory from my mind to Sterling's. Memories that would have a difficult time resurfacing because of the artistry I'd done over the years. His memories of me were always the most extensive, but transference was his only option if he wanted them back intact.

"Fine. I'll put it back," Sterling said. He kicked at the air in a bratty sort of way. He passed a coloring book with the word ELEVEN in bold letters. He next examined a price tag that read $11.11. He even passed a display of toys, where each row of figurines was arranged in sets of eleven.

The mind at this age was unreliable. There was a chance none of these details actually existed in the memory itself. The fact that they kept repeating was a symbolic sign. It represented his age at the time.

We shared a stream of disappointment. A slight drawback. I would feel my own emotions as well as Sterling's at the time. He really wanted that game.

"Don't get lost, Sterling! I don't want to look all over the store for you," Laurel hollered as he walked out of view. Sterling's curiosity was always a part of him, both then and now.

As he journeyed through the aisles, he anticipated what he might find. He reached an area filled with many types of Geotic technology, and like a child in a candy store, he felt at ease.

Something lured him here. An impulse he could neither question nor control.

An instinct.

His wrist and forearm itched, and he cursed before reaching to scratch it. He browsed the magazine and book aisle. His nose scrunched, and his hands lingered on a magazine with a woman on the cover. He flipped through it, stopping only at the pictures of the women in swimsuits. An outflow of arousal and shame surged between us. Perhaps Sterling found this part of the memory unfavorable.

I sat, cross-legged, just a few feet away from him. His body jerked in my direction, his face speaking volumes.

How do I know her?

Dozens of open publications sprawled around me in a circle. Acculturation had come in many stages for me, and at the time, reading and writing the language had proved the most difficult.

"What are you doing?" he asked, raising one eyebrow. He crawled over to me, but stopped when I turned to him. He knew that we knew each other, but not how we knew each other.

True Travelers. Even untrained, their minds just knew.

I'd spent weeks suppressing Sterling's ability to find me, but his shakti only tried harder. The greater the amount of time spent apart, the stronger it became.

"I am…" I started with a calculated pause. *"…attempting to learn new words."*

He laughed. Harshly, adult-like, and arrogant. Comfortable. He crawled closer to me, near an open video game ad.

"You talk weird," he said, grabbing nearby materials. "Need any help?" It was as if the time apart had never affected us. He didn't have to know everything. His heart told him what he needed and didn't question the rest.

We spent the time together passing materials back and forth. I would read aloud, and he would correct my pronunciation of the words most foreign to me.

This hadn't been our first encounter, but reliving it, I saw why it held significance to him. It was the only memory where his role was the mentor, the teacher.

This day? It was one of our fondest. It had been such a shame to wipe away…

Sterling

When I opened my eyes, I stopped seeing memories. I only saw Tetra. We'd met so many times in my life. A few times, we'd even spoken to each other.

The one thing that stood out? I got older, but physically, she stayed the same. She'd always been there, unseen and unheard, but now I remembered those moments. I'd never forgive her if she took them away again. They were mine and they were of us, and I wanted them to stay. It was comforting to know we were always there for each other.

Always.

"You will always struggle without me, Sterling. There is no you without me."

I woke up in a better mood. The return of my memories gave me the best sleep I'd had in weeks. I didn't think I'd ever *really* understand a bond, but I did know that without Tetra, I felt incomplete. I kind of wished I hadn't bonded with a chick, though. Especially to a girl I was attracted to. We made it work, but there were still issues that made things uneasy between us.

I always beat Tetra when it came to waking up, so this morning, I decided that she had earned a special breakfast. I wouldn't be winning any cook-offs anytime soon, but this was the best toasted bagel with cream cheese I'd ever made.

"Time to get up, Tetra," I said, poking the exposed part of her shoulder that wasn't covered by blanket. She rolled onto her stomach, pulling the cover over her head.

"Heh, nice try."

I pulled the blanket down, just enough to see her face. I couldn't explain why, but her bed always seemed more comfortable than mine. Maybe because everything on it was new, including her "required" satin pillowcases. Mom claimed Tetra needed them, but I still couldn't tell you anything about differences in hair texture. No matter what, Tetra's hair always looked great.

"Come on. Time to get up. Breakfast is getting cold," I said, laying it on the side of the bed. I stood when signs of hunger at this point were too difficult to deny. She ate breakfast in one sitting, leaning up, as she rubbed her eyes.

"Well?" I said with a smile. Tetra picked at food, so it went without saying she must've she loved my knack for the culinary arts.

"Your cooking is reminiscent of Laurel. I am as good as awake." She stumbled onto her feet and headed toward the door.

By fifth period, I was feeling extra-confident about the trig test an hour away. We had a sub in PE, so that meant I had a second independent study period to properly prepare for it.

Kip, Waverly, and various others amongst the Golden Ones spent this time talking about the remaining days before Homecoming and how they were going to go out celebrating after this week's football game. I was grounded for eight more weeks, so I didn't bother torturing myself by contributing to a conversation I shouldn't have been having. Grey, Tetra, and I used the thirty-some minutes to map out examples, go over notes, and quiz each other briefly on what might be on the test.

During football season, Grey had to keep at least a C average to play, and me? I had to bring my D+ disappointments up to at least a C before my folks would even consider renegotiating my punishment. Tetra rarely took notes but was somehow great at helping us with the things we didn't understand.

Wished she wouldn't have switched all her classes around. I could have really used her help in composition.

Time always flew during the easy classes. Pretty soon, I found myself back in the locker room changing into my street clothes.

Grey took off after the first bell rang. He might have said something about meeting with the student council, but Kip stayed behind, like me, not in a rush to get to the next class. I couldn't be late, but that didn't mean I wanted to be early.

Just as it was time to head out, Kip made it harder by blocking me by my locker.

"Dude, don't rush off. I want to talk to you for a sec." He pulled his shirt over his head and proceeded slipping on his sneakers.

"What is it? Is everything okay?"

He gestured for me to sit, and I prepared for the worst. People only wanted you seated when the world was close to ending.

"Relax, man. It's not life-threatening. Just hear me out." He hesitated, and that just made me irritated.

"Uh, could you make it fast? I can't be late for my next class."

He leaned across the locker in front of me looking…I don't know, embarrassed.

"So um…what's the deal with you and Tetra?"

I shrugged. "I mean, there isn't really a deal. We live together." No way would I mention being spiritually bonded to her. *He didn't need to know that, did he?*

"It's just you guys seem close. Are you into her?"

Frustrated, I rolled my eyes. Kip had asked me this at least three times in two weeks. "You know I like Waverly."

Although, sometimes there was something that drew me to Tetra that went beyond this whole bond thing. It felt strange to admit it, but for the first time in my life, I may have actually had eyes for a girl other than Waverly. Maybe it wasn't anything serious, but it was definitely there.

He took in a deep breath, his eyes darting to every corner in the room. "I just wanted to make sure I wasn't overstepping any boundaries."

I fought with my book bag, unsure of why he was still wasting my time. "Ookay."

He raked his fingers through his hair, either stressed out or overworked. I couldn't tell. "Dude, I dig Tetra." Him and half the senior class. "But the thing is, she won't even talk to me. Won't even look at me. But she talks to that Samir kid and even Taylor Humphries. Taylor fuckin' Humphries."

Taylor Humphries wasn't Kip's biggest fan after Kip had beaten him out of sophomore class president two years ago. Since then, it was Taylor's life mission to make Kip look like an ass at every available opportunity. The fact that Tetra had already chosen sides with Taylor had to be a blow to Kip's ego.

"C'mon, I know she must talk to you. I was thinking maybe you could talk to her for me. You know I'd do it for you."

Yeah, for every girl except for the one who mattered.

"Kip, I am *not* cornering her."

"I didn't say corner her. All I'm asking is for you to talk to her. I'm...ugh... I don't know what else to do." Kip never came to me or even Grey about girls. He didn't have to. There wasn't a time I could remember him actually working for a girl's attention, so I'm sure he was feeling like crap about it. *Welcome to my world.*

"What is it that you want me to say to her?"

He placed his hand on my shoulder, looking like something I'd never seen before. Desperate. "We're going out after the Homecoming game. Get her to come with you, and I'll handle the rest."

I pushed his arm away, holding my hands up to ward him off. "Uh, did you forget I'm still grounded?"

"Dude, still? Fuck!" He sank down on the bench with his hand shielding his face. "So sneak out, Wayfairer!"

This was why I hated being friends with people who could come and go as they pleased. They always made these outlandish suggestions as if I had plenty of options.

"Don't take this the wrong way, Kip, but bite me! I do that and I might as well plan on not leaving the house until I'm twenty-five. Here's an idea: just start the conversation by asking for her help with something. It's rare she turns anyone down needing her help. I speak from experience."

"Sterling, I'm begging you." Now that Kip had resorted to begging and pleading, I did what any good friend would do. I bartered with him.

"What's in it for me?"

Kip clasped his hands together with that used-car-salesman look in his eyes. You know the kind—the one that'll sell you a lemon but will convince you it's a sports car. "Waverly's going to be there…naturally."

I clucked my tongue, crossing my arms in front of my chest. "Nice try, but you're going to have to do better than that."

He snapped his fingers in an *aha* moment. "When you go in for your driver's license, I'll let you use my car."

"And...?" I knew I was about to push it, but he couldn't really expect me to risk everything just so he could make googly eyes at Tetra outside of school. The water had to be warm for me to dive in.

"Dammit, Wayfairer. That new laptop you keep talking about? It's yours."

"Brand new?"

"Of course brand new! Hey, let's get going." The second bell was only seconds from going off. We had less than a minute to get to class. "But just so you know, it's going to take a few days. I just replaced the stereo system in my car. My dad's going to lose it if I make another big purchase. Give me until the end of the week."

Details, details. "Get it to me the morning of the game, and I guarantee Tetra and I will be there at that game."

"Done."

We shook hands. The second bell rang as we parted ways.

I'd been nervously anticipating how exactly I was going to convince Mom to let me go to the Homecoming game. Kip's advice to sneak out? Not happening, unless I was confident enough to sneak back in without getting busted. I wasn't. It was best to have a smarter approach. One that involved asking Mom in a way that, not only could she *not* say no, she'd think it was her idea.

I interrupted my teen drama marathon in the living room to catch Mom as she was walking out the door. I met her in the hallway before she could go any farther.

"Mom!" I said, while she was securing a scarf at the nape of her jacket. It wasn't *that* cold out.

"What is it, Sterling? I have to pick up the pizza, so make it quick." Mom said with a level of malevolence that was only evident when she knew I wanted something. My mom had a stellar bullshit detector.

Pizza? That's right. It was takeout night.

"Did you have something to ask me?"

Five minutes ago, I may have gone with honesty, but it looked like I'd have to get my hands dirty.

"Mom, I have a proposition for you, but before you say no—"

"No."

"You didn't even let me finish!" I said, following her to the front door.

"Sterling, if you're even *thinking* about telling me anything besides 'I'm getting straight A's for the remainder of the school year,' I don't want to hear it. You have that 'I need to hang out with my friends this weekend' look on your face. Guess what? It's not happening."

Geez, all that in one breath. Was I that predictable? Sixteen seconds had to be a record for her to see through me.

"Oh come on, Mom, my grades…" I considered carefully how to end this sentence. "…are *kind of* getting better." That wasn't a total lie.

Mom rolled her eyes, edging closer toward the front door. "Ugh, I'm exhausted with having this same conversation."

I followed her out the door and to the car in the driveway. "Mom, seriously. It's our school's Homecoming game. If I don't go—"

"You'll live."

Mom closed the car door behind her. I knocked on the window, willing her to roll it down. When she ignored me, I had no choice. Was it a suicide mission? Yes. Was I evil for exploiting her only weakness? Probably. She had left me no choice. It was go hard or go home.

I threw my head back, sighed, and collapsed my hands at my sides. "I guess Kip'll have to look after Tetra then."

Mom finally rolled down the window. "I couldn't hear you. What?"

I leaned over the open window, trying to look casual. It was hard to keep from laughing while appearing equally uninterested. "Oh, Kip and Tetra are hanging out after the Homecoming game. I figured she would've mentioned it. But I guess, why would she? Seemed like a date." I studied my mother's sudden change in mood. A slight smile curved at the side of her mouth, but her crow's feet hadn't moved. Not a convincing smile in the least. First defense down.

"Oh. Well, I guess it's good Tetra is making friends," Mom said in a weak voice.

I averted my eyes, trying my damnedest not to look obvious that I was studying her face.

"Yeah. Tet wanted us both to go. I guess it would've been more, like, a group thing if I *could* go. Not that anything would happen…" I said, leaving the end of the sentence open. It didn't seem fair to throw Kip under the bus because he wasn't the type of guy to take advantage of a situation, but I knew Mom well enough—she thought he might.

"Kip…seems so…experienced," Mom said to no one in particular. I'd hit a nerve. Even though she was my mom, it wasn't a secret Kip thought she was a total MILF. Mom knew he was harmless, but try explaining all those burnt desserts while Mom got knee-high drunk in compliments anytime Kip came over for dinner.

Mom's eyes doubled in size, as if she were afraid to blink. Who knew what went on in her head, but one had to consider all outcomes.

"Sterling, I'm not in a good mood and don't make a habit of my generosity, but you can go to that game."

In a triumphant victory, I pulled back my arm in a fist pump.

"I like Kip. I really do. But Tetra can be naive sometimes. You can go, but only if you make sure Kip and Tetra stay out of trouble." She could barely finish before I was hugging her through the window. One girl down. If only Tetra would be this easy.

My phone buzzed. I leaned over, hiding the screen with my spindly, long fingers.

What'd she say?

As if Kip weren't annoying enough in person.

It was a quarter past seven, and I wasn't any closer to asking the one person who mattered. If Tetra didn't go, I wasn't going. After a half hour of strategizing, I decided that manipulating the facts had worked wonders on my mom. All I would have to do was convince Tetra that it was her fault I was grounded in the first place and she'd have to say yes, right?

With a laptop, a guaranteed shot at my driver's test, and alone time with Waverly on the line, I was willing to try anything. At best, the two of them would hang out and it'd be obvious they had have zero chemistry. Tetra would go back to ignoring Kip and everything would be back to normal.

Ugh. Being in the middle was exhausting.

I excused myself to butter the popcorn. I needed fuel to sit through that chick sitcom about…clothes, boys, and other stuff I would've completely ignored if the cast hadn't been hot.

There was no way she'd miss a midweek teen drama marathon. It started as a tool Tetra used to study the way people our age acted in *Geo*, but she'd become obsessed with how young adults were portrayed. Apparently *Geotic* teenagers were completely different from *Noban* teens. Big surprise there. Here we weren't exactly walking around with what looked like decorated underwear, and we didn't spend our childhood training our *shaktis*.

BEEP.

Melted butter, ready for pouring. I walked back to the couch, spreading my legs over the couch's arm. My head rested on Tetra's lap, something she didn't seem to mind.

It'd been weeks since Tetra confessed that our time apart restricted our physical boundaries. I was glad we got over that.. Her legs were strong, but it was amazing how they were also unarguably soft. Maybe it was just girls in general, but they made way better pillows. They smelled better, didn't deflate, stayed warm, and required little adjustment.

"I do not understand. Why is she upset with her?" she asked.

I pointed at the screen to the girl wearing clothes no teenager could afford. "You know Adam? That guy she likes? He likes Genevieve. But Abby is jealous of that because she's rich. Do you get it now?"

Tetra frowned, and her nose twitched. Another question was coming.

"I do not understand. If this Abigail is of affluence, what would cause her resentment toward Genevieve over a man?"

At least I knew this one. "Because, Gen's prettier," I said with a laugh.

This confused Tetra even more. "So you can rank lower in affluence, not require any skills or achievements, but as long as you are physically appealing, that is a reason enough for people to envy you?"

"Pretty much," I said with a shrug. She fidgeted underneath me. I readjusted my head, watching her stare into space.

"There is a saying in *Noba*," she started, before trailing off into a language I couldn't understand. There was a sing-song quality to it that sounded natural and fluid as it left her mouth. I sat up.

"What does that mean?"

She curled her legs in, her body toward me but her eyes focused on the TV. "It means, 'The one remembered for their appearance spends a lifetime motionless, bewitched by their own reflection.'"

"Well, most people around here don't have *shakti* strength or advanced abilities. It's not perfect, but that's how people judge who they like."

She swiveled toward me, curling her cold feet underneath my legs. "Or who they do not like. Perhaps that is why I am not well received. Because many find my appearance *physically appealing.*"

I shook my head, gathering my thoughts. "Tetra, you're not going to get any sympathy from me. You want to know why guys act weird around you? It's because you're pretty. You want to know why girls don't like you? Because you're hot. You want to know why people want your attention? Because you're amazing."

Wow. Did I say that last part out loud? Awkward. Waverly was the girl of my dreams, but any person with eyeballs could see everything Waverly had, Tetra did, too. They were both smart, ambitious, and super-hot. If I didn't watch myself, I'd catch myself falling for Tetra. Not that it would matter. No one ever got her attention. She mentioned a fling way back when. I kept thinking that maybe that unknown person held the keys to her heart. Bad news for Kip.

Which reminded me. I had to ask her about this weekend. It was the perfect time to change the subject.

"Hey, Tetra, you weren't doing anything over the weekend, right?"

"I thought I'd be spending it with you."

Don't get me wrong I liked having someone to share this burden with, but it was going on week three with no freedom. There were only so many cheesy teen marathons a guy could take.

"Well…obviously. But wouldn't you like to get out for a change? Have fun? You know, with other people?" I said, hoping she would catch a hint.

Her eyes reduced to squints. "If I don't have fun with you, why would I with other people?"

Anytime Tetra unknowingly insulted me, it meant her ears were open. I had her full attention.

"You've seen it at school. All the Homecoming stuff. Everyone's going to the game at the end of the week. You remember Kip, right?" I said, in my attempt to sound nonchalant. Tetra's lip curled in discontent.

"Vaguely."

I studied her expression the best I could in five seconds before going all in.

"A bunch of my friends are going, obviously. But Mom won't let me go unless you do." I knew it was a low blow, but I had to poke her sympathy button.

"Why don't you just ask her? She may surprise you."

I'm sure Tetra knew I was lying. Or she was better at reading me than I gave her credit for. This was going to be much harder than I'd initially planned.

"Come on. It's way better than watching…*Crescent Moon High*. You'll get to be around people. A lot of people. And just to be nice, I'll even throw in a crowd-loving corn dog."

Tetra just scrunched her eyebrows. "Nice? That doesn't sound like you."

"Come on, Tetra. I really want to go!" I know I sounded like a two-year-old, but too much depended on this. There wasn't any room to be proud.

"Why do you want to go?" she asked as I collapsed onto the couch. My back sunk into the pillow as our eyes met again.

"Because Waverly is going to be there. I really wanted to hang out with her," I said, defeated.

"Why didn't you just say that? I am already aware you possess a strong affinity for Waverly. If going ensures a favorable outcome for you, you should have said that from the beginning."

Tetra turned back toward the TV and continued getting lost in her "stories." I tried not to bounce up and down in a victory dance. The day couldn't have ended more perfect.

Tetra

Sterling and I surveyed the seating for the sporting event. There were a few empty seats on the high-rise end, providing an optimal view of the football field. It was puzzling how so many came to watch twenty-two people kick around a ball.

We were surrounded by fellow classmates, teachers, even people I didn't recognize adorned in blue and white from head to toe, CCI's school colors. The fanatics wore faces ornamented in a substance that resembled ceremonial paint, and those who didn't wave banners decorated with CCI's logos wore fingers made of foam with encouraging slogans.

Sterling wasn't in the best of moods. Peter misplaced his keys, and Sterling complained we were missing the pep rally, an event before the match. I was certain the pep rally was not his real concern. He'd said Waverly's name repeatedly the whole time he spent getting ready. When we found Sterling's friends, we sat directly behind Waverly and the girl with the face full of freckles, Margaret. I hoped Waverly's presence would lift his spirits. I knew he thought highly of her.

Once we got comfortable (or as comfortable as one could be sitting on a cold metal surface), Waverly offered a genuine smile and a slap to Sterling's knee. "I was just thinking about you guys. Hi, Tetra."

Margaret had a look of disgust on her face that seemed exclusively reserved for me, but when she spoke, she addressed everything to Sterling. "Look who decided to show his face in actual moonlight. How long will it take before your folks are passing out milk cartons, filing police reports for their missing child? Did you have to sneak out again?"

Sterling hit her over the head with a foam finger. She panicked and switched seats with Waverly, claiming it had taken an hour to do her hair. It looked the exact same. I couldn't understand why she would waste an hour's time on the same outcome.

The deafening discord of the pandemonium engulfed us. If the Homecoming game was supposed to hold my attention, it wasn't off to a good start. We were a smaller group than anticipated. When were the rest coming?

I poked Sterling. A dopey smirk lit up his face. "See, Tetra, I knew you were going to want nachos as soon as we sat down."

"Where are the others?" I interrupted. I didn't interact with Douglas and avoided Kip at all costs. Grey was the closest person I had to a friend outside of Sterling. We'd bonded last week over my skills as an artist. His presence had a calming effect on me and he was easy to please.

Sterling pointed to the field. "Douglas is 17, Kip is 32, and Grey is 09. We're not meeting up with them until after the game."

I tensed up. How did I let Sterling convince me to come here? I wasn't properly dressed for the sharp weather change.

"Just relax, Tetra. It has to beat sitting at home all day." I did my best to follow his advice, though *Geotic* athletics was something I might never be partial to. Why did they call it football again?

Sterling

When we got to the roller rink, it was flooded with people from CCI and victory banners that predicted tonight's victory. Everyone crowded around Doug, Kip, and Grey like they were gods. They'd probably be eating for free all night. For Grey, that was one of the only perks of being flanked by phony, vapid golden people. He couldn't turn down free food.

Tetra was waiting outside when Kip surprised me from behind. "Hey, um…is she here? Did she see me play?"

I didn't have the heart to tell Kip that Tetra had barely watched the game. She'd been preoccupied playing Solitaire on my cell phone. All I did was nod and avoid direct eye contact. It wouldn't take much for him to realize I was full of shit.

"She's outside, Kip."

Kip pushed me to the entrance. "Dude! What are you waiting for? Go get her!"

I was seconds away from flipping out. That wasn't part of the deal. I was supposed to convince her to come, not to do all the work for him.

"You asked me to get her here. She's here. Which took a lot of effort on my end."

Kip ran his hands along his face, resting them behind his head. "How do I know she's not going to just walk off the second I go up to her?"

I shrugged. "Not my problem."

"Look, if you don't do this one thing for me, I'm going to be up your ass all night, cock-blocking hard. Along with to-morrow, the day after, and the day after that…" he continued as he counted on his fingers.

"Okay, okay! Just don't say I never helped you."

"Hey, Tet, can I talk to you for a minute?"

It was kind of sleazy putting her on the spot, especially since she didn't look that interested. But if I didn't help him, Kip would somehow weasel out the deal. He was the king of renegotiating favors to fit his interests. Even with the laptop already safe in my hands, my driver's exam was months away.

He'd remember this moment when I came to cash in that favor and have no problem telling me to kick rocks if I didn't try. All he'd have to see was that Tetra and he had no chemis-try and there'd be no hard feelings.

"My friend Kip wants to talk to you."

Tetra rolled her eyes. "Sterling, there is never a moment your friend Kip doesn't want to talk to me. Or sit with me. Or partner with me. Or buy me lunch. Wherever I turn, he is there. I find his company vexatious. Why does he wish to speak with me?"

I shrugged, a slight grimace coming on. "I don't know, Tetra. I guess he likes you."

"In the way that you like Waverly?" she asked.

I was caught off-guard a little. "Yeah, I guess." She grabbed her arm at the elbow. "Don't feel like you have to talk to him just because I'm asking you," I added. Just thought I'd throw that in there so she wouldn't feel like I was pimping her out.

"I will talk to him…but only if you swear something to me."

What could I expect? No one did anything for free anymore. "Sure, Tetra. What is it?"

Her hand rested on my shoulder. She gazed at me with wide, rounded eyes. "I want you to talk to Waverly. Your friends seem to be your biggest distraction. I will see to it that at least Kip is out the way."

I nodded. She'd actually help me? I didn't deserve a friend like Tet. She didn't like Kip but was totally taking one from the team. She'd definitely be taking the "Wingman of the Year" award.

"Do not disappoint me, Sterling." Tetra stuffed her hands in her pockets and walked inside the rec center. She approached Kip, and from the look on his face, he tried to act shocked. Yeah, he wouldn't last too long with Tetra playing that card. They walked off together, heading toward the dining area. Now all I had to do was find Waverly.

Tetra

Anyone in my position would have screamed of boredom. Me? Bored would imply that I was engaged. I wasn't. How Sterling's friend Kip managed to make me aware of *all* his many accomplishments, dating back two years, in the last twenty minutes was a talent within itself.

He'd made varsity of all six teams he tried out for. For lacrosse, field hockey and rugby, he'd even been appointed captain. Since sophomore year, he'd helped bring four of them to nationals, becoming the proud owner of seven rings in various titles. While he was bragging about how many universities were interested in him, I decided there was only so much a person can be expected to endure. He had to be stopped.

"You speak a great deal of your achievements. Does your entire existence revolve around dribbling and shooting goals?"

I provoked a smile from Kip, but it was unreadable. "Okay, well, maybe I'm just trying to impress you," he said with a wink.

Did he really believe twenty minutes of mindless chatter would encourage an inspired reaction from me? His eyes locked with mine as he waited patiently for my next response. "I regret to inform you that your efforts have failed. These activities, they do not interest me."

His eyes widened, mouthing the word *Wow*. His body language faltered. Once bird-like with shoulders, back and chest out with the sureness of a *Noban*, he now sat there broken and defeated.

It was common to make someone aware of their faults in *Noba*. It was neither rude nor cruel. We took our ability to be critical and truthful in stride. Judging by Kip's expression, he was used to being praised and adored by his peers. Perhaps even lied to. He sat twiddling his thumbs, silent, trying to reassemble his confidence. It didn't appear to be returning anytime soon.

"Okay, well, we don't have to talk about me. Why don't we just join the others on the floor? Do you know how to skate?"

I winced. "I've never been roller-skating before."

His eyes lit up with glee as we made our way over to the rental counter. Towards this end of the arena, the earsplitting sound of the satellite radio made it hard to hear what the counterperson was trying to tell me, but overall I'd found that to be a good thing. I'd grown tired of hearing Kip speak. My only wish at this point was to get this time over with. I was missing a *Crescent Moon High* marathon for this.

I'd replaced my sneakers with a pair of pre-used skates, lacing them up as tight as my ankles allowed without constricting blood flow. Kip stood up in front of me, holding out his hand for me to take.

"If you've never gone skating before, it could be a little overwhelming trying to find your balance. I can give you a few pointers, or better yet, you can just hold onto me." I took his hand but only because it appeared rude not to. The carpeted floor that made up the lobby made it that much harder to move in these things but once we'd reached the smooth, hardwood surface of the skating floor, I'd found no difficulty in finding the suitable footing these skates required. *What was Kip saying about this being overwhelming?*

He caught up to me, skating alongside with a look of disappointment before he'd opened the floor to speak. "I thought you said you'd never skated before?"

"I haven't."

He laughed. "So what? You're just naturally good at something you've never tried before? I guess I'm just bummed I couldn't show you anything."

"I'm just a fast learner is all," I offered in an attempt to save the discussion from becoming too discouraging for him.

"It's okay, Tetra. Not a big deal. But since talking about me is off the table, tell me what you do for fun." The rhythmic blend of rattling wheels filled the space around us as skater after skater made their ways past us.

I blinked back in confusion. Fun? What did *Geotics* consider fun? I liked to Ride the waves of wide open seas, but I couldn't admit to that. Not without violating number thirty-two on the Complete Tetra and Sterling Living Guide. There was an exhilarating surge within me when I challenged both space and time and transported to other worlds... But I was sure Sterling wouldn't recommend that either.

"I am no fun," I replied. It was true. Based on *Geotic* standards, I was no fun.

All he did was brush away my question with a wave of his hands. "C'mon Tetra. Everyone has fun. I bet someone like you has tons of fun." His smile almost returned him back to his original cocksure self. "I want to know more about you so *again*, tell me what it is you do for fun. And don't worry about it sounding corny. I promise, I have an open mind."

I shrugged, unsure. "Why don't you tell me what you do for fun? Something that doesn't involve odd-shaped balls or an elaborate breakdown of plays."

He eyed me through squinted eyes. Eyes that were as nearly as dark as mine. "I thought we weren't talking about me," he said.

It was becoming a natural occurrence to roll my eyes in Kip's company. "Kip, you were the one to make this declaration. I stated no such thing."

He let out a breathy laugh, something he seemed to do a lot. "I have to give it to you, Tetra. You are a girl who says whatever's on her mind. *All the time.*"

I wasn't sure how I should contribute to the conversation, so I continued on in my skates, making good on my turn as I pivoted in the opposite direction to face Kip. Once you'd mastered the basics, simple tricks like skating backwards were almost as easy as skating forward. Besides, it proved difficult to fight the urge to be competitive with the ones who skated by. At least this way, my attention was centered on Kip.

"So…I suppose this is you now avoiding my question?" From a distance, a girl with dark hair hidden under a hoodie was headed our way only moments away from colliding right into Kip. Just seconds before she did so, I jerked Kip toward me, our bodies pressing against one another as the clumsy one with dark hair crashed into the hardwood floor.

This close to me, he'd given off a scent of clean-cut grass, something woodsy like cedar, and a trace of sweat. Separate, the smells may have been ordinary, but together they were rather pleasant. "You really want to know what I do for fun?"

I nodded. His lips tucked in, evolving into a smile. His eyes seemed to devour me once over, much like the first time we'd met.

"I pray for a chance to talk to pretty girls like you."

There wasn't a chance that anyone could be *that* mundane, but if Kip were being honest with me, his pastime made him just as deprived as I was.

"Then we are both no fun."

Kip was irritating, but his smile was infectious. At times it made me want to smile. Or laugh or give in to the craving of being close to him or even…

"Hey, Kip," Waverly yelled, in the company of an approaching Margaret. "We pitched in for a locker. Do you want us to hold onto your phone for you?"

Kip shrugged. "I left mine in my car."

Waverly pointed toward me, "Tetra?" Once I admitted I didn't have anything worth keeping locked up, Margaret and Waverly finally noticed neither of them had pockets.

Kip volunteered to hold onto the key, but Waverly insisted I do so instead. I made sure to tell her Sterling was looking for her as she and Margaret skated off, as I placed the key into my shirt pocket for safe keeping. I skated on ahead, and Kip made every effort to catch up to me, slinking in on my left of me until we were face-to-face.

"Look, Tetra, before I end up wasting both of our times, are you involved with anyone? Do you have a boyfriend?"

I considered the question. "Yes," I affirmed with the utmost of confidence. "Since my first day of school, I've made four boy friends. As far as I know, they all identify as solely male."

Kip's posture stiffened, his eyes exhibiting an incredulous look. "Wow, someone doesn't waste any time. I guess there's no point of us having this conversation then." He lowered, then lifted his head, a sympathetic look in his eyes. Dark eyes always told a different type of story.

"That bothers you? You're welcome to be my boy friend as well."

A bark of laughter escaped his lips. He stopped when he noticed I didn't find the humor in it. "I'm sorry. You're not serious are you?"

I crossed my arms in front of my chest. "You don't have to laugh at me. I'm perfectly fine with the boy friends I have. At least they don't tease me."

Shame unfolded in his expression. "I'm sorry, Tetra. It's just... I don't want to date someone who has, like, four boyfriends already."

"Who said anything about dating? They're just my boy friends."

He offered me a bemused smile. "*Right...* Who are your boyfriends again?"

Simple enough question. "Well, there's Sterling and then there's Grey. Erm...Taylor Humphries and Samir Ali."

"Do you guys go out on dates?" Kip asked with a narrow-eyed expression.

I shook my head. Not unless you counted eating together in the cafeteria or going over lines during independent study.

"Do you hang out with any of them after school?"

Of course I did. Sterling and I lived together, but to Kip, that didn't count.

"Have you kissed any of them?"

With that question, I gathered that "boyfriend" hadn't meant what I thought it did. I'd assumed it meant a boy who is my friend. From Kip's probing questions, it was must've meant something more… Like, lover.

"No," I replied. I knew that would change in the next few months. Samir and I talked of a kissing scene in the winter play, where I was his leading lady. Would sharing a kiss make him my boyfriend, then?

"Look, I really like you, Tetra. I don't know if you've heard anything about me and maybe you just don't dig guys with player reputations, but I'm just asking for a chance to get to know you better."

"To be a boyfriend?" I asked.

"No, to be *your* boyfriend."

Why was Kip so eager to know me? Would it disappoint him to discover there was not much to know, or rather, little truth that I could confide in him? *Noban* unions did not require us to know much about each other. I was certain my parents didn't know more about each other than they had to.

To be part of a union was not at all like bonding. Unions were used to further bloodlines and enhance status. They didn't require a high regard for one another.

"Before I agree, you have to promise me two things."

He nodded. "For you, anything."

We skated off onto the side to reach the lobby, where we sat down at a nearby table away from where the music played the loudest. After minutes of skating, I'd already missed the comfort of my sneakers.

"I wish not to be lied to." He agreed. It should have been a given, but *Geotics* lied at the smallest occasions. If you wanted candor, you had to forcefully request it. "The way you treat others, I do not like it."

His lips pursed to one side, highlighting their fullness. "Can I get an example?"

I compared the way he behaved toward his friends versus those who weren't. Taylor Humphries was abrasive but over-all? Harmless. It bothered me how Kip was unkind to him. While I knew Samir thought highly of himself, his character troubled no one. *Geotics* weren't built to endure harsh criticisms. I knew them both rather vaguely, but Kip's interactions with them often left them distressed.

"I can lay off Samir, I actually like the guy. Didn't realize anything I've said got to him. But Humphries? That's a lot to ask. The kid hates me. I don't screw with him just because. He always has to remind everyone how much smarter he is. He has no problem making me look like an ass."

I stood. If Kip would continue to be mean-spirited to others, especially ones who'd taken the time to make me feel at ease here, then he'd lost my attention. Kip reached for my hand and pulled me back before I could skate away. I sat down next to him.

"Wait, okay. I'll lay off Humphries if it means that much to you."

To be candid, it wasn't my concern how every person was treated. But it did concern me how the people I associated with treated others.

"Then I have decided, you are welcome to be my boy-friend."

Kip's mouth hung open, his eyes widening in shock. "Just like that?"

My brows furrowed in confusion. "Is that not what you wanted?"

In an animated fashion, he gestured yes. Enthusiasm shone through his eyes and lips. I hadn't noticed how magnetic I found those lips until I was close enough to feel the heat from his skin. I wanted to feel them on my lips. To taste the warmth of his breath. To give in to the sensation that pulsed through me at the thought of the two of us being intimately connected. My lips were only centimeters from his engaging his.

But…I held back. I should ask first. There was a chance Kip didn't want to kiss me. I bit my lip, building the courage to speak. "With your consent, I'd like to kiss you."

He let out a small laugh, wetting his lips before holding my waist in his arms. Even through his football jersey, his heartbeat was strong. It'd been so long since I'd been this close enough to another person. It was nice.

"For future reference, Tetra, you don't ever have to ask for my permission to kiss me."

The first moment of our kiss showed promise. Gradual and gentle. As the moment passed, I was forced to engage in what felt like a battle of tongues, a test of who passed on the most saliva. A pang of regret engulfed me, dreading the next time I would have to kiss him.

He leaned away. I was grateful it was over. Our kiss ranked well below my expectations. Kip, on the other hand, had trouble hiding his excitement. He kept licking his lips and smiling, most likely making it his next mission to see how far his tongue could go down my throat. If Kip kept kissing me like that, I wouldn't last.

"I can already tell I'm going to love you being my girl-friend," Kip said.

That confused me. "I'm not sure I understand…I am your girlfriend?"

Kip smiled a smile so large, it easily took up half of his face. "That's how it works, Tetra. I'm your boyfriend so that means you're my girlfriend. Is that *okay* with you?"

Between repairing my broken bond, the coursework at school, becoming Samir Ali's principal actress, and gathering clues that would lead me one step closer to that wicked *Naga*, I was spread quite thin. Now I'd have to be Kip's girlfriend?

I was forced to excuse myself—or rather—wasn't sure it was the proper etiquette to wipe off one's mouth while in the company of the person who had just kissed you. Being a girlfriend would be a challenge at this rate; it was a good thing a restroom had been in close enough proximity for me to take a break from Kip, and the noise.

The bathroom floor was empty; clean with white tile floors, and contrasting dark green stall doors that appeared to have been freshly painted. While I'd felt a presence of someone in the bathroom, I was grateful they were behind a stall. It would be difficult to explain how strange I'd look wiping Kip's kiss—or more precisely—his slobber from my mouth.

I suppose I should've been grateful that there hadn't been an after taste, or at least not a terrible one. In efforts to pull myself together, I leaned over one of the bathroom sinks and splashed the running water over my face to prepare me for next few tortuous minutes. I couldn't hide in the restroom forever.

The towel dispenser had been a few inches away from me, as I reached to take two and wiped my face off before throwing them in the direction of the garbage bin. I must be off tonight. I'd missed, but I couldn't tell whether it was because eventually I'd have to return to the rink floor, or something else I couldn't explain.

I knelt to pick up the paper towel, and out tumbled the key Waverly asked me to hold. The sound of metal gently tapped the tiled floor. I reached down to retrieve it, and noticed something peculiar.

While I'd known I hadn't been in the restroom alone, it came at a surprise when I noticed not one, but two pairs of legs underneath one of the dark green stall doors. That shouldn't have caused much alarm, but neither of them were moving. I finally became aware that I'd felt something.

A malevolent presence.

That itself rarely caused alarm on its own, but I forced my awareness to listen, smell, or feel for anything my eyes would betray to me. Then I heard it. A light hum. Nearly outside of a normal person's auditory range. But when I concentrated hard enough, it was almost like a breath. Only it came out as more of a…hiss.

I stood at once, prepared to take the stall door down if I had to. I'd definitely done a lot more with less to go off of.

A surge of raw energy ignited in the pit of my torso, as it traveled from my knee to my ankle, until I lifted my foot from the ground and kicked the door open with the force of the driving *shakti* at my disposal.

From that moment on, every second painted an image; a girl, as pale as snow. I couldn't decide whether it was from fear, or the fact her soul hovered outside her body, like a shadow that wouldn't connect. And another figure, one I wouldn't need further proof to know what it was. In the body of a girl—no—not just any girl. The one Kip and I passed on the rink floor. The one with the dark hair, who'd all but bumped into Kip.

Whoever she *was*, no longer existed. There were serpentine amber eyes bleeding out the sockets of what once looked like human eyes. An unnatural sound vibrated in the monster's throat, a strange combination of a growl and a hiss, as the soul that hung in limbo snapped back into the survivor's body. She gasped for air, as if she'd been underwater for far too long, as she stumbled against the seat inside and fell to the floor.

"Go! Now!" I yelled in her direction. At least she was smart enough not to hesitate at my instruction. The *Naga,* disguised as a human girl, slipped under the stall next to me, searching for an alternative escape route.

That was, until I slammed the door on its face before it could get the chance.

I only had a moment before it regained its footing and that door re-opened and in that split second, I braced myself when the *Naga* wearing the dark haired girl's face burst out just as reckless and disoriented as I was.

It tried to break past me, but I was bigger and heavier than the body that stood before me. Devouring souls appeared to have its limitations. Anytime I'd crossed paths with it before, while in human form, it could only do as much damage in the body it was stuck in.

It tried to head-butt me into a wall, but sidestepped out the way. It managed to tackle me, aggressively clawing at my midsection, forcing me to wrap my forearm around its neck to restrict its from breathing.

I reached my other arm around to strengthen my hold, but the *Naga* slammed me against the closest bathroom wall, knocking the breath out of me.

A scratchy tremble vibrated against my forearms, sounding more human than the entire struggle alone. "You can't—" It started to say, but I just squeezed tighter. Somehow it managing to keep talking. "Kill me. You tried this … last time. It is no use."

"I don't need to kill you." I strained to say, fighting against it as it tried to crush me against the wall. "Knocking you unconscious will do."

The hair color of the body I was strangling transformed to a ginger red, and body type grew with it as well.

The *Naga* tried to slip out of my grasp, hoping its new size would be enough to subdue me, but all it did was force me to squeeze tighter. It elbowed me in the stomach before I finally let go and the weight of someone twice my size charged into me, backing us both through the bathroom entrance door.

"What the hell are you doing in the women's bathroom you fucking pervert!" Maggie's was only voice a few inches away. I attempted to scramble against the break, but I hadn't noticed the shapeshifter had shifted into male form.

The *Naga*, now wearing a new face I hadn't seen before, took off into the crowd of people on the rink floor and that's when Waverly and Margaret ran over to me. Apparently, everyone planned to meet up to eat, and they'd required the key they asked me to hold. They hadn't expected to catch me in a struggle.

As I fought to regain both my breath and my footing, both Waverly and Margaret insisted on helping me. "Tetra, what happened? Do you need us to call an ambulance? Or the police—"

"No!" I interrupted Waverly. "I mean … I knew him. I … erm … we were once from rival schools." I hoped they'd accept my non-answer.

"Wow Tetra, you must take this CCI pride seriously." Margaret said. "What was your last school a boarding school or something? You didn't seem so surprised to see him. Why don't you want us to call the cops?"

As I grabbed my side, having forgotten how hard that wall and door had been up until now. "Are you accusing me of something?"

Margaret held out her hands defensively, her brown eyes wide against her fair skin. "No. I just wouldn't have taken you for a brawler at your old school. Did you see the size of that kid? You totally had him." She seemed impressed.

"I pegged you for the silent type kind, but between Waverly's voice of reason, my mouth and your brawn, we could totally rule Senior Field Day." She said, slamming her clenched fist into her other palm for emphasis.

"That's all you care about?" Waverly scolded. I didn't know what Senior Field Day was.

"Of course not! Come on, Tetra, if you don't want to press charges, the least you could do is let us help you." Margaret added.

Their help was the one thing I *didn't* need.

During our struggle, the *Naga* had shifted into three forms, and I hadn't recognized any of its faces. There was no way to know whether it had gained those forms before we'd encountered each other, or if they were new.

Next time, it could be someone standing right next to me, and I'd never know it. For now, I'd lost my chance. I wasn't sure when I'd get another one...

Sterling

After an hour of skating, my spirits soared to learn that everyone was planning to meet up in the dining area so we could finally stuff our faces. I scanned the tables but didn't catch any wind of Waverly or Margaret.

"Hey, where's Tetra?" I asked Kip, but before he could answer, Tetra joined our small group, followed by Waverly and Maggie helping her over. Kip and I stood, instantly concerned, when they helped her sit.

"What happened?"

Okay, so normally I wouldn't trust Maggie as a story teller, but when she jumped in and took the lead, she made a small deal seem *way* less small. She was half way through the story when Kip walked over toward Tetra and asked her was she alright.

"Yes. I'm sure many of you are thirsty, why don't Sterling and I get us some drinks." Tetra yanked me by the arm in the direction of the concession stand.

"Umm...thanks for offering my services." I said, pissed that I'd been pried away from hearing more of what happened because I knew Tetra wouldn't tell me. She was all types of antsy, or at least as antsy as it got for her. Maybe it was tied to the fact that the *ten* minutes I'd left her alone with Kip, they'd already managed to declare themselves a couple. I knew Kip liked her but *geez*, who works that fast?

She tried refilling one of the drinks, but more of the soda made it to the floor than inside the cup. Her hands shook unsteadily and it took her three times to put the lid on, only to tear the cup at the side so she had to get another one.

"Tet, is everything alright? You're trembling." She'd got the third lid on without any damage, but only because she was completely focused on the one cup. That was weird, even for her.

"Yes Sterling, I am fine, I just…" And there it was. The first time since I'd known her to lie to my face, or at least intentionally hide behind the truth by changing the subject. "How did things fare with Waverly?" she asked.

Since she obviously wasn't planning to share any details of what had gone on in the time she'd been alone, I thought it best not to waste the energy trying to get her to.

"I think the better question is, how did things *fail* with Waverly? Sure, we got a chance to talk a little bit, maybe even flirt but clearly, I'm underperforming compared to your success story. I left you and Kip alone for *ten minutes*, and you've already declared yourselves a couple." I knew Kip liked her but *geez*, who works that fast? Tetra wasn't even his biggest fan. "What the hell did he say to you?"

"It was simple, really," Tetra started as she fiddled with a lid to a cup filled with purple liquid. "Kip asked to be my boyfriend, I said yes. You shouldn't have any trouble in garnering a similar response from Waverly."

Yeah, okay. "It's not really that simple."

"Well, why not? You talk to her nearly every day."

This was one thing Tetra *wouldn't* get. Since her "arrival," she wasn't partial to anyone, but that didn't stop half the student body from ogling her. She was in a position to do what most girls did so well: reject. The idea of asking Waverly out seemed easy, but the rejection? The thought of it made me skip trying altogether. I was always afraid of ruining our friendship, so I settled.

"It's so easy for you, Tet. You're a girl. You don't have to do anything. People just like you."

Nothing I said the next few minutes got through to her. She stood there, lost in thought. Finally, she snapped out of her trance. "Gender… It plays an important role in many of the points you attempt to make. Even when choosing a mate. These are things that differ greatly from our culture."

"Well, what's it like in *Noba*?"

Tetra never talked about where we came from in past tense, and out of habit, I hadn't, either. Maybe in a way that was how Tetra kept it alive. Maybe *Noba* was still alive. I mean we were here, weren't we?

Tetra's lips pressed into a hard line. "The selection process is not decided by the individual. Parents—they arrange these matters. Their children do not have an opinion. There are its benefits as well as downsides."

What benefits would I have letting my parents pick out a girl for me? She'd probably be some nun with no experience and, like, zero personality. Maybe even well below my standards.

"So you have to date whoever your folks tell you to?"

"Sterling, you misunderstand me. There is no 'dating' in *Noba*. When your mate is chosen for you, that is your sole life partner. Similar to your parents." In different terms? Married.

"Gosh, Tetra, what are the benefits?"

She perked up from her slouching posture. "No daunting courting process as you are now experiencing with Waverly."

Hmph. I guess that was a benefit. Still…my folks having complete control of who I had to spend the rest of my life with? I had to be better off on my own.

"Do not allow fear to stand in your way of telling Waverly how you feel. Life? Time? Perhaps you believe you have more than enough of both. But trust me, you'll wish you had more of one when your time together is cut short."

It sounded like she drawing from experience. She rarely brought up her past when it didn't involve me. In fact, she didn't talk about it at all. I wish she knew she could talk to me. Nothing about our relationship could get any more personal than sharing a room, sharing a culture, and—while we were on the topic—sharing a soul.

She dropped the last cup she'd been attempting to refill but thankfully it was only filled with ice. Nothing a few paper towels couldn't fix. As I kneeled on the floor with her to clean it up, it became clear that she was *not* as okay as she claimed. She raked her fingers through her hair, pulling and tugging at the roots as her face strained in frustration.

"It was here." She said, as if I were supposed to catch on to what *it* was. Then it dawned on me. The reason she was so worked up. *It* was the reason we were linked in the first place. The evil that knew no end.

"I tried this time. I really tried. People are dying…and it's all my fault. The *Naga* continues to outwit me by taking on new identities, so many that now it's hard to look at anyone without thinking it might be an enemy. Everywhere I look, I see an innocent person who has a life, a family, succumb to this monster and I am powerless. Sterling, I ask so little of you but the time for games are over. I genuinely need your help. *Please*. I cannot take on this task without you." She hung her head down in defeat.

And things only got more serious with each passing day. As long as I tried to prolong harnessing these unwanted abilities, the time had come where I had to be of bigger help. The only thing I'd managed to accomplish since meeting her was making accidents happen. But this feeling inside me, this power, had a mind of its own. It was time to see what I was capable of.

Most of all, I wanted to be the *Noban* Tetra needed me to be.

CHAPTER 16

Tetra

If I learned one thing this week, it was that varsity jackets were far from comfortable. Wearing Kip's was an unspoken declaration that I was his girlfriend and that he was my boyfriend.

It brought a smile to his face every time we stole glances in the hallway, and I fought back the guilt I felt when I considered doing away with it. If it meant that much to him, I'd endure the hot itchiness.

I finally pieced together how just the presence of a name—in this case, Matherstein—almost instantly changed people's perception of me. The brand of his family name across my back resulted in boys, who before, had invaded my personal space on a daily basis, chose to avoid me altogether, and the girls? The idle talk of rumor that was once audible now became whispers accompanied with hawkish stares.

Such strange customs this world had.

I attempted to shove back the mountain of stress that formed in my consciousness. Even an hour of early mediation didn't help. I refused to sleep, I could barely eat. Somehow, I needed find the time to bring Sterling to at least an apprentice level of his required development. Until then, I'd look at everyone I passed at school as a potential victim. Unfortunately, I was in no real position to guide him. Not until I fought back the rainstorm of doubt inside of me. It would take me more than a few hours of daily mediation to work through this most recent failure. Maybe even more than physical training itself.

What I required was a diversion to take my mind off the current situation but at this moment in time, I was lost for suggestions. At least until the two girls from the other night, Margaret and Waverly surprised me at my locker bearing plans of engagement.

"Hey, Tetra. You coming to my party tonight?" Waverly placed her arm around my shoulder and leading me toward my first class as we carried on the conversation.

Physical contact. I was still adjusting to being touched in a casual manner without prior consent. It was innocent and allowing it to happen was a vital part of being Sterling's definition of normal, but I couldn't lie and say I felt at ease.

"Erm, I am not certain. A party, what does one do there?" Waverly and Margaret laughed, looking back and forth in wonder.

"Geez Tetra, what did you go to a boarding school or something? Because I mean, that would totally explain the whole bathroom beat down. Those places are all work and no play. You *so* have to hang out with us tonight." Margaret said.

"Yeah, I mean I know Kip is probably going to be down your back all night but still, that doesn't mean you can't kick back and have a good night out with your girlfriends. He's my cousin and all but personally, I think you can do better than him."

Sterling had mentioned it before. Waverly and Kip were blood relatives. They both shared the same golden complexion and dark eyes, as well as prominent facial deformities, commonly known as dimples. But Kip didn't share her epicanthal folds. That and something else …

"Didn't Kip mention my party tonight?" Waverly trailed off. Although Kip and I were now what the senior class had deemed "an item", we hadn't spent much time together unless it was during our lunch period. Margaret leaned against me, close enough that I could see the brown flecks in her eyes.

"If Kip is being an asshole, you can always ride with me. Give me your number. If you need it, my dad could give you a lift."

The day started out like any other morning, but by fifth period, I had new friends, and an invitation to a party. The regretful news? I hadn't a clue what to do with any of them.

I'd always looked forward to my independent study block as it was the one portion of my day I could spend as I pleased. When I wasn't overwhelmed with legions of coursework, I would often find myself perusing the school's gymnasium or weight room to brush up on my neglected forms and muscle group-tailored routines. However today, I was in no condition to fully focus and as a result, the person who'd thought it clever to sneak up on me had regretfully met the soft give of a workout mat at the end of a grapple. I pinned him down only realizing my blunder when he took hold of my forearms, his eyes widening in shock. It was Kip.

"Wow, Tetra," he strained underneath me. "Sometimes I forget how friggin' strong you are. Not for nothing, though. It's sort of hot."

"Why were you sneaking up on me? I asked, still in defensive mode.

"I was trying to surprise you, but now I know that you and surprises don't really mix. A little help." I stood, taking his hand in mine as I hauled him up.

He'd had this way of closing in on the distance between us that I was beginning to become accustomed to, but during the only available time I had to train during school, I found his presence distracting.

"Did you want something?"

Kip laughed. "Honestly?" He led me to the room's studio mirror, and it was then I remarked on how aesthetically compatible we appeared together. The contrast of hue, height, and facial features were what many people found suitable on *Noba*.

"I … want … you," he said, placing a kiss on my neck with each word. I was grateful he avoided my lips. Kissing Kip always felt like kissing a fish.

"You want me … to do what?"

Kip spun me around until I faced him. His face was pleading. "Tetra, we, like, never hang out. Or at least not outside of school. I was hoping we could change that." He leaned in, bringing his mouth close to my ears as the heat of his breath sent fluttery bristles to the core of my stomach.

"I was thinking if you weren't doing anything and it was okay with Sterling's folks, that maybe we could go out tonight. Have some real … I don't know, fun."

I broke free of his hold to head over to the pull-up bar that sat in the center of the room, but he only followed. From my waist, he hoisted me up, carrying on the conversation without letting my last fifteen minutes here go to waste.

"I have plans. Waverly invited me to her party," I said as I performed a pull-up.

"Yeah, well, I thought it went without saying that we were going to go together," Kip said.

I did another pull-up. "Well, you didn't mention it to me. I assumed you wouldn't be going."

Kip rubbed his brow bone, looking as though he was considering his next words. "Look, I didn't want to rub it in Sterling's face if he couldn't go."

I considered Kip's statement. While Sterling was under extreme surveillance, limiting his activities to just home and school, that didn't sound like the whole story.

"So should Sterling attend, you, Grey, and I will all go together?" I asked.

Kip rubbed his neck, wearing a look of dread. "Yeah … that's a full car. I kind of didn't want to be 'the ride' just in case we decided that later we wanted do our own thing. You know, just in case we want to be alone."

I did a few more pull-ups, thinking that over.

"Let's just see if Sterling can go first," he added.

I nodded, already eager to change the subject. There was one thing I still needed to know. "By the way, what is a party?"

Sterling

My day had gone exactly as planned. That was, until seventh period trig.

You see, I was going to my seat like I always do. You know? *My assigned seat.* And who do I find sitting in it? Kip … next to Tetra … in my seat. There had to be rules against this. Having Tetra as my neighbor was the only reason I was even passing Trig, and as far as I knew this was Kip's best class. Would I look like a jerk if I told him to move?

I was too disgruntled to be excited when Waverly waved me over to a seat next to her.

From the outside looking in, "Ketra" made sense. But I knew the parts of them they didn't know about each other. Ten bucks said they didn't make it past the week.

Kip whispered something to Tetra as her mouth curved in a way that resembled a smile. The pencil in my hand snapped. Dammit, that was my only one.

"Jealous much?" Waverly whispered, laughing. She scooted as close as she could without causing a safety hazard and laid another pencil on my desk.

"Do you think they're serious?" Waverly asked. A soft snicker left her mouth, and as if on command, Kip reached for Tetra's hand. All I could do was slouch in my chair and try not to look jealous.

"What am I? The Kip and Tetra police?"

Waverly giggled, leaning in far enough for me to feel her breath on my skin. It gave me goose bumps.

"You know what everyone's saying, right?"

"Should I?" I was curious, but gossip was rarely good news.

"Geez, Sterling. You're a little slow. Anyway, people are super-confused. We all thought you and Tetra …" Waverly trailed off, wearing a big grin on her face.

Snap. There went another pencil.

"What? Because we live together?" I said. I couldn't believe that *I* was the subject of gossip.

"Well, you know, it's not just because you live together. You two are rarely apart. The trio formerly known as you, Grey, and Kip appears to have a fourth member."

Okay, so maybe Tetra and I were always around each other. But she had her own acquaintances. Samir and Taylor were always down her back. How come no one accused them of being more than friends?

"Well, we live in the same house. We're friends."

"That's it?"

"That's it."

Waverly slumped back into her chair, letting out a huge sigh before leaning her elbows back onto the desk. She started coloring in her name on the top of one of her notebooks. "Coming to my party tonight?" she asked, grinning, as if the answer wasn't obvious.

"Duh." It was a secret to no one. Waverly threw the best parties.

"Well, I guess I'll see you there."

I spent the entire ride home contemplating ways to convince my folks that I needed to go to that party. Tetra was going. Definitely an angle I could use, but would it work a second time? It was worth a shot.

Kip pulled to the front of our house. I reached for my bag, securing my headphones inside. As I leaned over to open my door, I caught a glimpse of Kip leaning into kiss Tetra. His lips barely touched her face before she hopped out of the car, leaving him tumbling onto the passenger seat.

She didn't look at him as she spoke. "Sterling, are you coming?"

I didn't want to gloat. *I had to*.

I patted Kip on the shoulder and smiled. "Smooth. Catch you later, man."

Dad was working late so the only person who would need convincing was Mom. I was prepared to resort to long-winded toadyism, but there was just one problem with that.

It was Mom's night to cook, and I couldn't find anything nice to say about my mom's cooking. Tetra sat at the kitchen table, which was good timing on my part. My mom couldn't say no in front of Tetra. She cared too much of what Tetra thought.

"Mom, can I go to a party?"

An incredulous look spread across my mom's face. "No 'Hi, Mom. It's nice to see you.' No 'Hi, Mom, do you need any help?' As soon as you walk through the door, it's just: 'Can I go to a party?'" Mom's tone was mocking.

I sounded nothing like that. "Well, can I?"

Mom stirred a pot of something that smelled slightly edible, making me hope that dinner wouldn't suck after all.

"Tetra, were you going to this party?" Mom asked.

Tetra perked up in her chair, knowing damn well she held the fate of my mom's decision. "I'd highly considered it."

Mom sighed, clearly defeated. "Fine. Sterling, you can go. But only after *all* your homework is done. Trust me, I will check."

I was already halfway up the staircase. Homework finally had a purpose.

"Ugh! Why does everyone keep hanging up my shirts? I can never find anything," I said, scanning my closet for something to wear.

Tetra entered the room, finding a spot on my bed. *"As opposed to on the floor?"*

"As opposed to on the floor?" I muttered in a mocking tone. She climbed under my blanket, making herself comfortable in a bed I'd spent half an hour making warm.

"Hey, Tetra, are you doing okay? These past few days, you've been kind of off and I'm worried about you. You said we were going to get into this whole training thing and I mean, while I'm not exactly looking forward to it, I just don't want to let you down."

Part of me wondered whether Tetra was still up for the whole training thing. Every day I brought it up she brushed me off with a response that wasn't quite her usual self. A few days ago, she was ready. Now? She just seemed preoccupied.

She offered a small smile.

"You will not let me down. While it is true that you may not reach my current aspirations for you, I'm certain you will follow through with what I will teach you." At least she was back to low-key insulting me again. That was the first step in knowing the old Tetra was back.

"Are you sure you're up for this party? Because we can stay home if you want to." I really hoped she'd want to go.

"Perhaps this party will be just the distraction I need to work my way through this rut. I will go. Especially since I promised the girls I'd be in attendance."

"Great! So, which one—the green or the red?" I asked, holding up two shirts for her to consider. I hoped she picked the green. It was my favorite color.

Tetra wrinkled her nose, then pointed to the burgundy sweater.

"Geez, Tetra, you barely looked at it."

Tetra sat up and curled her legs underneath her. "You've never asked my opinion on clothes before, nor have you ever given yours on mine."

Slumping onto the mattress, I waved my arms upright, resting the shirts on top of my chest. "That's because you'd look good in a trash bag."

I'd never seen Tetra in a trash bag, but I imagined she'd make it work.

"Well, in my opinion, I've always thought red suits you."

I stood to face the mirror with both my options, tossing the green shirt on the floor. Red it was.

Tetra

Loud pulsating bass assaulted my eardrums as strobe lights danced around the room in a fashion that made my eyes dizzy and disoriented. Was this what a party was?

Even in a crowd of a hundred, Sterling wasn't difficult to spot. I caught up with him, grabbing his wrist before I lost another person in this mob of swaying teenagers. He stopped lowering a bottle from his mouth, his lips curving into what could only be described as a sly smile. The music was so loud he had to yell in my ear for me to hear him.

"Everything alright, Tetra?"

"What is expected of me now?" I asked. He shrugged and I was met with Sterling's answer for everything.

"I don't know, Tet. Just do what everyone else does." With that, he was swallowed by the crowd. I scanned the room for recognizable faces. The boy with the pale skin and contrasting tattoos. Rebel? He was the first person to make eye contact.

When he noticed me staring at him, he smiled and waved. In the midst of returning the gesture, a stranger wrapped his arm around my shoulder. The harmonious blend of sandalwood, cardamom, and ginger meant it could only be one person. Grey.

He led me into the kitchen, letting go once when we reached a table with cups of liquid lined up on its surface. "Having fun yet?" he asked. He picked up a cup, then went for another I assumed was for me.

He held it out to me. "Do you drink?"

"Drink what?" I asked. He laughed placing the second cup down.

"That just means you don't."

Grey leaned against the wall, bringing the half-full cup to his mouth. We were scanning the room, exchanging comments, when Waverly and Margaret approached us passing out tubes and plastic jewelry.

"You guys made it!" Waverly shouted over the music. They pulled me in for a hug, and for the second time today, I didn't feel uncomfortable.

"Where's dickwad?" Margaret said as they walked back around the table. Waverly held out a tube and a bracelet.

"Face paint or glow-in-the-dark bracelet?" Waverly asked. I reached for the tubing with "Electrifying Green" boldly printed on the label. Unscrewing the cap, it smelled of inorganic chemicals.

"I'll take a necklace. Green's not really my color," Grey said, placing a blue fluorescent ornament around his neck and then making his way back to the deafeningly loud main room. I backed away from the table and bumped into Kip.

"What happened, Tetra? You just disappeared on me," he said with frustration in his eyes. I pushed the metallic green paint to the top of the tube and rubbed it between two fingers.

"I didn't know you were looking for me."

"Well, I didn't think I'd have to spend all night chasing you."

"I apologize, Kip. I've never been to a party."

Kip's defensive stance relaxed. He crossed his arms over his chest. "C'mon, Tetra. Seriously?"

I nodded. A silent "wow" left his mouth.

"Oh. I didn't realize your parents were so strict. I'm sorry."

It was then I realized the tube of paint was meant to be decorative. Ceremonial markings were cosmetic but told many stories about an individual. I wondered how Kip might look wearing traditional *Noban* markings. I beckoned him to lean forward and my fingers moved skillfully across his face. I highlighted his aquiline nose and dominant cheekbones, threading three dots over his brow, a horizontal line under his left eye, and a vertical line underneath his lip. His markings symbolized strength.

"How does it look?" Kip smiled, his eyes glowing with intensity. For the first time since I'd met Kip, I saw him in the way everyone else did. He was … handsome.

The main room grew irritating fast. The sporadic light show hurt my eyes and the music was too loud to enjoy, yet somehow the way the paint highlighted the masculinity in Kip's facial structure made me forget I was even here. For the first time in days I'd let my mind wander to another subject other than Geo's destruction. *This* … was the very thing I needed to get my mind off all things catastrophic.

When a slow song played, Kip twirled me. Never had I seen so many people being so openly intimate. Physical intimacy was not a common practice in all worlds. *Noba* was one of them.

It was indulgent, selfish, and a sign of weakness to give in to unworldly desires, but I'd always thought it was something

Nobans were miseducated about. Yes, it was selfish; yes, it was indulgent; but there was something about intimacy that taught you things about yourself that you never knew were present. I was fortunate to have experienced such things with a True Traveler in my past, and I wanted to remember what it was like to feel those sensations again. But not with Kip's need to control. We needed to work together, or I would never want to be that close to him.

Kip's lips grazed my shoulder, and it was the first time I hadn't found what he did with his mouth unpleasant. Sterling had given me only one guideline for the night: "Do what everyone else does."

Before I could change my mind, I surprised Kip with a kiss on the lips. He pulled away from me, smiling, leaving the remnant of distilled spirits along the flesh of my lips. "Let's go upstairs" was all I managed to read from his mouth over the music. He grabbed my wrist, pulling me toward the staircase, away from the madness.

Sterling

Finding Waverly in a house full of drunk kids was no easy task. I managed to bump into Douglas, but he was already ready to go home.

It was my first real taste of fun since being grounded, and surprise, I wasn't having any.

I saw Grey in the corner but didn't approach since he was busy flirting with Brittany. No way was I messing that up. That girl had it hard enough with her brother playing attack dog all the time. Plus, she was hot and geeky just like Grey liked them. *At least one of us was scoring.*

The lights shut off in the living room, accentuating the fluorescent party favors passed out earlier. It looked sick, like a laser show, further proving that Waverly's parties were always unmatched. But it made it hard to distinguish faces, which made it that much harder to find Waves.

She had to be around here somewhere.

I bumped into Kip and Tetra, who were on their way up the staircase. Mental note: Erase all thoughts of Kip and Tetra hooking up. The patterns on their faces caused a flow of memories to surface. Suddenly, my head hurt. Damn, how much had I had to drink? I pushed my fingers down hard onto my eyes.

My eyes opened to smoldering flames and rainstorms of ash. Wherever I was, it wasn't Waverly's party. I blinked, hoping this new place would just die or go away, but it only became more real. More frightening.

People with markings like the ones Kip and Tetra wore ran past me, screaming, fighting…*dying*. A woman came at me, sword raised, preparing to slash. I pressed my eyes tight, opening them once more when I bumped into someone, reminding me where I was.

At a party. Waverly's party.

The relief was short-lived. I blinked, and returned to the place of nightmares. This was my past.

A marble-skinned serpent slithered past me. Or what felt like me. I willed myself not to move, fearing that even in a memory, it could still feel my presence.

It stopped. Its head was now several yards ahead, its body reaching immeasurable lengths behind. It turned around as if seeing something there for the first time. It raced back toward me, its amber eyes fading to blue in the distance. It stopped just seconds before passing through me.

"I will have you."

That was the last thing I remembered before passing out.

CHAPTER 17

Tetra

I waited for Kip in the empty room. It was sleek, spacious, and mature with a few family photos scattered around, which led me to believe this was Waverly's parents' room. I picked up one photo on the nightstand—a recent photo of Waverly and her parents.

It was just as I thought. Waverly's mother and father did not share the same phenotype. The photo only captured her mother's profile, but there was no doubt in my mind that Waverly favored her mother. Her father was paler with a different eye shape. The only thing Waverly took after him was his jawline. Strange. I hadn't seen a center-facing portrait of the woman in the picture, yet a sense of familiarity rushed through me when my eyes focused on it too long.

We'd never met. But there was something about her.

The door creaked open and in walked Kip. His face, now free of paint, hosted a sinister grin. A shame. The markings had brought out the symmetry in his features.

"So, where were we?" Kip said, accompanied me on the bed. He leaned in to join his mouth with mine.

While his lips were soft and full, there was something slovenly about the way they moved, the way he ran his tongue into my mouth without warning. If I continued saying nothing, I would *always* dread intimacy. At this point, I was losing all curiosity for it.

I pushed him away from me, wiping the moisture from my mouth. Kip plopped backward on the bed in a fit.

"Ugh! Tetra, you're so confusing!" he said, as he leaned up on his elbows.

"I do not like the way you kiss me," I said.

"Seriously? You're like the only girl that's ever said that."

I doubted the truth in that. I was just the first one to be honest. "Could it be that people are just blinded by your appearance? You are well perceived by many. It could be that no one wants to question your ability to do something." Kip turned away, but I reached out for his arm. "I apologize. I had not meant to offend you—"

He shrugged me off. "How am I supposed to feel? You just told me I'm a terrible kisser."

It was difficult to remember that the truth was not always seen as a favorable method of communication. Truth brought out anger and aggression, sometimes sadness. I could search Kip's mind to unlock what really plagued him, but it came at a price. One Sterling most certainly would not approve of.

Kip played with the tear in his jeans, staring down at his feet. I ran my fingers over his hair, reaching the temporal lobe of his skull, the part of the mind that comprehended language, retained visual memories, and dealt with emotion. Kip's emotions ran through me at once.

Tetra is so hard to impress. Why is it, when I actually like a girl, she doesn't give a crap about me? Urgh!

I ripped my hand away. His stream of thoughts flowed rough and unbalanced and only proved that, underneath his physical attributes, charm, and popularity, he was still insecure like others less fortunate.

"Kip … you try … very hard. I would enjoy your company more if you didn't try as hard." When he turned to me, I leaned in to kiss him the way I wanted to be kissed. The way I was taught to kiss. With not just my mouth, but my soul. Our lips took their time getting acquainted, alternating between soft and hard kisses that brought powerful waves of ecstasy. He leaned back, breathless, adding moisture to his lips by the lick of his tongue.

"I try because I like you."

I climbed onto his lap, leaning in closer as he lay down on the bed.

"But your way's *way* better," he said, biting his lip.

Our lips met again, in sync and on a mission as his hands fondled my back before resting at my hips. His heartbeat pounded against my skin in a way that made me want to feel closer to him, be closer to him, and that wouldn't happen through these clothes.

Intimacy as I knew it was the feel of a person's skin, the change in one's breathing, and the heat of two bodies, bare and touching. I attempted to lean back only to be drawn in closer.

"Am I doing something wrong, sexy?" Kip asked.

"I want to feel your skin."

Kip half-smiled. He tugged his shirt from underneath me, eventually pulling it over his head. His body was nothing short of impressive. He lay back down , pulling me closer to him.

"That better?"

My trail of kisses across his chest gave my answer. His skin smelled of cedar, fresh-cut grass, and sweat, and like other times, I found myself captivated by his scent. My tongue traced the skin leading from his ear to his neck as he trembled under my touch.

"Tetra, I'm going to sound like a total dweeb, but we can't go any further. I don't have any condoms," Kip said.

I nodded, respecting his wishes. He leaned back up to continue, his lips fighting mine in a game of tug of war.

My sacral *shakti*, where my back met my spine and hip, surged to my core and exited through my wrist. I ran my fingers through Kip's hair, once again tapping into his thoughts, which were now collected, calmer, but still flowing at a mile a minute. If his lips hadn't been busy, I was sure he'd be talking out loud. He felt so many things at once.

She's so beautiful... I'm horny as hell. I'm an idiot for not bringing protection... I've have to be the luckiest guy alive. I freaking love this girl.

Sterling

Familiar voices faded in and out. Who they were, I couldn't tell, but verbal clues made things simple to put together.

"Dude, what was in these drinks? They better not be laced." Questioning, accusing. Grey.

"He's probably faking. Find a stick and poke him with it. Bet he'd wake up then." Doubt, followed by a threat. That would be Margaret.

"You guys, shut up. This isn't the first time this has happened. There might be something wrong." Concern, pity, and stress. Waverly. My friends hovered over me, and even though my eyes weren't open, I could see them. Or sense them. All by the sounds of their voices.

I willed my body to move, my eyes to open. I needed to do something, anything. What I got was nothing. Then the memory hit me like linebacker.

I will have you.

My eyes shot open. I jerked up, frightened and a little embarrassed that all my friends were there watching me, varying expressions on their faces. Grey reached in and tapped me on the shoulder.

"You okay, buddy?" he said. I rubbed my head and nodded, hoping they wouldn't press further.

"See? Totally faking it. He's probably high! Let me see your eyes!" Margaret said, leaning in to invade my personal space. I turned away, rubbing my eyes too.

"So … this has happened before?" Grey asked, though it wasn't really a question. Of course, Waverly would rat me out. She meant well, but I really didn't want to be having this conversation right here or right now.

"No, I'm fine. I'm just … off."

Margaret shrugged it off, looking eager as hell to get back to the party.

"You sure, Ster? Because if not, I could call my dad, right now and—"

"I'm fine!"

Grey nodded and stood. He and Marge disappeared through the patio doors. I rubbed my face again. Not a good night.

"You sure you're okay? Because you can be honest," Waverly said. Why was everyone suddenly on me about how I was feeling?

"I said I was fine!" I barked, prompting Waves to hold out her hands in front of her.

"Don't get mad at me. All I asked was if you were okay."

Now I felt like a jerk. I was tired of everyone asking me, but the alternative was that she didn't care enough to ask.

"Sterling, this is probably reaching, but are you epileptic?" Waverly asked, twisting the fabric of her tunic. I clucked my tongue. I should've known. She volunteered at a hospital. Of course she'd analyzed me.

"No, I'm not."

"It's okay if you are. It'd definitely explain a lot."

There was more to what was happening to me than the seizures, but I wasn't going to tell her about it.

"I don't have epilepsy. And I'm not crazy, either," I said, regretting the words immediately. I could never be sure how much Kip told Waverly, but I wasn't about to pick today to start sharing.

An awkward silence fell between us.

"Some party," I said under my breath. Judging by Waverly's smirk, she totally heard me.

"It's just a party, Sterling. Our friendship means more to me than that."

I laughed. She *almost* sounded convincing. "I know you don't really mean that."

"Yeah, no, I don't."

We burst out laughing. At least she didn't treat me differently.

"Sorry for ruining your night."

Waverly bumped her shoulder into mine. The scent of her shampoo or something she was wearing reminded me of how sweet she was. Strawberries. Mint. Jasmine.

"You can't really ruin my night more than playing hostess does. Plus, screw you, my parties are awesome." She winked.

A sharp stab pounded at the right side of my head. "Ah!" I cried, caving to my knees as the pain traveled to the root of my chest.

"Sterling, are you okay?" Waverly asked. The pain made it hard to concentrate. It was no use lying—Waverly could see for herself. My chest burned. I only hoped it wouldn't worsen.

"Come on, Sterling, let's get you up." Waverly pulled at my arm, urging me to stand. She was making it worse, but how could I tell her that without making her feel bad?

"Let's find Tetra. We have to get you guys home," Waverly said as she dragged me back into the house. We walked up the stairs, squeezing our way through the crowd. I nearly fell three times before we stopped at a room at the end of the hallway.

Waverly opened the door.

In one blink, my eyes saw something I couldn't distinguish. Tetra was with a man; one I'd only recognize in memories.

I rattled my head, hoping to gain footing on what was really in front of me. It worked—Tetra and Kip lay on the bed, kissing. Waverly stormed over to their sides.

"Tetra needs to go!" Waverly said.

Kip pulled away from Tetra, sending his cousin a look of death. "What the hell, Waves, we're kind of busy—"

Tetra spotted me and got up, walking toward me with extreme concern. "Sterling?"

Her eyes widened when she reached my side. "We need to get you out of here *now*," she whispered. Fine by me, I was about two seconds away from collapse.

"Whoa, he doesn't look good. Do you guys want a ride?" Kip asked, pulling his shirt on.

Tetra tensed, looking more nervous than I'd ever seen her. "*No*! I mean … let me help him to the bathroom. I'm sure he'll be fine." She led me out of the room.

Once in the bathroom, I fell to the floor as Tetra locked the door behind her. She touched the side of my head and snatched her hand back as if she had touched something hot.

I curled into a ball on the floor. When I opened my eyes, blinding energy and fire tangled in my gut. Tetra flinched. She bent toward me, forcing me to stand.

"Whatever you do, Sterling, *don't* let go!"

There was no time to respond. One minute, there was pain in my chest. The next? My skin felt like it was being ripped off.

We fell to the ground, hard, landing several feet away from each other. It was then I noticed we weren't in a bathroom anymore, but a park. Tetra crawled over to me and cradled my face.

"Sterling, listen to me. All of what is happening is not without reason. Your body is trying to tell you something,"

I pressed my eyes shut. "How do I make it stop?"

She hesitated. "You don't. You can only listen, then release or channel the energy someplace else." What was she talking about? I didn't know, but I knew I couldn't take much more.

Hot tears rolled down my cheeks. "I don't know how."

Tetra placed her hands on both sides of my face. "Sterling, I need you to look at me. Nod if you can hear me."

I nodded.

"Calm yourself. This … is going to hurt." With that, she drew back her fist. I thought she was going to punch me in the chest, but instead she opened her palm upon impact. A throbbing, illuminating light moved between us.

The pain ceased.

Tetra fell onto her back, fighting back screams. I crawled over to her, watching her eyes blaze pure white, before releasing a raw beam of energy from her wrist toward the sky. Her lips parted and she heaved in a breath.

"What was that?" I asked.

She coughed, clearing her throat before she answered. "A message. I do not know what it means."

"*That* was a message?" I said, pointing to the sky.

She blinked, shaking her head. "Yes. Normally, I can interpret things like that. This time? I wasn't able to. In your voice, I kept hearing the same word over and over. Something that only has significance to you."

I tried propping her up. "What did I keep saying?"

Tetra hesitated. "My name."

And she slipped out of consciousness.

Tetra weighed more than she looked. We had exactly twenty minutes to get home before our curfew, and without that crazy *ticking* thing she performed earlier, I had to haul major tail to get home.

The weight on my back shifted, and I felt her grip tighten. Her cheek was buried against my neck, making every hair on my body rise as her lips contacted my skin. Maybe it was weird, but right then and there, I wondered what it'd be like to kiss Tetra, and not in my dreams. It probably made me a lousy friend, seeing as how after tonight, Tetra and Kip were more a couple than ever.

"You okay back there?" I asked. Tetra nodded, resting her head on my shoulder. It was nice. For a while, we were quiet, but I had questions that, if I didn't ask now, I'd lose the nerve to ask once we got home.

"Hey, Tetra? If we're supposed to be the same, how come your energy doesn't do what mine does?"

Tetra paused. "You're scared. Of what your power can do on its own. It's different for me. I grew up wanting this. Wanting to be exceptional, to be strong ... to be bonded. Your energy can become dark when not properly trained. Perhaps that's what's happening now."

I wanted to mention the part about the serpent, and the words that had filled my mind when we'd locked eyes, but she was already dealing with enough. I didn't want to worry her.

"We are wired to work as one. Until you truly understand what that means, you will never be able master your abilities as I do. I'm afraid that's all I know."

For once, I was actually okay with not knowing everything. I mean, what would I need it for anyway? Yeah, there was the *Naga* problem, but once it was out of the picture, Tetra and I could lead normal lives.

"May I ask something of you?" Tetra only asked questions she couldn't find the answer to herself. Which meant it had to do with something she found strange about the difference in culture.

"Okay?" It came out sounding like a question.

"What does it mean … to '*freaking love*' someone?"

I fought back laughter. I tried to imagine Tetra repeating that to someone. The thought was just as funny as hearing it now.

"Uh, you're going to have to elaborate," I said, leaving the statement open.

"Love. I have heard various declarations spoken to me, of me, in my lifetime. I wasn't sure what it meant to people here." It made sense. It wasn't hard falling for Tetra. She was special.

I shrugged. How could I describe what love was to another person? There were so many different types of love—where would I start?

"It just means that someone likes someone … probably more than they should."

A sniffle left her nose. She was crying.

"You okay, Tetra? Because if you want to talk …"

"It's nothing. I just … knew someone before the genocide. There's no way of knowing if they survived."

My heart skipped a beat, and I had no idea what to say. Have I mentioned lately that Tetra didn't talk about people from her past? Ever.

"Do you love Waverly?" Tetra asked.

Honestly? Half the time I wasn't sure how I felt. Blood rushed to my cheeks and I fought back an ironic smile, as I thought about the two most important girls in my life. One didn't notice me, and the other was with someone else. Man, did I sure know how to pick them.

But love … That was a strong word.

"I'm not sure."

"So you don't?" Tetra sounded dubious.

"No! I mean … there's a difference between the love you feel for a friend versus the love you feel for someone you feel is meant for you. Maybe that's Waverly. I want it to be. You just never know with these things until … I don't know."

I looked up, relieved to see we had made it home with two minutes to spare.

"It is good that you wish to love Waverly. There is something … different about her. She would make a good girlfriend."

Sterling

Man, the cold was excruciating. We might as well have been stuck in an arctic tundra.

This would've been the perfect time to laze around the house, eat nothing but junk and drink hot cocoa, but no. For the entirety of our ten-day break from school, Tetra made me travel from *City* to *Woodlands,* because it was a secluded area and the best place to pull against my *ticks*.

I liked *Woodlands* during the summer, when I wasn't forcing my eyes open against the painful blasts of cold wind against my eyes and cheeks.

Did I mention how freezing it was?

We normally followed the trails until we found an open space that also had soft snow.

"Tetra, can't this wait until spring?" I asked, shivering from the wintry breath that kept traveling down to my chest.

"That depends on whether you'd like to be in the presence of the wrong company the next time you *tick*." There was no need to be sarcastic. *I mean, it's not like you haven't had an extra decade or two to perfect this or anything.*

Tetra made materializing from one place to another look simple. We couldn't even be outside a certain proximity anymore without me being pulled, naturally or epically *unnaturally* in her direction. It wasn't frequent, but enough to make me want it to stop.

"I'm trying here," I called out, drenched in sweat even though we hadn't really done anything.

"Sterling, it is not without complication. You are so old." Standing just a few feet away, she had her arms crossed against her chest, wearing an expression that suggested she was completely serious.

Overwhelmed with snark, I answered back, "I'll be sure to bring my walker next time. I mean, if that's alright with you."

"Do not be ridiculous. I did not mean in the literal sense. You've lost your natural ability to control how your body, mind and the elements around you battle one another." She walked off, expecting me to follow her lead.

"Even as an infant, you showed a great understanding, but you were immersed in an entirely different culture. It is as if I'm teaching someone who isn't from our world."

"Well you could've just lead with that." I argued back, avoiding the fact she had a point. It wasn't completely my fault I sucked. She was my only teacher, and she wasn't exactly a patient one.

"An important thing to know about pushing against a *tick* is to clear one's mind of useless matter. I'm sure that'll be a challenge for you, but you'll learn that in time."

I squeezed my hand into a fist, clenching my jaw, resisting the urge to retaliate with something equally witty. I had to keep remembering this was *Tetra*. Her lack of inhibition for the truth was never less than … irritating.

Once we got to a wide-open space of earth, she stopped and turned, walking backward to head in the opposite direction. "I will show you an example of what it's like to clear your mind, compared to what it's like when you're preoccupied. Watch closely." As Tetra prepared herself in a static running stance and took off.

"Riding is what happens when you are in control." Tetra went on to say, as her voice grew louder despite the distance. "It requires both physical and mental concentration. But most of all, tru—" As her voice echoed into the distance, and her body began to convert and blaze into a colorless blinding light. She disappeared, leaving me standing in the middle of nowhere.

"Tetra," I called out, studying the plain around me, looking to see if she'd landed someplace in my peripheral vision. A minute must've gone by as I whirled around, surrounded by nothing but trees, with nothing but the sound of crunching snow beneath my feet. I walked in circles, looking for footprints, trees shaking, *anything*. There was nothing.

Did she end up in the wrong place? That wasn't like her, but stranger things had happened. Could she have been in another world? Or stuck somewhere? Man, I really needed to ask her about this kind of thing. It'd be good to know if *ticking* had *any* use outside of running away.

I was about to head back toward the direction of the trail when a gust of numbing, biting wind blew into my eyes, blinding me. Tetra collided into my chest. I tripped and managed to fall onto my back, Tetra on top of me.

If I wasn't an icicle before, falling into a bank of snow was sure to do it. "Ugh," I groaned in pain. "I'm so glad I could break your fall." Once she was on her feet, she brought her hand out to help me up. Something told me I'd need more than that if this was going to happen often.

"I admit, my landings can use work. It is much easier to connect to the ground than a person. It isn't likely to move, whereas channeling you doesn't mean I know your exact location. It's usually more of an educated guess."

I dusted off snow and held onto my back, massaging the outside of my winter jacket as if it'd help. "I wish guessing didn't involve me being pummeled to the ground." I stumbled left to right, trying to keep my footing.

"My strength relies on yours just as much as mine. The stronger you get, the stronger our bond will be. But that requires *discipline* and *training*." She pointed her index finger continuously across my chest. "So if you wish not to get pummeled, there is no way around it."

Tetra

Sterling's abilities continued to remain unpredictable.

I'd watched him run a dozen times during my instruction, and whenever he'd intentionally tried to use his abilities, he was unable to Ride. But any moment he was exhausted, he'd just … *tick*.

"I'm freaking freezing," he coughed into the air.

I ignored him for the eighth time, because it wasn't *that* cold. Likely Sterling thought if he complained enough, it'd convince me to return home. Luckily for me, I wasn't so easily persuaded.

"I believe I am going about teaching you with the wrong approach. It is not likely you'll master riding of any kind, if you don't even know what element you're connected to." I kneeled against the frozen, barren patches of soil underneath me, and placed a palm against the lake. A loud cracking sound echoed against the trees. "Perhaps if I were to show you what it was like to Wave Ride, you wouldn't fear it so much."

Sterling didn't appear concerned until I took off my winter jacket, and proceeded toward the lake. He pulled against my forearm, attempting to stop me before I went any farther. "Wait a minute, are you nuts? That ice is like, a week old. No way can it hold a *person*."

"Trust me, Sterling. I know what I'm doing." As he finally let go, I continued forward on the fragile ice, its center my destination. Sterling's fear was valid. Based on how long the lake had been frozen, my weight and the relatively warm winter night, the ice was very likely break underneath me. But I didn't need it to fully support me. I was in control.

Culturally, most worlds viewed water as a peaceful, calming source of power. But in *Noban* culture, our opinion differed greatly. Water was cold, collecting, unyielding yet destructive. It had both the power to drown you, and to crush you underneath its weight. For all its softer qualities, its power to destroy was unmatched. Wave Riders were formidable opponents, and viewed as dangerous. I suppose it came as no surprise I'd come from an entire legacy of them.

I feared a number of things, but to walk on water had *never* been one of them.

I heard Sterling screaming in the distance, his voice amplified by the empty space. Trying to assure him things were fine proved quite difficult once I lost my footing and the unstable surface beneath me gave in.

The moment I felt my foot submerge beneath the surface, my instinct kicked in and I ripped myself backward, to an area that melted into pure water. I should've sank, considering that the surface was no longer solid, but my arms spiraled out in a pushing and pulling motion, and the water underneath my feet carried me forward. I propelled myself, as if I were skating, but without the need or use of skates. The water melted and refroze beneath my weight, as I swayed my arms.

The ice cracked, making ice, losing ice. It slushed at my command as with incredible speed, I made my way toward the shore. With one last graceful leap, I landed neatly in the space behind.

"Whoa! I hope you don't expect me to do that!" Sterling said.

I lifted my jacket from the ground, dusting it off to rid it of snow and debris. "It is not a question of what I expect from you. When I mastered water, it was inevitable, because it had always communicated with me. I can teach you how to communicate with the water, but you have to trust me."

"Well, how will I even know I can communicate with it?" he asked, his expression displaying not only his uncertainty, but his fear as well.

"Trust me. You will know."

After a small push, or in Sterling's case, an *insistent* push, I guided him each step of the way to the lake's center. I kept my distance, though I wasn't far behind. "This doesn't seem like—whoa!" Sterling yelled, louder than I'm sure he'd meant to.

I took a light step, just a few paces behind him, so that our weight wouldn't be too localized. "I am right behind you. Should *anything* happen, I'm here. But you must take this as your chance to finally listen. Listen to the cracks, the water underneath, anything. It may be trying to communicate to you now, but you may not be paying attention—"

"I think the message is pretty clear," Sterling started in a state of panic. "It doesn't seem to like me very much!" At least he'd reached the center without falling. Part of me was sure he'd be too afraid to make it so far. He must've trusted my judgement more than I gave him credit for.

A series of cracking noises echoed in the air, and Sterling started to walk away from the center, unable to control his fear. "Tetra, I don't think I can do this."

"Just listen. Find a way to communicate, even through your fear."

But Sterling hadn't heard a word I'd said.

He shifted, swore and tried to balance himself in a grace-less lean. Then he took off at a sprint.

"Sterling, you are too heavy! I know you are afraid—" I tried yelling out to him, but then the ice broke, forcing him beneath the surface. There wasn't a moment to lose

I leaped forward—weight be damned—and dived into the mouth of the lake. The frigid temperature was unbearable. It was a good thing Sterling was not difficult to find. His flaxen hair greatly contrasted against the aquamarine water of the lake. Even under water, I felt his fright and desperation, made evident through his flailing and silent screaming. He would lose his air supply if he didn't stop.

I pushed my arms forward, propelling myself through the excruciating sensation of a thousand piercing needles. I reached out my hand to take hold of Sterling's wrist and bring him to the surface.

At least, that's what I'd planned to do.

Sterling wouldn't move. It was as if he were stuck, like a weight that couldn't sink nor float to the top. I tried to pull against his weight, as well as the lake's friction, but he would not budge.

I let go of his hand, backstroking to gain distance between us, so I had better use of my arms. The downside to riding *underneath* the water was that it required the same stances and the use of my arms. Riding the wave underwater was a much stronger challenge, especially due to the circumstances, but I could do it. I had to push against its stinging resistance, while still maintaining form.

Our bond told me Sterling was still alive. He floated idly, hovering in the same position. He appeared lifeless, with his mouth hanging open and his eyes closed, as if he'd already succumbed to a mortiferous fate. Gathering and working against the powerful current pushed the water around Sterling, though he himself would not budge. That was, until his right hand twitched and he opened his eyes.

A strange golden light began to omit from Sterling's eyes. He started moving—no, floating—rather violently. Like a big block of ice forcing itself to the surface. I worked fast to close the distance between us, my first instinct to take hold of his wrist in hopes of waking him from the trance he appeared to be in.

I braced myself for the possibility that his body might *tick*, ripping us in the direction of wherever his mind took us. His *shakti* felt as it were about to explode, as if his soul was trying to rip him from this eminent threat.

I kept hold of Sterling's wrist as we kept … ascending. One second we were in the water, the next, we cleared the lake's surface and kept rising higher and higher, until I feared we'd go past the trees.

Sterling's arm still stretched toward mine, but he remained unresponsive each time I called out to him. Suspended above the ground, he just kept … flying.

If I didn't stop him, once he woke up, he might not be in control anymore.

I brought my free hand up close to my body, and I felt the water's weight as I proceeded to draw it from its resting point. A foreign wind came out of nowhere, attempting to battle against the water's pull. I knew I'd succeeded when the icy liquid reached my ankle. I closed my fist, willing the water to freeze.

The sudden stop only made my grip around his wrist tighter.

Sterling's glowing, pupil-less eyes began to fade. Conscious, confused and petrified, he looked as if he were about to scream. I had one last thing to say before he went into a terror-stricken howl.

"Well, at least I know what your affinity is for …"

CHAPTER 19

Sterling

Man, this place looked way better in the spring. No ice-covered trails, no storm damaged trees and best of all, no half frozen lakes. I couldn't help but revel in how amazing a day it was, as the birds chirped a familiar song they'd waited all season to get a chance to sing again.

We'd trekked through a meandering dirt path, passing sign posts to the routes most commonly used. With the weather being so great, *Woodlands* had double the number of visitors, so we were forced to go off trail in order to find a spot offering more privacy. Really, it was just a private place for Tetra to scold me on my less-than-stellar progress.

It'd been months since I discovered my connection to wind. When I thought about it, it explained why I sometimes got chills during even the most scorching hot summers. Growing up, there had always been instances where things would knock over for no reason at all. Or times where my hat or notebook flew out my hand even when I wasn't the least bit clumsy.

All this time it was just the wind trying to communicate with me and because I didn't know what to look for, I always ignored it.

There was one benefit in all this. In the time we'd been coming here, I finally managed to control my *ticking. You know, to an extent.* But still, it was a huge improvement from waking up on the front lawn every so often only to be awakened by the cold rush of water.

Tetra surprised me when she took a seat on a patch of dry grass at the edge of a tree, midway through her instruction. Tired, maybe a little frustrated. Half the time it was always hard to tell with her. No matter how many times I asked, she always assured me she was alright.

I sat beside her, nudging her shoulder as I attempted to lighten the mood with a very sad attempt at a joke. Lately, with the way teaching me seemed to drain her, she hardly seemed in the mood for anything anymore.

"Geez, Tetra. We don't have to go so hard today if it's taking so much out of you. Let's face it. This whole communicating with wind thing, it hasn't happened in a while. Is it possible the ability just comes and goes for Wind Riders?"

"Don't be absurd, Sterling. These affinities we possess, they do not come and go. Something is blocking your connection. Fear, perhaps. Uncertainty, definitely. It would help to know what triggered the initial incident in the first place. What were you thinking of at that moment?

"You mean other than not drowning?" I bit back. When I gave it more thought, all I could remember was hearing these voices, although I'm not even sure I could call them voices. They were more like whispers. They didn't sound human.

"If you want it so bad, then why are you down there?" they'd asked me. The second I trusted the feeling, I opened my eyes and all of a sudden I was floating. The voices hadn't come back to me since. For now, I wasn't sure what that meant.

"Unfortunately, I am not skilled enough to help you connect to it. Wind riding was a talent I have yet to master as I am part of the *Oerban* tribe. If I had experience with wind riding, I would be pleased to pass on that knowledge but for a Wave Rider who has no real grasp on how the wind communicates, the concept seems foreign to me. What you need is a Wind Wider. What I need is a Wind Rider."

Just great. "Gosh, Tetra. Do you know any?"

"Yes and ... no. I have an acquaintance. An old ally from my time spent on *Noba*. However, they are not of this world. Which means we are at a loss until—" She stopped. It didn't need to be said. Saying the words out loud only meant one thing. That one day, we might actually have to leave this world, leave *Geo*. What would I tell my friends? Hell, what would I tell my parents?

The idea made me wonder if this whole tapping into my abilities was even worth the trouble.

"Hey Tetra, random thought. If we have the ability to manipulate time and whatnot, what's stopping us from going back in time, y'know? Putting the drop on The Day of Scar before it happens? Preventing all this madness in our current lives. I've been thinking about that for a while now. You have to admit; it'd probably save us all this extra time in the long run."

Tetra glanced at me, eyes blazing. I thought she was about to give me a good scolding but her response was calm and centered. Almost practiced as if she knew eventually I'd ask such a question.

"It is critical that you know that it is not orthodox nor is it encouraged to back and alter actions in your own time. Terrible things happen. Events you are not able to change. You must accept this fact and move on. Attachments are what makes it harder, which is why they are not urged."

Well there went that idea. Why in Geo were we granted these powers but limited in decisions how we used them. It just didn't make sense sometimes.

"Another vital lesson is that time moves differently in other worlds. The ones we do not belong to or have built an attachment to. Those are the one exception. Since you've made no connection to the world, by technicality, you do not exist there. But altering your own timeline comes extreme consequence. If you take anything from what is taught from my instruction, that is the most important.

When I suggested we get a head start at getting home before it got too dark out, I was thrilled when Tetra agreed. She didn't even subject me to one of her infamous lectures.

It was going to be a long walk from *Woodlands* to *Suburb*. Thankfully Tetra broke the silence with some decent news. A weekend off from all of this.

"By the way, Sterling. There's a chance I'll be unavailable to train with you for the next few days." She cringed, a cross between a frown and a smirk. "Margaret and Waverly asked if I would go dress shopping with them. I'm afraid it will take an unpredictable length of time."

A part of me should have been more excited that Prom season was quickly approaching. The great thing was that I wouldn't need to talk Tetra into it since I was no longer grounded. I wanted to go; all my friends would definitely be there, but I wasn't entirely sure if I'd go alone or with a date.

For the longest time, it'd been my dream to go with Waverly but … *ugh* there didn't seem to be any point dwelling on that fact

"So this Prom matter everyone keeps speaking of," Tetra started and from the times we'd spent together, I could already take a guess what she was planning to ask me.

"I have questions. Kip, well, he assumed I'd go with him because of our association with one another. When I asked him to explain the purpose of Prom and what it was one did there, he laughed and commented on how humorous he'd found me." Tetra's lips thinned. Another addition the many things she wouldn't understand about this world.

"Prom is like a dance. You know? A party. Pretty much one of the last things kids do before we leave high school. It's fun."

"*Is that all?*" she asked in confusion. "Everyone seems to make it out as grander than it sounds. As if it mirrored a coronation of some sort."

"Coronation?"

"Forgive me, it slips my mind sometimes that you don't remember mine. When I initially joined your family, I was ordained. You were too young to take part in the ceremony but it was scheduled as soon as you were old enough. It is what stamps the final seal of a bond. You can't be fully recognized without one and if you aren't fully recognized you cannot become a *Rishi.*

"There seems to be only one advantage to this Prom proposal. Kip has been everything but willing to take our courtship to the next phase. He promises the night of Prom he'll be more open to progress into a more sexual relationship."

Suddenly walking in silence didn't seem so bad after all.

"Kip's actions are much more contradictory than the boys I've witnessed on my list of television programs. This behavior, is it customary? "

"Yeah, Tetra, that's because that's a TV show. Not real life. And FYI, not exactly a topic I feel all that comfortable talking to you about."

I tried telling myself it was because I didn't want to think of my friend in that way. *Both* my friends in that way. But the real reason was I sort of resented their relationship. When Tetra and I got into this whole bond thing, I was sure it would always be just the two of us. When that changed, I convinced myself that I could never warm up to her low-key insults and abrasive criticism. Was it weird that it had actually grown on me?

We were different in every way that counted but she was all I could ever think about these days. Maybe that was just the drawback to our relationship with each other. I wanted to be happy for her, but it was just as equally hard not to feel jealous that whatever she'd experience with Kip, would be things she'd never experience with me.

"You question why I ask these things of you as if it isn't perceptibly evident. There is no one in this legion of galaxies I trust more than you. The others, Margaret, Waverly, even Kip, they are who I consider dear friends. But you. You are so much more than that. Endless. What we share is eternal. If it continues to make you uncomfortable, I do not wish to bother you with it. I only thought … If I cannot come to you with things, who can I talk to?"

I was going to regret this.

"Listen, Tetra. There's nothing wrong with Kip. He's an idiot sometimes but the thing is, he's not used to working hard for girl's attention. I think he's just afraid he's going to screw things up. He really likes you."

Unfortunately, he wasn't alone in that.

Tetra

Prom was supposed to be a big event. It was a rite of passage for most youth on *Geo*, a moment most of them wanted to cherish. It seemed simple, nothing like any rite of passage I would have had to endure in a past life.

There were four weeks until prom. Just four weeks …

Somehow, here I was, picking out dresses with Margaret and Waverly.

"You're not supposed to pick out dresses with your boyfriend. That's what we're for!" Margaret lamented.

Shopping with Kip, shopping with Margaret and Waverly—it didn't matter to me either way. I didn't enjoy one's company more than the other. If this was something I was supposed to do with girls, I would conform.

"Ugh! Could you help me with this zipper, Tetra? They only had it in a smaller size, and I can't get into it!" Margaret said.

I walked over as Margaret tried to zip up the dress. She was right, the size was too small for her. As far as her proportions went, where she was angular up top, she was dominant in the hip area. The zipper was not going up.

"That dress does not fit you."

Margaret laughed and tried to zip the dress up again, swearing when the zipper broke. She should have listened to me.

"Do they have anything that'll fit a real body?" Margaret asked. Waverley laughed with her.

Waverly was the tallest of us and the leanest in terms of proportions. The only problem she had was that everything that covered Margaret and me looked significantly shorter on her, particularly in the legs.

"Waves, get me that size eight dress in hot pink?" Margaret asked.

Waverly's eyebrows scrunched, meeting the middle of her face. "The one with the corset bodice?"

"Hell no! I'm not trying to look like a slut like Cameron."

Slut. I'd heard it on television. In hallways at school. Even to describe me as I walked by, but I'd never asked what it meant.

"Margaret?" I asked.

"Yeah, Tet?" she said as she attempted to squeeze out of the first dress.

"What is a slut?"

Margaret's face broke into a mischievous smile. "Duh! It's someone who sleeps around."

I was perceptive enough to learn "sleeping around" didn't actually mean "sleep". Hearing my friends use it in context with this word "slut" made me curious.

"Is sex immoral to you?" I asked.

I tried on a yellow dress that Margaret had to pull over my backbone. It was much too tight. *Noban* attire was revealing, but it wasn't meant to restrict movement.

"Eff you, Tetra, and your D-cups. What—do you have a bedazzled va-jay-jay, too?" Margaret attempted to pull the dress farther up my torso, but it had already gone as far as it was going to go. I wasn't exposed, but I could barely move. "And hell no, sex isn't bad."

"Then why do you shame someone for enjoying it?"

Margaret's eyebrows furrowed, and a heinous laugh followed. "Because I don't like her. I can't think of another word to describe her."

Waverly rolled her eyes. "Yeah, but Tetra's got a point." She whipped around, her eyes widening when she saw me. "Okay I know which dress I *wanted* to try on, but now I can't."

I didn't like this dress. The fit was awkward, and uncomfortably tight. "It is alright Waverly. It is yours if you believe it'd flatter you more. I do not have the body type for a dress like this if I plan to do more than sit."

Waverly laughed, placing the silhouette of a dress over the front of her physique as she studied her reflection in the mirror. "Imagine what it'd be like to switch bodies whenever you wanted. I bet you every dress would fit if I could do that." She smirked.

"What did you just say?" I couldn't help but ask abruptly.

Waverly laughed, and her features softened against her smile. "Tetra, I'm kidding! Geez, you're usually better at catching my jokes. Or at least making some witty comeback about how *you do not get, that was not funny.*"

Margaret turned away from her own mirror and countered, "You're really *not* that funny, Wave." As Waverly hit her over the shoulder, and I decided to ignore my intuition for the time being.

There was something about what she'd just said. I couldn't help thinking—No. I'd overlooked former suspicion before. Until I was sure, I didn't even want to *think* how I'd finish that sentence …

I should've known today would be an unsettling time. I hadn't slept well throughout the night, and foreboding hung over me the entire way to school.

The clouds were darker than usual. It rained, if only lightly. I was forced to tie my hair up. Getting it wet left it too responsive and I didn't have time to worry about that. I didn't normally grouse when it came to rainfall. The earth cried for it, a necessity that was unavoidable. That is, if it were a natural occurrence.

I didn't have a reason to assume otherwise, until I spoke to Margaret.

Margaret took botany. She enjoyed it since the course's final consisted of cultivating and cloning a plant root to grow into a new one. She joked that her project was a cross between something illegal to use and something distracting to look at. Today she was frantic.

Margaret was animated to begin with, so it was difficult to find her anger genuine most times. Something troubled her.

"I'm going to rip them apart, separate their body parts, and use their legs for a coffee table," Margaret said in an exchange of huffs.

"What's wrong?" I asked.

"My fucking final! Some idiot destroyed *everything*! *Everyone's*! All the plants were wilted. If this is someone's idea of a senior prank—"

Wilted. That struck a chord. Everything Margaret said before and after blurred. This morning there was rain. That might've been a coincidence. Now there was this?

"Can you show me?" I interrupted. Margaret shrugged, but led the way. When we reached the botany lab, teachers and students crowded around it, making it difficult to reach the front. They speculated that maybe an artificial light had been left off or the heat cranked up.

This was no slip of a light. *Geotics* didn't share the same connection to their earth *Nobans* did. They didn't know what it tried to tell them, the remnants left behind. These plants weren't wilted. They looked as if they were screaming.

The *Naga* couldn't hide long without feeding. The plants wouldn't sate its hunger for long. Soon, it would be looking for a new soul.

Sterling

Today was the day. There were only three weeks until prom. If I was going to ask Waverly, it had to be today. Any later, and she might have another date. Any earlier? I hadn't had the courage before today.

I should've practiced beforehand, but Tetra was no good at pretending to be Waverly. She seemed distracted anyway. Even Kip couldn't get her attention. Not that I was stalking them or anything.

Poke.

A pencil met my ribcage. It was Waverley's. It must've been a sign. We met eyes and laughed. Smooth.

"What's Tetra's deal? She's been on edge since fourth period."

As if I was supposed to know. Tetra was withdrawn, but anything could've gotten her there, so I'd learned not to ask.

"Have you studied for the trig final yet?" I asked.

A grimace stretched over Waverley's face. "Somewhat … Kind of … Not really," Waverly said with a laugh. "I'm not doing anything after school. If you need a study buddy, I wouldn't complain."

Waverly was asking me to study with her? If this wasn't the day, what would be? It was settled. After school, I'd ask Waverly to prom.

There was an advantage to studying with Tetra. By comparison, she was focused, more patient. It didn't help that Waverly and I got distracted every other minute with a network update on social media. We were going to fail. It wouldn't matter once I asked her.

You're stalling, Sterling. The worst she can say is ...

"So ... Waverly ..." That was about as far as I'd planned. Dammit. I should've practiced with Tetra.

Waverly rolled her eyes and laughed, leaning over the table. "Ugh! I knew studying with you was a bad idea. We have too much fun together."

An instant renewal of my confidence. She offered a bemused smile, a sign of now or never.

"Enough fun to go to the prom together?" I asked, stumbling on the last two words.

Waverly's eyes widened, and it got quiet. She wrinkled her nose and avoided eye contact. This was a mistake.

"I meant as friends, y'know? I didn't mean like—"

"Douglas already asked me. During eighth period. We're only going as friends, but I kind of said yes because no one else asked me."

Waverly studied her phone, and I shrugged it off. "No, it's okay. I just ... It's no big deal—"

"If you would've asked me, like, in trig or something, I would've said yes. I'm your friend, too. I was freaking out about prom being only three weeks away so ..."

Of course someone would ask her. She was Waverly. I was an idiot. "Really, Waves. It's okay. I didn't want to go alone either. I'll just ask someone else," I said under a smile.

I hoped it was convincing. I was crushed. Completely crushed. I checked my cell phone screen. It was fifteen past five anyway.

"Listen, Waverly, it's getting late. I have to catch the train and bus, but good luck on the final next week."

Waverley nodded and gave me a small wave. Looking back only made it harder. She would've said yes. She … would … have … said … yes. Nothing could make me feel worse than this.

It started pouring again. Rejecting that ride from Kip had its downside. With a bullshit forecast and no umbrella, I could've swam home and I wouldn't have been any less drenched.

It was just good to be home.

The house was quiet. The TV was on, but no one was watching. If Dad wasn't working, he'd be upstairs, taking a nap before dinner. Mom might be out, but the car was in the driveway.

I threw my keys on the counter and my book bag near the stairs. I raided the fridge and was lucky enough to find the last birch beer and a slice of leftover pizza. I was more depressed than hungry, but devoured both before heading upstairs.

The weather was still rough, adding an atmosphere to the silence. Things at home were never this quiet. Something wasn't right.

I froze at the top of the staircase. My eyes better be lying to me. Tetra was walking out of my parents' room, closing the door behind her.

"What were you doing in there?"

Tetra flinched, caught off-guard. She ignored me and walked past, disappearing into our room. I followed her. She wouldn't. She had no reason to. She promised.

"Tetra, I know you weren't doing what I asked you not to—"

Tetra held out her hands defensively, but refused to face me. "Sterling, don't. I do not have the time or patience. Definitely not now." There was an icy tone to her voice. I couldn't believe that *she* was mad.

"Tetra, we had a deal. I didn't tell you. I *asked* you. I asked you to stop. We're not subjects or experiments that you can keep altering what we think. Especially me and my parents."

Tetra threw her hands in the air out of frustration. "Sterling, I am under so much pressure. I'm asking you. Do not press this."

"*You're* under a lot of pressure? What kind of pressure can you possibly be under? Your life is perfect. You have a perfect life, perfect grades, a perfect boyfriend—"

"The idea that you think at a time like this, that I would allow something so minuscule to—"

"Then what? What do you have to worry about? Why would you need to manipulate people? After I asked you not to!"

"They're not your parents!"

The room grew dangerously quiet. There was no way I'd heard her right. "What did you just say?" I asked.

Tetra crossed her arms over her chest defensively and bounced on the balls of her feet. "You are not their son. Not biologically, anyway."

"You're … you're lying," I said. My heart sank deep into my chest. She had to be lying. Why would she make up something like that?

"The *Naga* expected me to be in the presence of an infant. I left you with the Wayfairers because … I knew they would root you. Suppress your ability to Ride."

Tetra paused, waiting for a reaction. For a response. I hadn't heard a single thing. Not until she started speaking again.

"That is why we needed to be separated, Sterling. There was no other way. When we first drew each other out, I thought you'd remember me, but rooting you worked. I always felt familiar to you, but not at the risk of you knowing you weren't Peter and Laurel's biological son. When you started to resonate, you referred to me by my given name. I *had* to manipulate you, but most of all, Peter and Laurel."

Tetra's eyes burned on my skin, but I couldn't look at her. My chest was so tight words wouldn't come out.

"Laurel rejects the change the most. She is harder to manipulate. Her mind has no memory of giving birth to you."

Tears spilled down my face. I felt like such a kid. I was sad. I was confused. I was anxious. But most of all, I was upset.

"You'd better be lying to me, Tetra. Because what you're telling me …" I didn't finish the sentence. I didn't know where it'd go, and those words would be like poison if I let them come out. Tetra reached out, closing distance between us, but I backed away.

"If you're not lying now, what you're telling me is … my whole life has been a reconstruction of some game you've been playing, and that doesn't sound like you. I don't want that to be you because I *trust* you. I *care* about you. People who trust and care about each other don't do things like that."

It became harder to fight the break in my voice. I rubbed my face and paced. Tetra's eyes grew dull and wet, but she stood her ground.

"I had to, Sterling. I ran out of options. It was stay together and die or separate and have a chance. I wanted to tell you. I was going to tell you—"

"*When*?!" I screamed in a fit of rage. Tetra eased back.

It was the furthest apart I'd felt from her since we'd been here. I didn't know the person who stood before me. She didn't deny it. But that wasn't the same thing as telling the truth.

"I don't even know who I am when you're around me," I said, as a state of sickness engrossed my body. "I keep thinking this is supposed to happen, we're supposed to happen. But ever since you came here, you're like the worst thing that's ever happened to me, and I can't …"

I left the room and didn't look back.

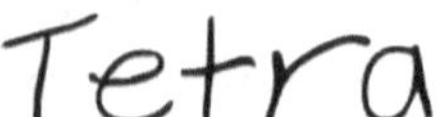

Tetra

K ip jumped at every creak, every sound or threat of motion in the house. He was nervous. Being in a room alone had never been an issue before—why was it now? I'd called him after Sterling left.

I had ways of finding him if I wanted to, like before when we called to each other. But he was upset. He might never forgive me if I manipulated him again, so I'd called Kip.

Sterling wouldn't answer messages I sent, but I knew he might with Grey or Kip. Grey wasn't the best at answering his phone or messages after midnight, so Kip was my best bet.

"He's asking why *I'm* asking where he is," Kip said. I pulled at the skin of my hands. I wanted to ask so many questions, but Kip was a better texter. I was too descriptive and detailed. It gave my identity away.

"Ask him if he's all right … or … No, tell him you're just curious to know where he is. So you know where to pick him up tomorrow."

Kip faked a smile. "I'll put, 'Can't Sleep. Just Up.'"

See? Much better texter. I waited for the thought bubble to complete at the bottom of his screen.

Grey's.

A pinched expression spread across Kip's face. He looked back down at his phone and typed the letter *Y.* He must've been asking why.

Dunno. Sterling's response back. Sterling was vague, but if he were at Grey's, he was safe. He'd gone somewhere familiar to him. A place of security. I was disappointed. For now, and for however long, it was not with me.

"Did something happen?" Kip asked.

What was I supposed to say? I'd been keeping things from Sterling, but I'd lied to everyone since coming to *Geo.* I couldn't tell Kip why Sterling was upset with me. I couldn't tell him how sorry I was that I'd hurt Sterling, that I hadn't meant to, that everything I did was to protect him.

I couldn't tell my boyfriend the truth. I hid my face between my legs and wept. Kip leaned over to hold me. I didn't object. "Do you have something to tell me, Tetra?" Kip asked. What did he mean by that?

I put my arms around him, running my fingers through his hair. In a moment, all his insecurity ran through me. Sometimes, he was threatened by Sterling. He was afraid to say it. Kip wasn't a keeper of secrets—except for this. Small things never intended to deceive. A fear his girlfriend and best friend were lying to him.

"You are my boyfriend, Kip. I care about you. But I care about Sterling, too. He is upset with me. If I'm being honest, his feelings are valid. But it's not what you think." I sat down on my bed. I curled into a ball and didn't want to come up. Kip stood. I didn't want him to go.

"Please … stay."

Sterling

It was a long night. The longest of my life.

Don't get me wrong. I loved Grey's siblings…most of the time. But there was no *envy* there. Being one of six must've been a nightmare. Grey probably got the best sleep of his life last night. His siblings loved new meat.

At fourteen, Sami played her music low enough not draw attention from the parentals, but loud enough to find its way through the reverberating safeguard that was *supposed* to be Grey's wall.

Remy and Ren, the twins (or the evil twins, courtesy of me and Kip), could have taught an online course on how to strip people of their dignity. They wanted tears, gore, complete warfare. With the promise of fresh blood, Grey wasn't a target and also a lot harder to be caught off-guard. Me? I could only hope the magic marker mustache and smell of months-old sprayable cheese would wash away with a vigorous shower. I was traumatized and paranoid by five in the morning, curled into a ball, with one eye open.

I wasn't mad. This was their normal. It reminded me why we always preferred Kip's house. But there was an advantage to tonight. It left me so distracted I didn't remember why I was here in the first place. Why I avoided thinking, so as to not feel so empty.

Mom and Dad. They weren't my birth parents.

It was the first time I'd thought the words since walking out. The people I'd grown up with. Raised me. Loved me. Protected me. Weren't my parents.

I'd never wondered why they weren't in my *Noban* memories. Or why I didn't look much like either of them. I never considered where I got my pronounced nose bridge, fuller lips, or my hollow-as-hell cheekbones. I thought I took after a grandparent or something.

I didn't know who my birth parents were, but I desperately wanted them to be Peter and Laurel.

Tetra lied to me.

Who was I really?

Tetra

K ip spent the night with me. I felt shame for misusing the faith the Wayfairers entrusted in me, but last night I hadn't wanted to be alone. It made me forget the wedge I'd driven between Sterling and I.

I'd done the right thing. Decisions were hard to make in the case of survival. The stability needed to survive this world was one I couldn't provide. What I'd done had taken true sacrifice. I'd known it would impair my own abilities, but he was my *Noban*. I would've done anything to ensure his survival.

Since we'd bonded, accepting his faults was my nature. Protecting him was my nature. To be one was *our* nature. Separating had consequences. We were no longer one, but it was my call.

I didn't have cherished memories. My past had been nothing but suffering, tragedy, and uncertainty. The selfish part of me wanted new memories to replace the old ones. So I let this world ground me, weaken me. I'd formed unnecessary attachments. Attachments I would, in time, abandon.

But it was a sacrifice I'd been willing to make. I would miss my friends. I went from having none to having more than I'd ever had. The time would come when a decision would need to be made, but unlike the past, it'd be one we'd be forced to make together.

Without Sterling, the urge to wake for school was burdensome. Kip had only left an hour ago but was still my ride. Peter and Laurel didn't object to him taking the time to wake me. He kissed me on the nose, followed by the mouth, finally unleashing an outbreak of tickles. The penalty would get worse if I didn't make haste, so off I was to the shower to prepare for school.

Kip and I rode there, hand in hand. I decided it best to cease riding Kip's mind. He shared so much willingly anyway. More than I could say for myself. My ability allowed me to understand, influence, and peer into a living thing's mind, but it had the power to hurt people. I didn't want to hurt Kip. I cared for him. I only wish I'd seen that before I had hurt Sterling.

Sterling

School sucked. Tetra spent the whole day avoiding me. I guess I was doing the same. But a part of me did want her to approach me. I didn't expect an apology, but I was tired of all the past excuses.

"I was protecting you," "I didn't tell you for your own good," or my absolute favorite, *"You weren't required to know."*

If I wasn't required to know my entire life would be different if I just knew the truth, what *was* I required to know?

In PE, she'd occasionally glance my way, only to move her focus back to our friends. If she missed me, she didn't show it. I wondered if my face screamed my longing and the burning need for her attention.

I wanted to arrange something through our mutual ally, Kip, but I didn't want to give him the wrong idea. Kip already had a hunch that I had a soft spot for Tetra, but the constant denial and reassurance from Tetra always kept his suspicions at bay.

To be honest, Tetra was someone I genuinely really liked. More than I should have, considering. All the time we'd spent this year, getting to know each other. How could I not? But that didn't mean I wasn't supportive of them as a couple. It wasn't like I was the kind of guy Tetra would take a second look at.

Noban culture had taught her the power of selection. Obviously, compared to Kip, I wasn't much to brag about. I knew I wasn't meant to be that to her anyway. I was beginning to understand the way bonds worked.

Unconditional understanding. Companionship. Maybe even love. Even if not romantic. I should've hated her, but it took too much effort. I wanted us to be on speaking terms again. I couldn't help it. She called to me.

"Tetra. Can we talk…alone?"

Kip gave a pained look of confusion, but my attention was on Tetra. Her expression was vacant. For a minute, I thought she'd tell me no. It surprised me when she excused herself from Kip, agreeing to meet in the hallway. I didn't know what we were going to say, but it was good to be talking.

Tetra

"I plan to stay at Kip's house tonight. Perhaps longer."

Sterling's gaze appeared feverish. He curled his arms over his head. "You're what?"

"You need some time. I'd feel better knowing you were at home, safe with your parents."

We stared at each other for too long to consider it a moment.

"They're not my parents."

I didn't know what to say. I turned on the ball of my foot, but Sterling blocked my path, taking both my hands.

"We haven't talked. Are we going to talk? I wasn't... I didn't... I don't want you to go," he said in a pleading tone. The pain and anger that boiled inside him surged from him to me at our joined hands.

"Sterling, you are not ready to talk to me. You need time." I paused, struggling to get the words out. "Goodbye, Sterling."

With my arms crossed over my chest, I turned in Kip's direction. I was the better one at standardizing my emotions, but I was overwhelmed in solace. He wanted to talk. It meant he was open to listen.

Sterling

I lay on my bed, lifeless. How could Tetra just leave me here alone? Nothing about this house, these people, and this world felt the same anymore.

I wasn't Sterling Wayfairer. Not really.

The only thing that felt familiar in this place was her. And she wasn't here to help me make sense of things. All the times Mom hadn't recognized me or was afraid of me, I'd been the cause of it. I'd resented her, called her crazy, questioned her love for me.

Turned out I'd never belonged to them anyway.

I didn't belong to this world. I didn't belong to Peter and Laurel. Maybe I didn't belong anywhere.

A soft tapping sound echoed at my door. I didn't answer, but Mom let herself in anyway, finding a cozy spot at the foot of my bed. She patted my leg until I faced her. She offered a weak smile.

"Doing okay, sweetheart?" she asked in a soothing tone. I didn't know what Tetra had told her, but she still sensed something was wrong.

"Tetra told me what happened with Waverly and your prom plans. Do you want to talk about it?"

Not really. I appreciated that she cared enough to ask. Before the truth, even at her worst, I'd never questioned my role in this family. I couldn't help that they were the only family I'd ever known. I still wanted to feel connected to them.

I didn't keep track of how long we talked, but it was the first time in a while. You know? Talking for hours with your parents? By the time I'd turned eleven, I'd outgrown it, but now? It was just nice to talk to somebody about anything and everything.

Mom had the crazy idea that I had feelings for Tetra. I spent ten minutes denying it, but I don't think she bought it.

Whether or not Laurel Wayfairer was my birth mother, she knew me. She knew how I thought, how I reacted to situations, how things affected me. I wondered how long I would have with her. How long would the rest of this fairytale last? I needed Tetra to help me understand. I needed answers. Most of all, I needed Tetra.

Tetra

The Wayfairer home was a world of clutter, knick-knacks, and keepsakes—useless memorabilia distribut-ed across the house, proving their existence there. Even Waverly's home was showered with remnants, memo-ries, welcome mats, or family photos that brought personality to each room.

Kip's home featured none of those things.

The furniture in the living room was minimalistic, yet expensive. It reminded me one of the houses in Laurel's *Dream Décor* publications. The only pictures on the wall were paint-ings, nothing hinting at the people who lived there.

Kip dropped his bag in the kitchen. I followed him as he opened a cookie jar and pulled out a knot of money that might've covered the entirety of the Wayfairers' monthly expenses. And that was *only* if they were lucky.

"There's money in here for food," he said, before I sat down at the island in the center in the room. Kip wore a hard expression in his eyes, one hard to interpret.

"Kip, where are your parents?"

He averted his stare from me as he answered. "My folks go away a lot. My dad works in finance and my mom...she just likes to go away. It's cool, I guess. Everyone complains about curfews and stuff. I don't."

He made a great effort to hide it, but it bothered him. By *Geo's* standards, I didn't have a functioning relationship with my parents either. Kip and I had more in common than I'd thought. I reached out to hold his hand.

"Why don't you give me the grand tour?"

The grand tour was more of a...brief tour. The second stop was his room, and well...we never made it past there. I spent the next half hour exploring my curiosity with Kip's body. His heartbeat pounded double time, and while it wasn't a popular thing to marvel at, it was my favorite part of being so close to him.

He remained adamant on his "no-sex-before-prom" conditions, but we found ways to be intimate. The moment was cut short, though, when he pulled away from me, resisting any flux of pleasure my lips sent through him.

"Tetra, can we..." He paused. "Can we just slow down a little? I want to get something off my chest."

Straddling him, I leaned up, watching his lips press into a hard line.

"What's going on between you and Sterling?" I detected a hint of jealousy from the way he stressed *you and Sterling*. "I hate to get in the middle. And you don't have to tell me everything, it's just…I asked you both about it and neither of you will tell me. He's one of my best friends, and you're my girlfriend. Why is it something I'm not allowed to know?"

In *Noba*, we held bonds over everything else. Things expected of us vastly changed the moment you became a part of someone else. It wouldn't be easy for Kip to understand. It would be difficult to accept the complex relationship that Sterling and I shared.

"It's nothing you should worry about. Our problems are not *our problems*. Things will work their way out in time." I leaned back in to kiss him, but he stopped me.

"Tetra, do I have to worry about you? I'm probably making stuff up, but I feel like…there's something there." Kip was right. There was something between Sterling and me. But it wasn't anything illicit. Sterling had feelings for Waverly. I respected that. I'd never go there with Sterling for reasons too complicated to admit.

"Kip, have I ever lied to you?"

His jaw clenched. He averted his eyes. "I don't think so."

"So you trust the things I tell you?"

He nodded, worry and doubt staining his features.

"Sterling and I are friends. We have been for a long time. He was there for me when I had no one else. We are close. But we are nothing more than what you see. Friends. All right?"

He nodded, leaning up to kiss me on the nose. A bell-like gong traveled through the house. The doorbell.

"I'll go get the food," he said, before disappearing into the hallway.

We'd been too wrapped up in each other for me to notice much about his room until now. Posters of athletes and girls on the wall. A jersey in a frame. Trophies in cases. None of it interested me more than the photographs by his bedside. A woman with brown skin, black hair, and a contrasting eye color. A fairer man, with Kip's snake charmer eyes and light brown hair. And a boy in a football uniform. Kip.

It must've been his parents. It was the only picture of all three of them. The rest of the photos featured Kip with another family. I recognized Waverly in all the photos, as well as her parents at different stages of their lives. The same veil of familiarity clouded my judgment. Waverly's mother. There was something unearthly about her. I couldn't explain why, but…

Kip walked in, his hands full of bags. Stealing a whiff, I was relieved it smelled edible. Much like takeout night at the Wayfairers, it was the only day I looked forward to eating.

"Thank you for letting me stay here, Kip."

He smiled. "You know I can't say no to you."

I wasn't sure which times he spoke of. He had told me no *all the time*. I gestured to the picture of his family. "Your parents look pleasant."

He shrugged, shifting noodles around with his fork. "They're okay." His way of saying they weren't.

"Are those Waverly's parents?"

His eyes lit up at the mention of them. "Yeah, that's my uncle Steve and my aunt Mina. You met my uncle at the play, but Waverly's mom spends a lot of time away managing her father's farm. You might meet her in a few weeks at graduation. There's no way she'd miss that."

Interesting.

I'd slept over at Waverly's house a handful of times, but I had yet to meet her mother. There was something strange about that. I promised myself I'd look into it later. Right now, takeout sounded good.

Tetra

What would I say to him? How would I say it? I prepared all morning for the inevitable encounter with Sterling. His history had always been *my* truth. It'd always been *my* truth. A burden I bore for things to move forward. I knew he wouldn't understand it *now*, but in time, maybe one day he'd try.

I was best at this. Appearing strong, when I did not want to be. It was the *Oerban* in me. Neither the *Fava*, the *Beru*, or the *Aina*, our neighboring tribes, knew our vigilance. Our strength. The *Oerba* mirrored the water—reserved on the surface, cold deep within. I spent my entire existence fighting warmth. I was impulsive. Unpredictable.

I was Sterling.

We were different, yet the same. His eyes witnessed the differences. The surface. If only he knew how similar we were, he'd know … how sorry I was.

The first three periods moved by in a blur. The senior class was dismissed early, so by fourth period, we were all rounded up for a CCI tradition: Senior Field Day.

Kip dedicated much of the bus trip to filling me in. If I understood correctly, it was a feast of grilled food, loud music, and sporting events that gave students a chance to bond. It'd end in an annual senior game, split into two teams. The game was determined by the year's football MVP.

I was proud to say that this year, Kip took that honor.

When we'd first met, I saw Kip as an arrogant braggart. With time, I'd seen how hard he worked, how underappreciated he was by those who mattered to him. We'd gone about it in different ways, but I…I wasn't a stranger to the feeling.

Grey was the football team's main striker, but Kip was the backbone. Grey wasn't shy about giving credit where it was due, in a long-winded, ten-minute speech.

I had a better understanding of *Geotic* sportsmanship, athletics, and camaraderie from becoming Kip's girlfriend. Once I was reluctant to wear his letterman number, but today I wore it with pride.

Sterling

Another sleepless night. I spent most of it contemplating how to approach Tetra, half the time convincing myself that I shouldn't. Everything about our bond seemed like a test. To bring out discipline, maturity, restraint?

I admit I didn't know much about Tetra's past. I didn't know her parents' names or much about her upbringing outside of what she'd told me. I didn't even know what it was like when she first met me. All those things crossed my mind on the bus ride to *Meadow* Park.

She kept her distance, and it was mega-confusing. My mark burned, but I hid it under my sleeve.

"Hi, Sterling."

Waverly surprised me. I hadn't been paying attention to much else today, so we hadn't crossed paths until now.

"Hey, Waves." It came out nervous and shaky.

She circled me, reaching her arm around my shoulder. "So Tetra's already found her way to the dark side. Totally siding with Kip. Grey and Kip can't both be on the same team, and you know Grey's going to pick you."

If only she knew how wrong she was. Grey'd want to win. There'd be no room to be loyal. "I guess we'll see."

In case I hadn't mentioned it, I despised rugby. It sucked that everything that screamed school spirit about CCI had to do with getting pummeled to the ground. Did I mention how much I hated rugby?

Guess it could've been worse. Last year, CCI's MVP drew Capture the Flag and set up an elaborate search out in friggin' *Woodlands*. More kids got lost than had fun. I'd say we got off easy.

Grey and Kip got team captain picks. Grey's team the Whites; Kip's, the Blues. Why didn't it surprise me that Tetra was Kip's first choice? Loyalty must've been more important than I thought, because I was Grey's first draft, a choice that surprised everyone. It was cool not being picked last, but it meant that talk I'd planned to have with Tetra wasn't happening anytime soon.

Grey scored a pretty sweet lineup. Other notables on his team were Doug, Waverly, and a few other Goldens. He chose Samir, but it could've just been that Kip didn't want him after that kiss he and Tetra shared during the winter play.

We took appropriate colors to wear over or replace our current shirts, and the Whites huddled up for a quick rundown of strategy. Each Golden One went back and forth on where we should focus our efforts.

Grey was adamant to listen. "I'm hearing you guys, but Tetra can dance circles around most of you. You're focusing too much on Kip, Maggie, and Aiden. What Tetra lacks in strength, she makes for in speed. Any ideas how we're going to deal with that?"

Silence. Maybe I wasn't as athletic, but I had an idea or two on how Tetra operated. It wouldn't mean much coming from me, because Golden Ones only trusted their own.

"Girl's no joke. Speed's untouchable, and she's got a mean right arm—" Douglas said.

"I wouldn't say *untouchable*," Waverly said with a hint of arrogance.

Calculating the odds, Grey chose where to spread the manpower.

"Sterling, Lopez, I'm making you a lock forwards. I'm going to need height in the second row. Waves, can I count on you as a back?" Waverly offered a quick nod, as Grey pointed to two other players. "Glover, you're loosehead. Ali...I' m going to regret this, but I'm making you tighthead."

Most of us didn't need an explanation on how rugby was played. It was the main sport one of our reoccurring subs chose when our PE teacher was on leave or took a sick day. Only the objective about the game changed. Kip would play to Tetra's strengths, so she wasn't the main objective. She was the *only* objective.

"Let the games begin!"

Just as I predicted, we got demolished. We didn't score one try in the game's first half and not for lack of trying. The Blues were just better. We were grateful for the ten-minute rest before the start of the next half. Forty minutes of getting slammed to the ground deserved more than a measly ten minutes. Just when things couldn't get worse? It started to rain.

Didn't it occur to anyone to check the morning's forecast *before* the MVP hat pull?

"Woo...you guys, we've got to restrategize or something," Grey said, taking a large gulp of a bright-colored sports drink. "We're not going to last another five minutes, let alone a whole half."

Everyone agreed. We were already losing, so it wouldn't hurt to switch numbers.

"Glover, Wayfairer, I'm switching you to halfback. Sterling, you've got fly-half."

Just great. There went any energy I had left.

The downpour continued another twenty minutes into the current half. The upside? The Whites were tied with the Blues. Where the moxie had come from, I didn't know. Maybe the rain had been good for something.

Waverly pulled some spunk out of nowhere. While everyone complained about not being able to use their legs tomorrow, she'd be found closing in on the possessor of the ball. She was fast. *Scary fast*. More than once, Tetra had to kick the ball to escape the holy mess of a five-man tackle. The real surprise?

How I stacked up.

I didn't stand around and wait for magic. I made the magic. When teammates passed, I caught. When enemies came for me, I dodged. It was like I knew where to be and when to be there. I skated past players with infinite ease as my feet entered the goal line for the third time. Now the Whites were in the lead.

As the rain let up, a dropkick from yours truly reset the game. Grey and Samir were in pursuit of the ball. I put distance between myself and rival players. Just by being a top scorer, I'd made myself a target. No one said it in words; it was all in the way they peered at me. *More manpower on Sterling,* their eyes said. No matter where I ended up, there were no less than three players on me. It felt good knowing I was someone to worry about.

Man, I should've tried out for some sport teams.

In an impressive catch, Samir took possession of the ball. He then passed it backward to Grey unscathed. Blues were on Grey hard before he tossed it back to Waverly. Call it an instinct, but it's like the wind told me exactly where I was needed. Waverly scanned the field. I was in the position to do something game-changing. Before I could register the thought, the ball flew in my direction. With less than eight minutes left in the game, I took off.

Sidestepping was not an easy feat when you had five guys gunning for you, but every time the wind blew, it guided me. There was no stopping me. And then it happened.

My wrist started to burn in that freaky kind of way, throwing me off my game. I couldn't let anyone see! Or worse, risk anything crazy shooting out. A body hit me and I was on the ground, four Blues tearing into me. I let go of the ball, happy to be rid of its weight.

Kip and Grey began fighting over the ball.

When I didn't get up in record time, Coach Ruiz called for a stoppage. Everyone crowded around me.

"Hey, Wayfairer, everything alright? You want to get checked out?"

"I'll be fine. I just need to sit the rest out. Sorry, guys." I attempted to stand but immediately regretted it. My legs felt like they were going to collapse under me, and my head throbbed with the hugest headache. Waverly and Tetra swooped in to flank both sides of me. Guess I'd be paying the emergency room a visit after all.

"Hold on, let me get my keys. I'll drive," Kip said. He patted himself down and swore to himself. "Forgot I didn't drive here."

Douglas swung his keys around his fingers. So glad *someone* had some decent news. "It's cool, Matherstein. I got this one. But my whip won't fit all y'all, so Sterling, you got a decision to make."

Without even thinking, I blurted out Tetra's name. Tetra glanced over at Waverly. "It's okay, Waverly. I've got him. Enjoy the rest of the game."

Waverly rolled her eyes and laughed. "You guys *are* the game." We faked smiles as Waverly wished me luck and ran over to the halfway line.

Douglas hesitated. "You guys, I'm just going to hit up the bathroom really quick, but I'm right behind you."

"Come on," Tetra said as she led me to the *Meadow* Park parking lot.

On the way to Douglas's car, Tetra lifted my jersey, and her eyes widened in shock. She pulled it down in a quick tug, as if hoping I didn't see it, but I saw it. Just in time for the real pain to set in.

The left side of my torso was entirely bruised purple. There was no way I'd gotten slammed that hard.

"Tetra. I don't think I can walk that fast. I need to stop. Just for a minute."

But she didn't stop, she sped up.

Black spots began dancing in front of my eyes from the pain. "Come on, Tetra, please. Just for a minute."

"We can't. Your injuries." She hesitated. "It bit you. It's spreading."

As we walked, Tetra explained that the *Naga* had to be on that field. How did I not notice? I couldn't even remember who I'd come in close contact with. If it didn't hurt so much, I'd be able to think clearer, be more helpful.

"If the poison gets to your heart... Never mind. I have to stop it before it does. I *need* some place private. *Now!*" Tetra urged.

There'd been a ranger station we passed on the way here. I must have passed out, because the next time I opened my eyes, we were there.

I was propped up against the wall, freezing and shirtless, while Tetra sat meditating a few inches from me. The words leaving her mouth were a language I'd heard before but didn't understand. It was more of a chant than a conversation. *Noban.*

She leaned in closer. A twitching shot of pain crawled through me, and I felt the burn of something sharp slide across my skin. It was a ranger's station, so it could've been a pocket knife, or something else equally as sharp. But when I looked down, vials of black liquid poured from the skin over my ribs. I screamed.

"I'm sorry," Tetra said, wearing her own version of panic. "There's just no other way for it to come out. I need to break the skin to help you."

When she stood, a flick of her wrist compelled my body to do the same. Her eyes burst open, devoid of color, exuding only energy as she moved her hands in an alternated pushing and pulling circular motion.

Graceful and full of purpose.

Looking down at my chest, I saw she was right. The poison had spread, and I had a strong desire to hurl. She zeroed in on me, her hands wild, like a conductor. The poison was moving to the point of the excision she'd made a moment earlier. She was extracting it, the same way she controlled the waves.

The surge of pain got stronger, the closer it came to my ribs. Instead of a series of small widespread pangs, it became an agonizing block of torment. An eternity later a stream of black liquid writhed out of my ribcage and glided toward Tetra's hands, her body absorbing the toxins. Doing what with it, I didn't know. At that moment, I was just grateful it didn't hurt anymore and my body looked normal. The ability to Ride waves *must've* had perks.

My excitement died down when I saw Tetra faltering. Something was wrong.

"Tetra?" I said, my voice full of worry. The dark mass traveled from her hands to her neck, turning her skin a poisonous black. She fell to her knees, clawing at her neck, but I caught her before she could hit the ground. The light in her eyes fled, as the tears streamed down her face, stained with black ichor. *No*.

"Tetra!" I cried.

And then she stopped. Stopped moving. Stopped breathing. Just stopped.

"Tetra!" I called out again. This wasn't happening. She was always so good at this stuff. I was useless. How could I possibly help her?

I pulled her close and, in the silence, heard something slight that gave me hope. Her heartbeat. She wasn't gone. There was still a chance to save her. I hoisted her on my back. I wouldn't stop until I found someone who could help. She was always willing to sacrifice for me. I couldn't lose her today. Not today. Not ever.

My legs burned from running. It'd stopped raining, but the soil underneath me was so wet and slippery, I almost fell a few times. I didn't want to let Tetra down. Not when she needed me. Yesterday, all I'd thought about was how my life had been a lie. Now I'd give anything for Tetra to insult me.

As long as we were together, we could do anything.

Tetra must not have gotten all the poison out. As I ran, my vision blurred. I was seeing things, like I was high or something. I saw stars. Not just eye floaters and flashes. I mean, *real* stars.

I kept running, but then that ripping feeling from before… That time at Waverly's party. I felt in control, but my body was being wrenched in the opposite direction. I was lost in a birthplace of stars. Intergalactic rows of worlds encompassed in an ocean of emerald emptiness. It was…cosmic.

If Tetra was still on my back, I couldn't feel her. I kept trying to follow the stars. Follow them to the light up ahead. I willed myself to stop, but the light…

I wanted to see.

I darted toward the opening. The air sucked right out of me. I was fading. What did that mean for Tetra?

I opened my eyes. Rebel was backing up on me hard, the ball coming in our direction. The scoreboard clocked the time at the 8:09.

That couldn't be right. I was back on the field guarding Rebel exactly where I'd stood fourteen minutes and thirty-two seconds ago. How did I get here?

Wasn't I just…in the parking lot?

My forearms were tender, the right wrist matching my left. Faintly glowing markings shone back at me. Maybe I'd dreamed the last fifteen minutes. The way Tetra looked at me, all wild-eyed and antsy, I knew I'd done something to cause a shift in the air. Wait, Tetra was okay. That was great! But…if I'd been here a few minutes ago and nothing had happened even though I *knew* it did, it only meant one thing.

I'd ridden time.

I thought it'd be different—painful, maybe even nauseating. *Sickest ride ever* were the only words worthy of describing the experience. I couldn't believe I'd done that by accident. It already felt like ages had passed, and I was dying to do it again.

My body moved to catch a pass, but my mind was on autopilot. The next time I looked at the scoreboard, there were still twenty-six seconds left in the half, and I was wide open. The ball was coming at me, and I knew I was going to catch it. It sounds weird, but the wind told me so.

My eyes locked on my target as I prepared to seize this ball and haul ass. That is, until someone slammed into me, knocking me hard into the ground. This time it was Tetra who tackled me.

"Do us both a favor and sit the next half out," she spoke lowly. "I know what you did. Your *shakti* is unstable. I can feel it. Do not make yourself a target twice."

Coach Ruiz's whistle blew, calling time on the next quarter. Tetra climbed off me and, in one forceful tug, hoisted me up on my feet. She was small but far from weak. She had nailed me on that tackle.

"My word might mean little to you now but trust me—"

With her hand still in mine, I pulled her in closer, my lips only centimeters from her ear. "I won't, but we have to talk."

She nodded. "Tonight. We will talk further then."

She attempted to move away, but I pulled her back in earshot. At this point, I didn't care how we looked to others.

"Promise me," I pleaded.

Her eyes regarded me. "I promise."

Content, I nodded as we separated, rejoining our teams. As per her advice, I sat out of the next half despite it pissing Grey off. This time nothing happened. The remainder of the game went on interruption and injury-free, with Kip's team beating ours 22 to 16. That hurt.

Grey, Doug, and I played decent together. It made me regret not going out for any teams in high school. By sitting out, I had held up my end of the bargain. In the distance, I could see Kip swallow Tetra in his arms, a kiss shortly following. When the two came up for air, Tetra whispered something to him. He didn't look mad. All he did was nod and pull her in again for another kiss. They parted ways as Tetra began walking in my direction, fulfilling her end of the deal.

Sterling

The walk home from the bus stop was awkward. There were so many things I wanted to say, but didn't know where to start. Tetra made things easier when her fingers interlocked with mine. Here went nothing.

"Tetra, the things I said before? I didn't mean them. I was angry … and scared. I guess I'm trying to say … that … I'm sorry. Are you mad?"

I hadn't expected to walk in silence for as long as we did. We were only feet away from home by the time I stopped staring at my feet.

"I was never angry with you. The truth about your lineage … It is a difficult truth to accept. I apologize for keeping it from you for as long as I did. Are you upset with me?" she asked.

My lips pursed as I stopped in front of her. I let go of her hand, searching for the right words. "I was. But I know why you did it." She nodded.

We made a detour to the backyard. It seemed like a night better spent outdoors. Tetra had a fascination with the way stars moved across the sky. I never asked why, but there was something about the way a shooting star calmed her. We sat on the grass, facing the sky in silence. It was easy to forget your problems when you were trying to keep track of all the stars in the sky.

"When we rode together for the first time, I didn't know where we'd end up. Time Riding was my weakest affinity, so I trusted you. I remember being so afraid. So uncertain how things "You must know that I only altered what their life was like before you. Their memories of you, the time you've all spent, their love—all of those are *real*. They did not *have* to love you. But they did. I can't make people feel things that aren't there. They are still very much your parents should you choose to see them that way. In *Noba*, when we come of age, we choose our family. I was a part of yours then. As I am a part of it now."

"Nothing seems real anymore," I said to no one in particular. Her hand squeezed mine. "I get that you've tried to protect me all these years … but can we get to a place where there are no secrets between us? I think …" I considered my words carefully. "… that is the only way we're going to get through this. I love my parents, but one day, it'll be just you and me. I don't want things to come between us again."

Tetra was quiet for a while. I wasn't sure if she was going to acknowledge what I'd said, but the atmosphere around us was calm. Maybe it didn't matter if she answered me. Maybe it only mattered that she was here. She turned to me, and we met each other's gaze, both with wet eyes, demeanors tired and broken.

"Okay."

<hr>

Tetra

An unsteady balance struck deep within my soul, pulsating, pounding my inner light. It was sharp enough to wake me from a comfortable sleep. My wrist seared with a scathing impulse. Energy hurt—always—but most times I had my grip on the burning sensation.

Unless it wasn't coming from me.

Sterling sat on the floor, hands outstretched and dancing across a page. There was paint all over him. I crawled to him, reaching out, only to find an entranced shadow of a person. I shook his shoulder, which prompted his eyes to finally open. An eerie glow of white—blank, yet full of purpose.

He was resonating.

He might not be aware of his current state. It was common to resonate when one unlocked an ability for the first time. The way his fingers glided down his canvas, the detail used, a creation outside his own realm of talent—were all signs Sterling was remembering. It was hard to know if this was good or bad.

Aurous flecks within slightly hooded eyes. Precision streams of crimson and gold over light brown skin. A soft black braid snaked across one shoulder, each detail marking familiarity. It was a woman.

Sterling gasped as he was adding the finishing touches. His eyes emitted one last glow before transitioning to their normal state of blue. He appeared disoriented, reaching out to touch his face.

"My head's spinning. Tetra, what happened?" he asked, noticing the moisture transferred from his hands to his face. "There's paint on my hands. Why is there paint on my hands?" he asked, but my concern was drawn to the artwork. Was it coincidence? Was it intentional? Was Sterling's mind looking to itself for answers? One could only speculate. I picked up the picture and held it before me as a look of panic washed across Sterling's face.

"What's wrong? Is that the *Naga*?"

"You don't know who this is?" I asked. Sterling shook his head. His abilities were forming, and now that he was of age, I couldn't stop it from happening. His mind was gaining strength. Older memories were surfacing. At the rate he was developing, there was no way of knowing how much time we'd have before we were found out.

"Should I?"

I hesitated. I didn't know where to start. "This is Hue Fan-Serafina. Sterling … this is the woman who gave birth to you."

Sterling

Each time my eyes took in the page, nothing else mattered to me. It was like my world stopped again. This was her … Hue Fan-Serafina. Serafina. My birth mother.

I didn't pay attention to much in class most days, but today I was even more distracted. I took the picture I drew last night everywhere, hiding it in my locker, my textbooks, my binders. I couldn't go more than ten minutes without studying it.

My finger caressed the detail in her eyes. The power in her expression. She had features I didn't have. In some ways, I resembled Peter and Laurel more than her.

I had her ears. Her lips? I touched my own; those were hers for sure. My jaw? I didn't get that from anyone else. But outside of bone structure, we didn't really resemble each other. I was blond; she was dark-haired. My eyes were blue; hers, a dark hazel. I was pale, but her skin was golden as if kissed by the sun.

It didn't matter to me whether we looked alike. She was just … beautiful.

I spent the day thinking about her. Imagining the way her voice sounded. Trying to picture how she smiled or what made her smile. Was she short, like Tetra? Or was she taller, like me? Was she kind? Was she timid? Was she rigid?

Was she still alive? Did she think of me the way I did her? Did she love me? Tetra didn't know much about the survival rate of that day. That day she referred to as the *Day of Scar*.

I was so caught up in thought I didn't notice Holly sitting next to me.

"Who's the babe?" she asked, low enough for only my ears to hear. Normally, a comment like that would've made my face turn beet red, but come on. She was my mom. Not a babe!

My notebook shut, and I murmured some excuse about an art project. I prayed it was enough to change the subject. When class finally started, Holly wasted no time getting down to business, which was great. Past that point, she didn't pry.

Hol was still my chem partner, even after the new semester. Outside of school, I wasn't sure how she spent her time, who she spent it with, or how she saw me. I put a lot of thought into what I was about to do. There was no way of knowing whether it'd create a serious meltdown or a rift between us.

"Hey, Hol. Want to go to prom with me?"

Holly snapped the pencil tip into the desk. "Wha-wha-what?" she stuttered.

"Prom? Did you plan on going?" I asked, casual yet confident, a smile forming.

Her bracelet became the most interesting thing to her. She kept snapping the row of beads against her skin like a rubber band. "No. I mean, no one asked me."

"Did you *want* to go?" I laughed.

Holly looked down at her notes, finger-combing the stray fringe of her ponytail. "Don't get me wrong, Sterling. I totally think you're cute. I just … see you as just my friend."

She must've thought she was hurting my feelings. She wasn't. It didn't bother me that I wasn't her first choice to prom. I wanted to go as friends, nothing more. "Come on, Hol. We're seniors. It'll be our last night to have fun together. I'm asking only as a friend. Do you want to go?"

Her lips pursed to one side. "Of course I want to go."

I shrugged. It was a no brainer. "So then let's go. As friends. By now, all my other friends have dates. And I want to go, but not by myself."

Holly huffed, crossing her arms across her chest. "This isn't a pity invitation, is it?"

I resented that. If Waverly was no longer an option to me, asking someone else wasn't a pity invite. I only wanted to ask someone I already liked, even if just as a friend. "Holly, I wouldn't have more fun with anyone else. You've been putting up with me all year. Let me take you to prom."

Her head swayed cheerfully from side to side. "It's, like, a week away. I don't have a dress."

My shoulder playfully brushed hers. "So get one. Me, Grey, and Kip already have a limo. And because I'm your date, I'll buy your prom ticket as a graduation gift. I'll make prom memorable for you, I promise."

"Okay. I'll go with you," she blurted out, full of excitement. "But only if it doesn't bother you that my parents'll take tons of pictures. They'll probably think we're getting married or something. Ignore that."

So, I wasn't going to prom with my first choice, but still … at least I'd be with a friend. She wasn't Waverly. She wasn't Tetra. But … I didn't know how much time I had left here. I wanted to enjoy each day like it'd be my last.

I couldn't wait for the last bell to ring. I wanted to update my friends on my prom date status. For weeks, they'd been trying to cheer me up after … you know. They'd be happy to know that my RSVP had gone from a maybe to a definite yes.

I caught up to Grey and Kip, and there was a bunch of tension between them. Even with my prom news, Kip kept moving, like he hadn't heard it. Or worse, didn't care.

"What's your problem?" I asked.

Grey made an animated number of warning faces. "Dude, ix-nay on the prom-stay.".

Kip wrestled with his keys, dropped them, and started yelling profanities. "Ugh, I don't want to talk about prom. It's not like I'm fucking going."

He sank onto the ground by the back of his car. Grey excused himself, patting me on the back. He muttered a final, "Good luck, man. Spent all of eighth period trying to get through to him," and then he was gone. I kneeled down but decided to sit. I didn't know how long it'd take to figure things out. "What's up, man?"

Prom was all Kip had talked about for three months. What he was wearing, what Tetra was wearing—it was prom this, prom that. What could have happened since I saw him this morning?

Kip ignored me, but he couldn't hold out forever. Not with all that frustration, irritation, and anger locked up inside. "Kip, did something happen?"

"Why don't you ask Tetra?"

Huh? "Dude, you totally lost me."

He stood. "You want to know why *I'm* not going to prom? Because Tetra dumped me, that's why."

"Wait, what?" I asked, barely hiding my shock. That sounded insane. Who breaks up with someone a week before prom? Tetra didn't do things without reason. There had to be more to this. Something bigger than this situation made it out to be.

"Kip, let me talk to her. I'll find out what her deal is, but until then …" Kip had his back to me, but I hoped he'd at least listen. "Don't do anything rash. Prom is our last big party before … Just promise me you won't make any decisions before I talk to her."

Kip couldn't read Tetra's mind. But maybe I could.

I don't know what I expected when I got home. It was one crazy situation after another since Tetra had gotten here, so I don't know why I expected anything normal this time. My mouth dropped at the sight of our room. I tugged at my hair, my vision getting dizzy.

Tetra sat in a pile of items, one of which she was still carving. A spear, a stake, even a makeshift bow and arrow were scattered next to her, keeping her company. My head was about to explode.

"Should I even be asking?" I asked, so frustrated it came out as a yelp.

"Please do not disturb me, Sterling. I am busy."

I bent down and nudged her shoulders, so she would stop and look at me for once. "I thought we weren't doing this. No lies, Tetra. That's what we agreed to."

Tetra finally faced me and dropped the weapon she was carving. "Sterling, I am trying. I don't have time to be conscious of your feelings right now. Normally I would, but I'm tired. I'm afraid. I'm upset. I'm running out of time—"

"What are you talking about?"

"You may think growing stronger is a good thing. And it is. In any other situation, it would be. But your *shakti* manifesting right now? Is not good. I should've seen it when you rode time. We leave stamps, signatures, proof of our existence every time we do. And you are leading the *Naga* right to us!"

My heart was racing so fast it was about to explode out of my chest. This definitely explained Tetra's recent paranoia. She'd shown signs before our separation, but just from this morning, I could tell she hadn't slept since she saw the picture I'd drawn of Hue Fan.

I was causing more trouble, even if it had finally started making things clear for me. Couldn't I have a second where I was happy for once? My head was getting dizzy, and if I hadn't been kneeling down, I would've fallen to my knees. "Me? I didn't mean to, Tetra—"

"I know you didn't. I'm not blaming you, but riding has its risks. Even more so now. Now that we can be tracked because of it. On *Noba*, we were a race of many, far too many to distinguish us from one another, but here? It's why I tried to suppress your abilities for so long. We were safe as long as you couldn't leave spiritual markers on the world."

"But I was only gone for fifteen minutes—"

"That is *more* than enough time to change everything. The rainstorm at senior field day? It was just a mirror image. *Geo* trying to tell us the reflection of who the *Naga* is."

My eyes widened at the first decent news I'd heard since I got home. "You think it was someone on the field?"

Tetra broke eye contact, shrinking behind a perpetual slouch. There was more to this.

Why was Tetra hiding this? Wasn't this what she'd planned for? What we'd been expecting? "Tetra, tell me who you think it is!" I steadied her by the shoulders, and she laid a comforting grip on my forearms. "No more lies, Tetra. No more lies."

She lifted her head to face me. Her look told me she didn't think I could handle it but was about to tell me anyway. I hoped the guilt trip was worth it.

"Waverly. I believe it is Waverly."

And just like that, my world came crumbling down.

Chapter 24

Tetra

Sterling must have asked "are you sure?" a dozen times. I tried to handle the situation delicately. I knew how much she meant to him, how much she meant to me, but it didn't change things. It may not be what he wanted to hear, but something had to be done.

"Sterling, I know this is sensitive for you. But you must know, anyone who becomes a part of that thing … is no longer your friend."

Sterling wept onto my shoulder as I held him close. His shoulders quaked as he held tighter, but I let him take everything in at his own pace. Better to get emotion out now. Emotion was the last thing one needed to be objective in a harsh situation.

"How do you know?" he asked, in a flat, monotone voice.

I pushed him upright to face me so my answer wouldn't just be words. "I'm not sure. But you saw the field. It would've had to be someone close enough to you not to cause alarm. The first victims are always strangers, but the closer it comes to your scent, the more likely it'll entwine with someone close to you to force you out. You don't emit the same spiritual scent when you are idle as you do when you resonate. The person it devours the next time *might* be you."

Sterling sniffled, cheeks puffy and red from crying. A dazed stare covered his features, and I assumed I hadn't gotten through to him the moment he opened his mouth.

"We have to go to prom!"

I prepared myself to speak, but Sterling interrupted me before I could.

"Listen, Tet. I know you probably think prom is a bad idea, but if it's ..." He couldn't say the name. That was fine. I wasn't able to at first either. "Then we'll just be leading it into a room of drunk and high teenagers with zero inhibitions. It'll be the perfect hunting ground. You'll never be able to track it if it takes another form."

I didn't want him to make sense, but he had a point. "If we were there, the least I could do is make sure it can't take another soul," I said, nodding.

Sterling took out his phone and handed it to me. "You need to call Kip."

"And tell him what? That I may have to *kill* something that resembles his cousin?"

Sterling had Kip's number dialed. "No. You *need* to go with Kip. We need a reason to all be together. You think breaking up with him all of a sudden isn't going to cause a red flag? What if it knows you know?"

I hadn't considered that. "I can't just un-break up with him—"

"No one is telling you to. But Kip won't go unless you go with him. It can be just as friends. But if you want Waverly at that damn prom, swallow your pride and ask him. Up until now, I've done everything you asked, expecting it would prevent this from happening." Sterling choked on his guilt, his words heavy with remorse. "Waverly was my friend. I want to make things right. But if we're going to …"

There was a tightness in his eyes, cold and hard.

"We *need* to be at that prom."

A replacement dress proved difficult to find a day before prom. My original dress had been sold at a tag sale, but with my build, I couldn't wear fit any dress. The places left that had dresses were upscale boutiques, which wasn't in the Wayfairers' budget. Instead Laurel and I decided a secondhand shop would be best.

Sterling laughed at every dress I tried on. At least he found something amusing at this point. He'd become a different person over the past few days. He should've looked forward to a benign prom experience. But our only concern at this point was for appearances.

Kip agreed to go with me, but my intuition didn't want either of us there. He was still my friend. I wanted to protect him, even if it was too late for Waverly. It could be my last night alive. So much might change that night.

By the eighth dress, I was exhausted. Laurel insisted on me finding the right dress, but I wouldn't find it following another person's trend practice. We'd been going about dress shopping the wrong way. In *Noba*, we made our own clothes. There was nothing I would've worn that I hadn't made with my own hands.

There were two bargain dresses in the color I favored. With Laurel's blessing, we bought both. I would have all night and tomorrow morning. I just needed shoes.

Sterling

Sleep was rare the past few days. I tried to be strong in front of Tetra, but I was freaking out. It was hard to be optimistic. I'd been putting on my game face, the one I wore to pretend my problems didn't bother me. I'd had enough practice. I'd need it tonight more than ever.

I had less to worry about than Tetra. She worried about more than just prom. She worried about everything. Now she had dresses, hair, and makeup, which was not her strong suit. I studied myself in the mirror. I'd rejected the traditional tux and bowtie for grey slacks, a vest, and a burgundy button-up. Mom and Dad agreed I should lose the jacket. Best advice I'd ever been given.

A knock came at the bathroom door. I knew it wasn't Mom or Tetra; they'd been too busy getting her ready.

Dad walked in, and for a moment, we just stood there, looking back at our reflections. Dad broke the silence when he slapped me on the shoulder.

"You look good, kiddo. You look good."

Dad had never been good at expressing himself. I knew part of him felt helpless that he'd never been able to do more for Mom. "It's been a rough couple of years, but I want you to know I'm proud of you, Sterling. I … don't know what I would've done without you."

He embraced me. It felt like the first time in years. I felt…good calling him my father. There may have been someone out there I looked more like, but as far as I was concerned, Peter was the only real dad I ever had.

"Knock 'em dead, kiddo." He ruffled my hair before making his way out the door.

It took forever before Mom or Tetra made an appearance. Dad and I small-talked downstairs until Mom finally emerged. She gushed and squealed about the job she'd done on Tetra's hair and makeup.

"You've got to see the dress. I can't take credit for that one. She created a miracle out of a mess."

Mom called out to her once, and Tetra made her debut at the top of the staircase. I had to stand for this one. I didn't know how she'd done it, but she'd combined two of the ugliest dresses into a masterpiece. The way it curved over her body and fishtailed at the end. She looked …

Beautiful.

"Tetra," Mom said, "where are your shoes?"

As Tetra made her way down the stairs, she held two strappy heels in her hand, promising to put them on before we left. Tetra stood in front of me, face to face. She gave me knots in my stomach, more so than ever before.

"You look … nice."

We stared at each other until Mom broke the connection. "Time for pictures!"

Tetra

Sterling appeared nervous, withdrawn, no doubt because of what might unfold before the night was through. He eased up when his parents started taking photographs of us. Laurel was camera-happy, not content until she had about a hundred pictures.

We stood in for each other's dates in the pictures. Laurel kept mentioning how cute a couple we were, even though he was going with Holly and I with Kip. Sterling looked so much like … someone I knew. Before. When things were different. Sterling *was* handsome in his own way. It was just something I chose to ignore.

We took a group photo. The Wayfairers seemed happy in this moment. It was an honor to be included in it.

We were the first stop the limo made. Grey and Brittany were the next. Interesting how that pairing had found each other.

Even from our first encounter, Grey had always been someone I related to. Out of all of Sterling's friends, he had accepted me first. His friendship made me question how worldly attachments could ever be such a bad thing. It pained me to know someday he would forget me.

It wasn't long before we reached Holly's. Sterling was once again subjected to taking a mountain worth of photos. We still had one more stop, but the group was too polite to interrupt. It was good Holly made it clear that if we didn't leave right away, there'd be no time for Prom.

Our last stop was Kip's house to meet up with Kip, Douglas, and the serpent wearing Waverly's face.

Nothing about *Megalopolis* changed. Its overwhelming population, its wide range of attractions, its glittering skyline. All of that made the district a pleasure to view. Especially at night.

It'd been the first stop we'd ever made upon coming to *Geo*. Back then, it had bustled with both oddness and conformity, and even a girl carrying an infant on her back never caused suspicion. I was glad to find a new appreciation for it.

Banners lit up for us. *"Honk or holler if you're happy it's prom!"* hung boldly on the hotel front. People honked. People yelled. The city was opening the welcome mat.

Sterling

I couldn't wait to get out of the limo. We'd finally reached the *Megalopolis* Metro Hotel, and the last half hour had been the worst. Douglas was a no-show. Waverly—or the thing that *looked* like her—did a bang-up job of portraying outrage. Without a heads up, I would've totally bought her being upset about being stood up.

Her bad mood rubbed off on Kip, who'd already been sensitive after his and Tetra's break-up. They were at it from the minute they were in the limo until pulling up to the hotel. Needless to say, Tetra and I kept our guards up.

I held Holly's hand in mine, my other friends close by, as we took turns gawking at the gala that stood before us. It was hard to put in words. The prom's theme was "A Starry Night," and it looked like a planetarium on speed.

Above us hung a ceiling of white string lights against a dark purple background, replicating the motions and cycles of the sky. The tables were something out of a black-tie party. In the center of each sat a bursting star centerpiece on top of fancy tablecloths and surrounded by silverware.

It reminded me of the night I rode time. The stars, the colors. I looked over at Tetra. She seemed equally impressed. I half-smiled. It was hard. Tonight might change everything, but all I kept thinking was … how pretty Tetra looked.

Tetra

"You've got to be kidding me. Is that a new dress? What happened to the yellow one?" Margaret asked. She batted away my reply with a wave of her hand. "It doesn't even matter because you look *gorgeous*! What's the deal with the corsage?" She held my decorated wrist, observing it with contempt. "Kip got you a fake corsage? What the hell?"

I tucked my hand into the other, hoping Kip hadn't overheard. I was never a fan of cutting flowers just to give them away. I thought it suited me better. At least this one wouldn't die.

"Where's Waves? They're taking prom arrival pics. I wanted one with us all together," she suggested.

I warned her *Waverly* wasn't being herself tonight and that Douglas stood *her* up. Margaret and Waverly were close. She'd unintentionally be my second set of eyes should *Waverly's* behavior seemed suspect. It'd be easier to be on my guard if she wasn't on *hers*.

Sterling

My two goals for the night? Keep an eye out for any-thing weird. And make sure Holly had a perfect night. She cleaned up nice. She was cute, but to-night she looked hot.

After a nonstop hour of dancing, Holly confessed she needed a break. I offered to fill her punch cup, looking for some time to myself, too. The panoramic view of my friends was cool. Any other night, things would've been so awesome.

At least Grey and Tetra were having fun. That put a smile on my face. It was too bad Douglas had bailed, otherwise the group would've been complete. I would've liked seeing *all* my friends, even if things turned south.

It was depressing watching Kip mope about. He spent most of the night with his teammates, and as long as he didn't cross paths with Waverly, he was good. I cared about his feelings, but I couldn't go five minutes without looking at Tetra.

She looked so … her. But better. The different shades of blue suited her, and the combined dresses contrasted one an-other. I kept thinking about how I'd missed my chance with Waverly. If I'd only told her how I felt, I could've protected her. Done more. But Tetra? She was sitting right in front of me. I know she and Kip had a history, but … I'd always wait-ed my turn. That never got me anywhere. People didn't know how you felt unless you told them. Maybe I'd choose tonight to tell Tetra how I really felt about her.

Someone bumped into me, but it was probably my fault. I should've paid attention more, but it was hard around Tetra.

"Dude, the tux." It was Grey.

"Sorry I was just …"

"Let me guess. Looking for Tetra?"

I shrugged. "Am I that obvious?"

"Yeah. Kind of." Grey laughed under his breath before punching my shoulder.

"I feel like a friggin' sleaze."

Grey took a sip from his cup, eyes darting from Kip to Tetra. "You are a friggin' sleaze. But come on, you and Tetra? Before there was Kip and Tetra, I always knew you had a thing."

"We never had a *thing*."

"Look, I'm not saying your *thing* is the same as Kip and Tetra's *thing*. But the way you look at each other, the way you talk to each other. There's something between you two, and I've been your friend long enough to notice this stuff." Grey held his neck, finishing the remains of his punch like it burned. "This punch has officially been spiked."

He filled his cup back to the rim, as I gestured to the punch bowl that hadn't been tampered with.

"What would you do in my situation?" I asked, lost as ever.

Grey burst into tears laughing, leaning his weight on my shoulder. "You're my friend. There's no point in lying to you. I wouldn't want to be anywhere near your situation. But if it were me? I'd do what felt right." He sounded like a cheesy rom-com movie. "If I were Kip, I'd be mad, but I'd understand. Eventually. Give him *some* credit. He's been a better friend to you than that."

Grey walked away. Tetra and Samir shared a dance together, and all I kept thinking was how I wish it were me.

Sterling

It was hard keeping Kip and Waverly apart all night. Neither of them were having fun and both would explode upon contact. Kip I understood. He was under a lot of pressure with college, football, plus the recent break-up. It probably didn't help that he was nominated for prom king and he was a shoo-in. He already felt like crap; more spotlight wouldn't be welcome.

But tonight was a different Waverly for sure. Even with the blaring music, she brought attention to herself, and it seemed like only a matter of time before … something happened.

Waverly looked as if she were about to rip Kip's head off. The way he came at her, she just might have. Tetra seemed to materialize out of nowhere.

"I do not like this. Kip is provoking it. I have to get it alone," Tetra said in barely a whisper. She smiled, laughing as if I said something funny, and I followed suit so as not to bring attention to us.

Tetra squeezed my wrist with force as we witnessed Waverly slap Kip in the face. "Screw you, Kip," she yelled, "For the record, *I* didn't dump you!" Waverly started crying, and my heart sank. "You're being fucking horrible. You know that?" She turned on her heel and stormed off.

"Help Kip," was all I could muster before rushing off to Waverly's side. Tetra caught at my arm, looking more concerned than I'd ever seen her.

"*Do not* confront her, Sterling," she said urgently.

"Don't you trust me, Tetra?"

"I trust *you*. Not your feelings for Waverly. It can use that. You can't go at this alone—"

"But if you're with me, I'm as good as dead anyway. It hasn't caught on to me all this time. I just want to be sure. I won't do anything stupid, just … *please*. Let me be sure."

She breathed out hard, finally letting go of my wrist. "You better not die. Or I'll kill you myself."

Tetra

K ip, how much have you had to drink?" His breath smelled of alcohol. No question he had been drinking.

"Just two," he said, holding up four fingers. I helped him stand. He wasn't fit to do so on his own. "Why do you care anyway? It's not like you've given me the time of day all night. What—did your fan club get bored already?"

"You're upset. And highly intoxicated. Let's get you to your room so you can rest." Kip had booked a room at the hotel in advance. It was supposed to have been our night, but it worked out better for him this way. I had to get him out of here. He handed me his key, allowing his arm to go over my shoulder.

We navigated through the crowd with everyone staring and pointing at us. I was in no mood for games and didn't want to add humiliation to Kip's night. I willed people to clear the path, but it wasn't going to happen. When Margaret and Grey approached, I relaxed.

Unfortunately, their presence only invited chaos.

"Where do you two think you're going? You just got voted prom king and queen," Margaret said, pulling us toward the stage.

"How? I withdrew my name from the nominations," I asked, easing a staggering Kip onto the stage.

"An overwhelming amount of write-in votes?"

Brittany approached, crowning me, while her brother Taylor crowned Kip. This was not good. I couldn't just leave, but I worried for Sterling. He was smarter than I gave him credit for, but he was also a fool. He wasn't strong enough to go against a *Naga*. At least I had experience with one.

He'd told me to trust him. I had to believe he wouldn't do anything to put himself in harm's way. Right now, I focused on Kip. I'd broken his heart, and he seemed to be in the best spirits he'd been all night. If I owed him anything, it was this moment.

We were supposed to commemorate our win with a dance. Kip led me to the center of the dance floor, where we were obligated to sway to the soft sounds of a classic song. My head rested on his chest, finding comfort in his heartbeat. Most times it beat so fast; tonight was different. He was relaxed, calm.

It was only for a song, so soon afterward, others joined us on the dance floor. Kip's lips kissed my shoulder, sending wintry, sharp chills through my body. Why were his lips so cold?

"This right here … was all I ever wanted. I never imagined we'd be this close."

Thump … thump … thump …

Kip's heartbeat. It was different. Off.

"This couldn't be any more perfect." The way he touched me was alien. His hands … Had they been gloved all night?

"Can I tell you something, Tet? You promise not to freak out or anything?"

I nodded, my heart racing with anticipation.

In a soft breath, he whispered, "I liked you better when you were Sai-Liber."

Sai-Liber. My family name. The name that held my true identity. Only Sterling knew my family name wasn't Pierce. The only way Kip would know that was if …

I struggled to free myself from his grasp, but his grip on my only tightened.

"Uh-uh, Sai-Liber. Not so fast. We wouldn't want to make a scene," he spoke in an icy tone, reserved for only me. "We've got a conversation to finish."

Kip …

"When I pull away to look at you, you're going to smile. Like I said something sweet."

Weighing my options, I answered him—*it* back. "And if I don't?"

It paused. It didn't try to pretend anymore. "Then it'll be me," it said slowly, with eerie purpose, "who'll make the scene."

I hadn't survived this long by playing hero. I did what was asked of me. It smiled, wearing Kip's expression.

"So … how'd I do?"

I didn't answer. It took all of me to guard my mind.

"How long?" I asked, my voice breaking unexpectedly.

It smiled with all its teeth, a smile that would've made me smile had it been the real Kip. "A day." He held out one arm, displaying himself with bravado. "He's a good fit, don't you think? Strong. Pretty. Undetectable. And used to be yours."

My mind drifted to the moment Marge had criticized my corsage. It wasn't a real flower. A real flower would've wilted at its touch. It wore gloves. Its hands would've felt cold without them, an easy thing to overlook. But it was the heartbeat that finally gave it away.

Whatever I was staring at … it was not Kip.

"You've gotten strong these past years. You resist me so well. Your little boyfriend here wasn't that strong." Its first attempt at a jab struck home. It wasn't like taking a physical hit to the face, but it hurt just the same. A kiss planted on my forehead, and I had a sudden urge to vomit. I wanted to cause this thing pain. *Now.*

"So I guess that hotel room is out."

Another blow. But I was better. Stronger. All it needed was one opening. I wouldn't let it get that far. We danced and I planned my next move. Given the chance, it'd kill me. But as long as it was *with* me ...

"C'mon, Tetra. Don't you like me anymore? Don't I *matter* to you?" it said, taunting me.

"You're stalling. If there was no use for me, I would be dead."

It held back, a cryptic curve at the side of its mouth, channeling Kip. "I'm listening."

"I'm either stronger than you or ..." I laughed, triumphant in a small victory. "You don't know who I'm bonded to."

The smile that once swallowed its face crept into a deep-set frown. It forced a breathy laugh. "The downside to *Nobans* bonding?" It leaned close to my ear and teased in a whisper, "You taste better together."

It sent a chill of fear down my spine. I persevered, staying passive, trying not to show how it affected me. It leaned back, facing me, wearing an unreadable expression. "*Geotics* ... they're a nice substitute, but they don't fight. Not like you do. They go easy. Only souls that fight suffer pain—"

"You wouldn't know *because* you don't have one," I sneered through gritted teeth. The pressure squeeze at my wrist grew tighter, seconds away from breaking it, triggering my birthmark to glow.

"I don't know how it's being done, but something about this world is blocking me. Don't think for a minute that I haven't looked for him. I thought it was this one." A revolting curve burned the side of its mouth. "Certainly fit the part, right? But outside a grief-stricken heart and a washboard set of abs, I came up empty, Tetra. You did this. Now he gets to spend his eternity with me."

Tonight was it. This might be my final fight. There was no way we'd both leave this room alive.

"Don't make this hard, Tetraphrimaporticheeq. We have a history, so I'm going to give you three options …"

"Three? I would've given you two," I shot back, watching its lips curl into a curve of ugliness.

"How about we cut it down to one? You get the chance to play hero tonight. I'm going to *let* you go, and you're going to return with that True Traveler of yours."

It hesitated, considering what to say next. It loosened its grip on my waist. I stepped back, studying my exit options between dozens of students and the marble door.

"And if I don't?"

"Then consider yourself an executioner. Because for every minute you're gone, I'll kill one person in this room. Trust me when I say it won't be the painless death I gave your boyfriend."

A lump formed in the back of my throat. I had no choice.

"The clock starts now." Eyes dark, cold, and filled with evil intent.

With no time to waste, I scanned the crowd and ran.

Sterling

Waverly had been hiding in the hotel's fitness center. What a jock. Everything about it looked, sounded, and breathed the same as her. It probably wouldn't help, but I brought a few things just to be sure. Parties were full of bouquets. I did my best to creep up unnoticed, but I gave myself away the minute I started throwing loose flowers at it.

"Sterling, what the hell?"

The flowers. They didn't wilt. I had a plan B but hadn't thought I'd get this far or close to it. Her. Tetra said plant life never survived close contact. The *Naga* couldn't be her.

"I'm sorry, Waves, they just … slipped," I said drowning in a sea of embarrassment. A sigh of relief followed. She was still … her.

I kneeled down in front of her, resting my hands on her lap. She wrapped her fingers around them, using her other hand to wipe the tears streaming down her face. "I came to check up on you. Are you okay?"

She shook her head. "You're a good friend, Sterling," she said, offering a faint smile. Even with raccoon eyes, she was beautiful. And alive.

"Waverly, I just wanted you to know …"

She didn't give me time before she leaned in and kissed me. Her soft lips fought fiercely with mine, making me forget where I was. Who I was. All I wanted was to kiss her, touch her, breathe her.

Kissing Tetra. I'd waited my whole life to do this—no, wait … I opened my eyes. She was Waverly, not Tetra.

Not Tetra.

This. This wasn't supposed to happen. I loved Waverly, but I couldn't get my mind off Tetra.

"I'm sorry," Waverly said, edging away.

"No. It's okay." I laughed. A girl had never apologized for kissing *me* before.

"It's because of Tetra, isn't it?"

Afraid to meet her gaze, I nodded. "For as long as I've known you, I didn't think *that* happening … would be like this." I bit my lip, hesitant to continue. "Everything around me is changing. I wish it'd stay the same, but I don't think it can."

Finally, I had found the courage to admit I'd always felt something for her. "I just wanted you to notice me."

She covered her face, hiding behind her hair. "I did. You never said anything. I'm not a mind reader. But either way, I knew." Her lips pursed to one side, and she played with the ends of her slick red hair. "But now, the way you look at her … I don't know. I'm totally jealous. But you're both my friends. I can get over it."

We laughed about it. It wasn't supposed to be this way, but I felt at peace getting out the truth.

"Since we were kids? That's a long time to be shy, Sterling. You might not want to wait that long to tell … *Tetra*?!"

A loud crash brought us to our feet. Her form was clear though the glass windows of the gym door. It was Tetra, kicking something with all her might.

Electrical sparks spilled to the ground. We ran over, yanking on the door's handle. Tetra. She was locking us in.

"TETRA!" I yelled through the glass. "What are you doing?"

She held her hand to the glass and gestured for me to do the same. A rush of silent words ran through me, jumbling through my thoughts.

This is goodbye.

No, don't leave me.

I've already put you at risk. I don't have time. I just needed to see you.

She ripped her hand from the glass and took off in the opposite direction.

"Tetra! Wait!" I yelled, frantic, banging on the glass. Her last words. *I just needed to see you.* Whatever was going down, I had to get out of here.

"Sterling, what the hell was that?!" Waverly screamed, eyes full of shock and wonder. I'd forgotten she was there. Whatever she'd witnessed was too much to explain. I wiped the warm tears rolling down my cheeks.

"Tetra's in trouble. Will you help me?"

A look of panic washed over Waverly's face. She stormed away and I couldn't blame her for getting spooked, but she came back with a ten-pound dumbbell and a medicine ball.

"Well, are you going to just sit there or help me break this glass?"

Tetra

I closed my eyes. I imagined a place of peace. Something to center me. Calm me. Him.

Sterling was safe. That's all that mattered.

I'd been so sure it was Waverly that I'd let my intuition become clouded. Kip had only been taken a day ago, so it must've been someone else before that. Someone close. People in their circle I should've been watching.

In the time I'd been gone, the ballroom had grown quiet, the silence deafening. The crowd parted as *it* waited for me, all eyes switching between me and the room's center. *It* wrapped its arm around a boy's neck, Kip's friend, a nameless person I'd never known from the lacrosse team.

"Seventy-four seconds," it said, taking a long, dragging breath. "You're late."

I circled it, ignoring the whispers around us.

"What's going on?" one girl said.

"Is it a prank?" asked another.

The *Naga* fed off the fear surrounding us. A wide smile settled on its face. The boy in the headlock struggled. It laughed, unaffected.

"C'mon, Kip. Stop playing around," the boy said. The creature reached down, whispering in the boy's ear. It wiped the smile off his face. Its glassy gaze caught me, void of empathy, blank, ugly. Not at all like Kip. That would make this easy.

"You're alone." It shook its head. "So you've already made your decision, Sai-Liber Tetraphrimaporticheeq?"

I took in the captive boy. There was little I could do for him now. "This battle is between you and me." I crossed my arms across my chest.

It stood there, cynical, considering. It snapped the boy's neck, dropping him to the ground. The crowd of teenagers roared into a raging frenzy. "You *suck* at negotiating." Grabbing a girl from the mob of screaming kids, it held her neck even tighter.

"You got twelve seconds."

Sterling

If there was one thing I wish I could un-see, it would be witnessing a murder. It was something I'd probably never forget …

What made it worse? Being forced to watch one of my best friends do it.

It was easy to see that whoever stood there, center stage, challenging Tetra, was no longer Kip. She'd been wrong about Waverly, but this? This wasn't *any* better. How long had Kip been Not-Kip? What kind of friend was I for not noticing? Had he suffered?

I couldn't sit here, watching whoever that was wearing Kip's face threaten to kill innocent people, but what else could I do? I needed to know more. There had to be a way I could help, even if it was just to buy Tetra time.

I left Waverly under a table with some other group of kids and scanned the room, looking for any familiar face I could get to unnoticed. I crawled from table to table until I reached the one closest to the ice display. A girl sniffled underneath the tablecloth, and if my guess was right, it was probably Holly. My hands covered her mouth, muffling her screams she would have made.

"Shh! It's only me, Sterling," I whispered, before taking my hand away from her mouth. She wriggled away, unsure who she could trust. I held my arms out, surrendering. "It's okay, Hol. It's only me."

Holly reached in to hug me. With all that was going on, I needed a hug. "Holly, this is going to sound weird, but I need you to tell me everything that's happened up until now."

Holly's lips stretched into a thin line, but she didn't hold back. She told me everything she could remember, but before she could finish, a collection of screams filled the air. Something hard hit the floor—another victim of the killer's hand. I couldn't just sit here watching people die, not when I knew *Kip* would stop after he had me.

The room became suddenly motionless. I turned to Holly and warned her to get to one of the tables near an exit. If at any time *Kip* got distracted, at least she'd be one of the first ones to make it out.

I took a deep breath, pressing my body to the floor to see what had caused everything to go stock-still, and it was then that I had the air sucked right out of me.

The *Naga* had locked its arm around the neck of its third victim.

Grey.

Tetra

My face told it all. I knew it, but worst of all, the *Naga* knew it. I'd lost the upper hand. The first two it would have killed anyway, no matter what I did. But *it* knew I wouldn't just let Grey die. He was my friend. Worldly attachments made you weak—it's what we grew up learning in *Noba*. In this moment, I couldn't help finding truth in that lesson.

"Kip, I don't know what I did … Whatever's wrong, we can get you help. I just …" Grey stopped, beginning to cry. It hurt to hear his pain. "What will people tell my family?"

Warm tears fell down my face. I tried to keep calm, yet failed. I was too scared for Grey.

"Wait. It's not him."

With cold, dead eyes, *it* snapped its head in my direction. "Well, if it's not him, then who?"

Sterling ran from under a table, arms flailing, repeating the words "It's not him, it's me" over and over again. He should still have been locked in the gym, but instead he was here, putting more than one life at risk. How could he be so foolish, so reckless, so …

He'd come back for … *me*.

I stood there, arms spread between the *Naga* and Sterling, trying to gain the advantage.

"Don't! It'll just kill both of you!" I screamed, but Sterling wouldn't listen. The stranger wearing Kip's face looked slightly amused.

"You don't look like a traveler," it huffed, examining Sterling while keeping its grasp on Grey's neck. "How do I know you're not just protecting him?"

Desperation filled me. "It isn't either of them! I'll tell you who the True Traveler is. Just let everyone else go."

It dragged Grey toward us, looking Sterling over with curious eyes.

"You resist me," it directed at Sterling. "You might be telling the truth. Only a *Noban* could display such a natural immunity to exploitation of the mind."

It looked from me, to Sterling, then to me again.

"But that doesn't mean you and he are bonded. If I kill him, Sai-Liber will lead me right to …"

"No!" Sterling shouted. He stretched out his right arm as *shakti* surged out of the mark on his wrist. It was a perfect hit, and the monster flew back, losing its grip on Grey. There was no time to think. I had my opening.

Sterling

Grey was in shock. Together, we watched Tetra advance on the thing that looked like Kip. She channeled her *shakti* toward it, land hit after hit, and while it kept *Kip* far away, it also meant Tetra couldn't get close enough to do any permanent damage. She couldn't win this battle. Not by herself and with just *shakti*.

Grey looked at me, considering what to say next. "Tetra's dying out there. I can't believe I'm saying this," Grey started in a wild panic that suddenly calmed. "But any chance of that light show you did earlier being of any use to us?"

My skills as a "light shooter" were novice at best, but I nodded as we moved to a different spot for a better angle.

"Are you a good shot?" Grey asked, totally knowing I wasn't. "Because I was thinking that that … stuff that shoots out would probably be a *big* help right now."

"I suck at controlling it and it hurts like hell," I said, extending my hand. "But I'll try."

Nothing happened. "I can't do it. I'm afraid I'll hit Tetra," I said.

A devastating blow slid Tetra clear across the ground. My fear fled. Nothing made me angrier than someone hurting Tetra. She moaned, turning on her side as *it* stalked above her. The rage inside me kept building. Aggressive. Stronger. I tried tapping the window that linked me to Tetra, but I didn't know if it would work. The *Naga* pulled Tetra to her feet, mouthing words too low to hear. She clutched the sides of its face.

If only I knew its name. It was like she'd thought it out loud.

I was in. *Kip's* face distorted into a number of sour expressions. Something was happening. The connection between Tetra and me was slipping. Whatever she was doing, it was working, but it drained her. I ran over to her, this time not caring what happened to me.

"Tetra, stop!"

Her eyes glowed white as the air around us took on a life of its own. The *Naga* screamed as it was lifted several feet off the ground, rendering it paralyzed and powerless.

"I ... I can't hold it!" Tetra screamed as she broke the connection between her and the *Naga*. Its body fell to the floor. Grey ran over as I propped her head onto my lap, hoping the elevation would keep her conscious.

"Is she okay?" Grey asked.

Tetra lay still, but managed to open her eyes. They shifted from Grey to me as she reached for both of our hands.

"It's okay. I am ... all right. I ... I'm glad you are with me," Tetra said, attempting to sit up.

"I know this is a bad time..." Grey paused, laughing. "...but I need to know what the fuck is going on."

"Kind of time-sensitive, man. What do you want to know?"

Grey's face pinched, like he couldn't believe he was even asking. "What the hell are you?"

Tetra and I locked eyes. We both shrugged, speaking over each other.

"We're bonded—"

"We're spiritually bonded to each other—"

Grey sat there, pondered, and then finally said, "What, like, Kenya and Daja in issue #198 of *BM: Apocalypse*?" Grey had read so much speculative fiction that this was the perfect time to show him I'd been paying attention all these years, whether he knew it or not.

"No, no, more like issue #23 of *Colossus VP*."

Grey nodded. To him, it made perfect sense. He turned around and pointed to the limp body stretched out on the ballroom floor, the one who looked like best friend. "And *who* is that?"

Tetra sat up on her elbows, eyes wide. "You know it is not Kip?"

"Tetra, Kip has been my best friend for years. Whoever that *was* tried to snap my neck."

We helped her up to a fully seated position. Now was the time to get some clues on how to stop this thing.

"What just happened?" I asked.

Tetra took in a deep breath. Whatever she was about to say, she wasn't proud of. "That … is Naukar," Tetra said, pointing. "Or at least, that's what we called it. The ones that lived, we named, to distinguish them from one another. I learned as much when I rode its mind. I didn't have a choice. It was trying to devour me. I didn't even know we could Ride the *Naga*."

"So what next?" Grey asked, impatient.

"Sterling," Tetra said, placing both of her hands on my face. "I've never needed you more than I do now. To Ride the Phantom with something like that creates a bond I will not be able to break once it comes to be. I'll be in its head, and it will also be in mine. I'll be vulnerable."

Not good.

"What do you need?" I said.

Tetra's face softened. "A *Naga* can revert into any shape it devours, but it feels strongest in Kip's body. That is one advantage. As long as he's in a *Geotic* form, I *can* hurt it. Without the use of my *helstone*, I can't kill it, but if it shows its true form … its skin will be impenetrable. We must to keep it from reverting."

Grey fidgeted, constantly looking behind him. "Lot of talking going on here …"

"And how do we do that?" I asked.

"Grey, did you notice when the *Naga* posed a threat to me, Sterling's *shakti* resurfaced? He is coming into his power, and I …" Tetra paused. "I may need to borrow that energy and because our bond is weak … It won't be painless."

When did anything about our friggin' bond feel pleasant? Grey looked back and met our gazes with bulging eyes as his mouth dropped open. "Uh … guys? Whatever you plan on doing, it needs to happen now. Dude is moving."

Kip's body twitched in the corner of my eye. If Tetra couldn't kill it, would anything we did tonight even matter?

She grabbed onto me tighter and tensed. "I've never attempted to take this much energy from you before. I need you to relax, or the stress could kill you."

"And you think by telling me that I'll fucking relax?"

"Guys … no bullshit. Whatever you're going to do? Do it *now*!"

"Grey, I can't. He's distraught. What can I do to make him relax?" Tetra said, in a panic.

Grey shrugged. "I don't know! You're the one who's bonded to him! What made Kip relax?"

Without warning, Tetra pressed her lips to mine, kissing me with fierce, untamed possession. Something powerful coursed between us. To say sparks flew was an understatement.

"I *knew* you had thing!" Grey said presumptuously. He probably said something else, but kissing Tetra made me leave the whole world behind.

Our lips fought and fused together until finally the current inside me died out. Whatever Tetra was taking from me, she had it. My eyes shot open, and feeling lightheaded, I fell onto my back. I would feel that in the morning, but man was that some kiss.

Tetra

With no time to waste, I slashed the air around me. My affinity was for wave, but now the wind answered at my will. The force pushed Naukar on its back, giving me seconds to gain the advantage. As tempting as it was to ride from one spot to the next, it'd require more *shakti* and I couldn't risk losing control. In three soaring side-steps, I was suspended in the air, bringing me close enough to do major damage.

A vortex formed above my head as I summoned the air to either side of me, picking up everything in its path. This was unlike anything I'd mastered. It was Riding the *Wind*. Objects I'd deemed difficult to move became weightless. Under my control, dining tables thrust forward, momentarily pinning Naukar to the wall.

Now was the time for a fist-to-fist facedown. Naukar stood up, brushing dust and debris off himself, his expression nothing short of beastly. I couldn't kill it, but I could sure make things hurt.

I punched my right fist toward its chest, but it leaned to the left, catching me off-guard. It grabbed my arm, pulling so hard I thought it was going to wrench my arm from of its socket. I kicked up, but it twisted my arm in back of me, kneeing me to the ground. I brought my head crashing back into its nose. *It* let go.

The force of the blow left a throbbing twinge at the back of my skull. It kicked at my thigh when I tried to stand, and I landed on my stomach. I spun on my back, using my arms to catapult me up as my foot landed square on its face.

Two more kicks to the face sent blood flying as I bent my leg in and pushed my heel into Naukar's neck. It snatched my leg back, using unnatural strength to twist my ankle. I screamed, scrambling backward. I needed time, if only a second, to reset my ankle. I couldn't put weight on it until I did. Naukar didn't waste any time charging toward me. I would need to call on the wind again.

Clapping my hands together, I summoned a gust of air to blow it back. I rolled over, pulling a belt off a fallen student. He wouldn't be needing it anymore. I brought the leather strap to my mouth, bit down hard, and twisted my ankle to back into place. Tears streamed down my cheeks as a part of me realized this was the type of battle *Nobans* spent lifetimes preparing for.

Before the *Day of Scar*, run-ins like this were the product of lore. This was a death battle. Only one of us could win, and I knew it wouldn't be me.

I stood up. While it wasn't as bad as I'd feared, my bruised ankle limited my mobility. Naukar wasted no time, charging at me as soon as it gained its footing. The closest object that could pass for a weapon was a catering knife well across the room. The smallest in the set, but it would have to do.

I rolled away from Naukar's first punch in a move that brought me in arm's reach of my only known weapon. I only had a millisecond to dodge the next hit before I dug the knife deep into the *Naga's* left side and rammed the blade up the side of its stomach. It screamed, gripping the wound while a spout of black ichor ran down the side of its body.

This thing was all about offense. Its only goal was hitting me, so that left its weak spots right open. The *Naga* devoured every part of you, even the glitches. Kip's weaknesses were *its* weaknesses. If I were an expert in one thing, it was Kip's body. It fell to its knees, out of breath and exhausted. It screamed again and kicked out in pain. It cried. "Tetra … how could you do this to me? I … I thought you cared about me. Look at me."

I lowered to the ground and reached for my *helstone,* only to find it missing from my neck. It must have fallen off in the fray.

I crawled backward, keeping an eye on Naukar the whole time. What I saw was a miscreation in the costume of someone I once cared about. A lesser demon who, amongst many others, aided in the destruction of a place I'd once called home. But that's all I saw. *Look at me,* it said. I looked all right. And it was all the reminder I needed to put this thing into the ground.

We made eye contact. The face that had just been in tears twisted in a snarl, revealing its true nature.

"You invade our worlds. Eliminate the inhabitants. And expect us to take it? You take on easy targets, worlds like *Geo*. You want to know what your biggest mistake was? It wasn't declaring war on *Noba*. No…" I caught my breath. "Your mistake was thinking you could kill my boyfriend and get away with it."

It smiled, its face covered in the dark blood that still spilled from its side. Nothing about it looked like Kip anymore. "You think you're strong enough to kill me? I annihilate blemishes like you. And you know what? I'm going to break every bone in your body and peel off all your pretty skin before I devour you, hoping—no, *praying*—that your True Traveler's watching, and *then* I'm going to do the same thing to…"

Its words ceased and body tensed. A flood of black goo poured out of its mouth as it held onto its stomach, falling forward from the shock. Waverly stood on the other side with the hilt of a weapon secured between her two hands.

"You dropped this," She said, pulling out what looked to be a sword. My *helstone*. No longer a useless stone but a blade dripping with the creature's blood. There was no time to celebrate as she threw it in my direction.

"Waverly! Run!" I yelled.

Naukar slowly stood, turning toward Waverly.

"Ouch," Naukar taunted.

With no way for me to shield her, it pummeled Waverly to the ground. She'd been so close. If only she had aimed for the heart.

I wouldn't miss.

Waverly's lip trembled. Why was she still here? Was she trying to be brave? What she didn't need was bravery—she needed common sense. The *Naga* wrapped its hand around her neck, bringing her to her feet. The skin around her neck was already bruising purple.

"You know; I'm not feeling as generous as I was fifteen minutes ago. Give me one reason why I shouldn't snap your neck like the rest of your pathetic little friends."

Waverly gasped for air. It loosened its grip long enough for her to talk.

"Bite…me," Waverly spat.

Naukar tightened its grip on her throat. "Don't get cute."

Helpless to stop it, I searched deep inside myself, channeling my connection to the root of its psyche. It was a place I didn't want to go again, but with Waverly at the brink of death, I had no other option. Energy rushed to my crown as I navigated through the innermost depths of its mind.

I reached into its head, and it trembled, screaming, to its knees. I tried to stay on my feet, but the melding of minds with a *Naga* carried a heavy weight. My own tears were followed by screams. Its aura was so violent, so impure. I couldn't handle what that malevolence was doing to me.

I broke my connection and fell to the floor.

Sterling

I caught Tetra before she hit the ground, trying to see how badly she was hurt. A moan escaped her throat, sending a rush of relief straight through me. She wasn't dead. Grey and Waverly approached us, eager to help.

"What the fuck, Sterling?"

"I know it's a lot, Waverly, but there's just no time to explain."

The one Tetra called *Naukar* pulled at its hair, screaming in a voice that didn't match Kip's one bit. It fell to the floor, flailing and writhing, its skin mutating into an explosion of scales. It was everything Tetra warned about, and the only thing worse than seeing one in memories was seeing one *right* now.

It squirmed and slithered as its length stretched. I didn't think it was ever going to stop growing. It let out a howl so piercing that everyone tried to hightail it out of there while we could. I was suddenly reminded of how heavy Tetra was to carry. Everything was fine until we were inches away from the entrance. Then the tail of something massive blocked us in.

"I hate to be the bringer of bad news, you guys, but we are royally fucked," Waverly whined as she reached over to help Tetra off my back. Grey looked over his shoulder, only to fall back in fear.

"Oh *shit*. Sterling, watch out!" he cried, and just like that I was swept off my feet and slammed to the wall. Tears of pain washed down my face as a sense of dread swept over me.

Unlike Tetra, I wouldn't last five minutes against this thing. And if it pressed me any tighter, I was going to suffocate. Its head was the size of my torso, and it would have no problem swallowing me in one bite.

"Traveler," it hissed in a husky voice, peering at me with amber eyes the size of footballs. I wanted to throw up. It coiled its body around mine as it wormed me to the center of the room. I closed my eyes, ready to bite my tongue to brace myself. *Here it comes.*

It craned its neck, sniffing at me, no doubt able to smell the fear, doubt, and inexperience oozing out of my pores. I opened my eyes, and it leaned back to take me all in.

"It was…" It coughed. "…clever of you to hide behind such a feeble body. You were the last one I expected."

Remind me to flail around and swear excessively just to give this douche a hard time while it ate me.

"Your *Noban* deceives you. They believe what they like, failing to understand our true purpose."

"What the hell is your *true* purpose?" I asked, catching it off-guard. It lowered me to the floor and slithered into a pool of its own body. Hands formed, then arms, and legs until I couldn't believe what I was seeing. Football uniform. Wholesome. All *Geotic*.

Douglas.

"No… No way."

It nodded. "Since the beginning of the school year, Sterling."

It morphed into someone I almost didn't recognize. Curly hair with hazel eyes. Tristan. The first kid who'd turned up missing at CCI. I remembered his face from the memorial set up for him by the science lab. It didn't stop there. Before my eyes stood Kip again, all patched up and perfectly convincing.

"Now, where were we?" it said. It smiled Kip's most charming smile, but on it, it looked anything but handsome. This was not Kip. I needed to constantly remind myself of that.

"You *Nobans* have us all wrong. You call us…*devourers*. We prefer the term *merging*—"

"I think my friends would disagree," I said, having no idea where the two ounces of courage I had left were coming from.

"Maybe. I may not be *your* Kip. But I have his essence, his memories, his confidence." It paused with a dry, rigid expression plastered across its face that looked a lot like Kip's. "His fears…"

He says there's nothing between them…Then why does he look at her the way I do? Would my best friend lie to me? No, he wouldn't…Maybe I'm just seeing things…Or am I?

Kip's voice. It was inside my head.

My mind's defenses were breaking down. Anything *Naukar* wanted me to feel, I felt. Kip had always silently feared my feelings for Tetra. Every doubt he ever had about it, every word he'd ever thought about it, all rushed into my mind, hurting worse than any so-called death.

"I'm sorry. I hadn't meant to. You were my best friend. If you can hear me, I would've never hurt you with Tetra…"

Tetra

I was injured, but I still had something left. A battle was never over until only one person was left standing. My *helstone* worked, but I may only get once chance. I wouldn't be able to get as close as I wanted, not without drawing attention. I would need something long, piercing—something, as a huntress, I'd held a thousand times. What I'd need was a spear.

My *helstone* heeded to my will, transforming into a spear that would've felt heavy to another but not to me. It was the perfect weight. *Naukar* continued exploiting Sterling's mind, and I was proud to know that it hadn't broken through yet. Sterling's mind had a natural block, but he wouldn't stay guarded forever. Still, he was the perfect distraction for *Naukar*. Its focus seemed to be on nothing else.

I needed to aim for the perfect spot to pierce its skin but not hit Sterling. I took a step back and prepared my target.

We can be one world, one mind, one soul.

Whatever *Naukar* was doing to break down Sterling's defenses, it was working. I could already feel Sterling slipping from my connection. I had to move *now*. Ignoring the pain of my ankle, I twisted forward and launched the spear from my hand.

Everything happened so fast.

The spear punctured Naukar's back and ran clear through its body and dropped to one side. The *Naga* fell on its back, convulsing, black liquid pouring from its eyes and lips.

I limped over to the *helstone* as it willed into the sword I'd grown up sparring with. I crawled into the Naga's lap, drew my weapon back, and carved its heart out of its chest. Its face shifted between Kip's and something reptilian, belting one last cry.

It stopped its struggle and burst into a mishmash of black liquid and blue light. With the strength of a meteor shower, it sent everyone flying to the back of the room. Sterling landed just a few feet to me, crying out. When I looked up, I learned why. The room filled with dozens of freed souls—young, old, sad, and lonely. Over the years, its victims had reached unspeakable numbers, and now, they were finally free.

Kip's soul lingered, looking down at his hands and himself. He was free. Before any of us could say goodbye he began to fade. We had no time to mourn. I put my arms around Sterling and prayed he'd hold on tight.

Sterling

Tetra put her arms around me, and that sharp pull that tore away at every molecule in my body transported us back into my room in a messy landing. The impact sent me flying into the dresser, and with all that had happened, I began to cry. Tetra started toward me, but I held my arms out to stop her.

"I'm okay, Tetra. I just need a minute," I said. We both sat there, covered in the dark, rancid ichor of the *Naga*. There was so much I didn't do or could've done. The only thing left to do that felt good was to cry.

It was official. The only life I'd even known was over.

Tetra

There wasn't anything I could say to Sterling that wouldn't make him feel worse than he already did. The *Naga's* purpose was to end worlds, and tonight it had ended more than one. Sterling's link to this world was gone. He stood to lose more. Family, friends … memories. The words never left his mouth, but we both knew he was ready.

Ready to leave *Geo*.

Sterling wiped tears away, smudging black blood all over his left cheek. I crawled over to him, resting my back against the dresser. I could do nothing to comfort him, not now. I just wanted to be there, by his side, to reassure him that I'd be there always. His hand slipped into mine.

Before tonight, I hadn't thought I could do it—kill a *Naga*. But I had. The leaders of the newly formed *Noban* council who'd once doubted me would have to listen now. *Nobans* might face this threat long after we were gone, but until every last face-stealer was in the ground, we would see a lot of people die. How long would we have together?

We searched each other's eyes and both knew. This was our last hour in *Geo*.

Sterling

I took a shower and threw some clothes on, but I didn't think I'd ever be clean enough to wash away the weight of what had happened with a bar of soap and water. When it was Tetra's turn, I was glad to have a minute alone. I didn't want her to see how I couldn't pull it together, but I knew I wasn't fooling anyone.

On the floor lay a remnant of our crash landing: a photo of me, Grey, and Kip. Carefree, together, alive. If I could've changed the outcome of things, I would have died in Kip's place. Living in a world without my friends was a fate worse than death.

It hurt to think about what the lack of Kip's presence was going to do to us, how it would affect his family, what it was going to do to Waverly. I didn't think I'd ever forget the look on her face as the spear ended the life of the thing that killed her cousin.

Would she remember this moment for decades to come? I needed to know because, after tonight, they'd be questions I'd never get to ask again.

My wrist burned as the photo fell to the ground, shattering the glass securing the picture to tiny pieces. I dusted the photo out of the frame and watched myself fade from the picture. Panicked, I sought another photo of Grey and me as kids, and like the last, my image dissolved. Tetra crept up behind me and placed her hand on the small of my back.

"It'll be like we never existed."

I only had one last request.

"Can I say goodbye first?"

Tetra

Sterling sat on the edge of the bed his parents shared. Laurel tossed and turned, as if she knew something was changing. Sterling reached out to touch her face, but I stopped him. She might wake up, and that would make it even more difficult to Phantom Ride her mind. He nodded, picking up a photo of the four of us during winter holiday.

His fingers grazed the spots where he and I vanished in the photograph. I knew this couldn't be easy for him. Any remnants of his life spent on *Geo* started and ended with the Wayfairers. After I did what needed to be done, there would be no trace left of him. He would no longer belong to this world.

"Okay," he said.

I summoned all the *shakti* that would come to my call. My core temperature rose, energy rushing to the brand on my wrist. My Mark of *Noba*.

"Peter will be easy. Laurel?" I paused. There was no easy way to say it. "There will be a lot to undo."

Sterling

In an hour's time, Tetra absorbed a lifetime of memories that belonged to the people I'd once called Mom and Dad. Laurel's mind fought hers, and by the time Tetra was done, she'd almost passed out on the floor. She had just enough power left to Ride us to the place she claimed we needed to be. It hurt like hell, but she was right. You got used to it.

We landed in separate spots on an empty coastal plain. We really needed to get these landings down better. When I came to and found her, she'd been floating in a nearby lake, like an exhausted castaway. I plowed through the water to prop her up on my shoulder. With my help, she stood, but she walked with a limp.

"You all right?" I asked. She nodded. Our surroundings were none that I'd ever laid eyes on before. Were we still in *Geo*? She pointed to a cliff up ahead, some distance from here. Guess we'd better get started.

The walk up gave me some time to think. I'd lost so much the past year, and yet all I could think about was how things for Tetra and me were going to change. Would we ignore the kiss? I hoped not. For once, we might actually have the chance to explore a relationship beyond a friendship.

It seemed like we'd been walking forever by the time we reached the mountain's ledge.

"It will take both our *shaktis* merging for us to Ride. But I thought you might like to see what you'd leave behind."

From this view, I could see all the regions I'd ever been to. *Megalopolis. City. Suburb. Borough. Seaside.* Which meant we could only be in one place.

Outland.

I strained my eyes, looking squarely at the sun. What would leaving one world for another one be like?

"What we're about to do requires a lot of trust. This will not be like things you did by accident," Tetra said as she broke the silence.

"I trust you, Tetra," I said as she took a step away from me.

"No. It is not me you will have to convince. It is *Geo* you must prove your worthiness to."

Show *Geo* I was worthy? How was I going to do that? I'd done it before, but seventeen years could make anyone rusty. She had the skills, the knowledge, and the experience of having already done it. What would happen if *Geo* found me unworthy? Would I get left behind?

Tetra walked away from the cliff's ledge. I followed. Nearly a mile away, Tetra stopped and reached out for my hand. A spark ignited inside her chest, and when she opened her eyes, energy radiated from her stare.

"Don't fight it, Sterling," she said as I felt our energy flow through each other. And just like that she was recharged. Like a mad woman, she raced straight for the cliff, dragging me with her.

"Tetra, wait—what are we doing?"

Her pace quickened, and I wished right about now she still had that limp. Closer and closer, we approached that cliff. What was she thinking? That we'd just fly off? I tried letting go, but she was too strong. *It was nice knowing you.*

Tetra exploded into a radiant energy. It spread further between us as we materialized into a missile of blinding rays. We moved faster than anything I'd ever seen, traveling at the speed of light through *Geo's* atmosphere. We melted into a sea of dark colors and bright blaze. Millions of stars ran toward us in a kaleidoscopic display of blues, purples, greys, and greens. We burned brighter, we moved faster. We were a shooting star.

We'd done it. We'd ridden our first world.

Together.

There was no way to know how long we'd been traveling. It could've been five minutes. It could've been five months. I now knew why time meant so little to Tetra.

This was Time Riding.

An abyss of stars and space melted away to reveal golden sand and an orange sun. We didn't have time to think before we came crashing down on a hard, wood-like platform. *Ow.*

"Nowhere in our history together have I been good with landings," she said.

"Tell me about it." I reached down to pat my hip. She crawled over to my side, helping me up on my elbows.

"Sterling, whatever happens, whatever decisions we make? I will be with you…always. Remember that, alright?"

I nodded and looked around in wonder. Where were we anyway?

Dunes of sand reached to infinity, and signs of life looked nonexistent. In fact, I couldn't imagine why a place like this had a random platform in the middle of nowhere. It seemed so out of place. Tetra stood up, and I took it as my cue to follow.

"What are we waiting for?" I asked before she shushed me.

She squinted her eyes at something in the distance. I wasn't sure what she saw. This place seemed to be nothing but sand. She looked down at the sand below us. The platform shook.

"It's coming."

"What's—"

"Let me do the talking. They are a xenophobic people. They speak this language but will ignore you if you fail to present them with their mother tongue first."

I was confused. Before I could prepare a question, a bronze train steamed in the distance. We were at a train stop. But there was just one tiny little flaw. There were no tracks.

As the bronze train approached, I noticed the car was being propelled by wind power. It never touched the ground. For something so gargantuan, it moved gracefully and was too amazing to be real. It was a flying train.

A collection of steam released from the smokestacks. It came to a halting stop at the platform, pushing us back from the pressure.

A set of steps lowered, and a man I guessed was the conductor stepped down, signaling for us to board. He wore a long, elegant tunic that on *Geo* could've passed for a dress over a pair of dark pants. He looked at his golden watch, yelling something I didn't understand, but Tetra pushed me onto the train, the door closing behind us.

Some passengers closed their train cars at the sight of us; others rudely stared. Tetra pushed me into the first empty car she could find and closed the door.

"You must forgive this world. They know we are not from here, and they're not always accepting of foreign people in the outskirts. Once we reach the main city, it will be better. We will have a better chance of adapting once we get a change of clothes and are able to blend in."

Main city? I didn't even know where we were.

"Where are we?"

"A world called *Illuminata*."

I looked out the window and only saw a valley of golden sand. Tetra took my hand in hers, instantly calming the nerves I'd had since stepping foot on this train.

"It will be all right, Sterling. I know someone in the city. An ally who'll want to help."

I wasn't sure where our path would take us, but I knew as long as we were together, there was nothing we couldn't do.

GLOSSARY

PLACES

Geo – The world Tetra and Sterling landed in after their first attempt at Time Riding.

Noba – The world that connects all worlds.

Illuminata – The world Tetra and Sterling travel to after leaving Geo.

City – Region in Geo known for its blend of residential and urban areas.

Suburb – A region in Geo known for its wealthy residents.

Borough – The second-largest populated region in Geo.

Province – A region that borders City.

Country – A rural region of Geo.

Megalopolis – Geo's largest metropolitan region; also; Geo's capital.

Meadow – A region in Geo known for its parks.

Outland – A region located on the outskirts of Geo.

Seaside – A region in Geo that overlooks the sea, also referred to as Beach.

Woodlands – A region in Geo that is heavily forested.

Denom – A fictional world in a Geotic entertainment series.

Oerba – The place of Tetra's birth; translates to "waterfall" in Noban.

Fava – A territory in Noba; translates to "desert" in Noban.

Beru – A territory in Noba; translates to "mountain" in Noban.

Aina – The place of Sterling's true birth; translates to "mainland" in Noban.

PEOPLE

Aboriginal – A person who was born and native to Noba. They are born with abilities and only change if a True Traveler bonds with them.

Noban – Meaning changes depending on context. Includes those with ties to Noba—friends, partners, bonded ones, lovers.

Geotic – A person native and born to Geo.

Oerban – A person native to Oerba.

True Traveler – A person who is not born on Noba, but can be called to Noba at any time. Both they and their abilities awaken when they bond.

Rishi – A highly skilled Rider of all affinities.

Denominator – A fan of the famous Geotic entertainment series, A World Unknown.

ABILITIES

Shakti – The spiritual source of a Noban's power.

Time Riding – The ability to manipulate time and travel to other worlds.

Phantom Riding/Ride the Phantom – The ability to manipulate a physical system without physical interaction.

Wave Riding/Ride the Wave – The ability to manipulate bodies of water, moisture and at its height ice.

Wind Riding/Ride The Wind – The ability to manipulate air, wind, and pressure.

Ticking – The force of time pulling and pushing forward or background (often when unrecognized)

resonate – To come into power.

unrecognized – To be untrained.

bond – A metaphysical phenomena in which a True Traveler and Aboriginal exchange half their soul for the others. It affects each participate differently.

helstone – A defensive weapon with the ability to transform into any weapon the wielder has knowledge of.

CREATURES

Naga – A race of malevolent shape shifters with the ability to devour souls. Their true form is unknown, but they are named after the form they take in times of duress.

EVENTS

Day of Scar – An apocalyptic struggle between the inhabitants of *Noba* and the *Naga*.

ABOUT THE AUTHORS

G. L. Tomas is a twin writing duo and lover of all things blerdy, fearless and fun.

When they're not spending their time crafting swoon-worthy heroes, they're battling alien forces in other worlds but occasionally take days off in search mom and pop spots that make amazing pasteles and tostones fried to perfection.

They host salsa lessons and book boyfriend auditions in their secret headquarters located in Connecticut.

Want to know when *City of Falling Stars*, Book 2 of the Sterling Wayfairer series, will be available? Subscribe to G.L. Tomas' newsletter (http://smarturl.it/GLTomasRomanceNews). You'll get access to promotions, diverse book lists and more!

Tetra and Sterling still have work to do. Join them in their ongoing series and watch as they discover new worlds together …

Want to know how we saw *The Mark of Noba* characters in their heads? Check out The Mark of Noba Pinterest board. Think you can outdo it? Submit your works of fan art to us!

Connect with us via Facebook and Twitter to have hour-long conversations about *The Mark of Noba*. (Okay, maybe not hour-long, but send us a tweet anyway!) Let us know if you're #TeamTetra or #TeamSterling!

We want to hear from you! Write us at guinevere@gltomas.net to discuss your fave stories by us! Comments, Suggestions, even requests what you'd like to see in our next publications!

Also, if you loved this book, please consider leaving a review. It really makes an author's day to read them and they're so, so helpful in determining if this is the sort of read for the next reader who may stumble across it. And remember no review is too short!

ACKNOWLEDGEMENTS

This is our second edition of this release, so it requires a ton of new thank you's!

First, we want to thank all the lovely folks who've supported the first release. Whether you liked or disliked *The Mark of Noba*, we've learned so many things that we were able to make this re-release a success!

We want to thank our editors Rebecca and Jen! Thank you for working with us, despite how annoying we are ;) So much of the book's success is built on the strength an editor can give it, and for that we can't thank y'all enough.

To Julie, of JT Formatting. How can we ever format a book without you ever again? Our books always look so amazing whenever you're involved!

To our author friends Constance Burris, Kiran Oliver, B.R. Sanders, Lyssa Chiavari, all speculative fiction folk, all-inclusive writers. Without awesome folk like you guys, we probably would've taken a lot longer to realize the need for the relaunch. Lyssa, your covers inspired our leap!

Speaking of covers! A huge thanks to Mosaic Stock, Elise the lovely owner, and Larry the in-house photographer. You guys gave us life with our new covers! The concepts came to life so much greater than we ever could've imagined, and it couldn't have been without Mosaic Stock.

We also want to thank Kierra and Skyler, the models who breathed Sterling and Tetra to life, y'all are amazing! We screamed so much between the casting call to the final product, and if only you guys knew how close you look to the Stetra in our head, you'd understand why the shoot meant so much to us! To Brad the Dad! You're awesome! Hopefully your kiddo is telling you that all the time ;p

Excerpt from
The Sterling Wayfairer Series
Book Two: *City of Fallen Stars*

Cover coming soon…

Tetra

A lot can arise when your body is ripped from one world to the next.

It feels like only yesterday that I'd revealed myself to Sterling, embarking on a journey meant to strengthen us but also ensure our survival.

We were spiritually connected, Sterling and I. *Noba*, the spiritual common ground that connected all worlds granted our bond. It was up to both of us to not only protect one another, but find out what our bond really meant.

The last few months have been difficult for both of us. The loss of a life, the loss of a love, nearly losing ourselves. Those were the sacrifices we'd made keeping attachments. I was drained physically, spiritually; but I hadn't expected to be so emotionally gone.

Sterling slept through his pain. For this I was grateful, as I had no encouraging words to say to him. Even when he was awake, we didn't know what to say. He felt responsible for everything. He'd lead us to *Geo*, the world he'd grown rather attached to. He spent his entire adolescent there, that the stay had rooted him. I could see it in his face every time he'd open his eyes.

Why *Geo*?

For that I had no answers. All I knew was how strong our energy was then. It'd allowed a *Naga*, a common enemy we knew so little about, right to us. I wondered how our *Noban* brethren had held up throughout the worlds.

The train ride was long and we weren't expected to arrive at our destination anytime soon. "Tetra." Sterling mumbled, as he tossed around against his seat, and rubbed his face against the fatigue.

Though we were out of eminent danger for now, I feared our journey was *far* from over…

OTHER YA TITLES FROM G. L. TOMAS

Best Friends. First Loves. Unforgettable Times.
Neighbors and best friends Paul and Felicia hoped they'd be
friends forever.
But as they change, so does their friendship.
She shouldn't have kissed him...He shouldn't have liked it.
Starting school changed everything.